RYDER'S ARMY

Brian Finley

DEDICATION

This book is dedicated to Wendy for putting up with me when I'm lost in Ethan Ryder's world. Thanks Boo. To Garett and Kyle who inspire me to try for greatness, and treat me as if I have achieved it even when I fall short. And to my Mom and Dad who instilled in me a love for reading and writing, and provided invaluable input and editing.

"Every day is a journey, and the journey itself is home"
– Matsuo Basho, 17th Century Japanese Poet

PART I – Old Home

Chapter 1

I had the crosshairs centered on the soldier's thigh. I began to gently apply pressure to the trigger. Anger was heating my face against the cold day. I'd watched this scene played over and over for the past year and I was not about to let it happen again. The boy had just been wandering aimlessly up and down the block for hours, occasionally sifting through the rubble of the burned out homes, now and then stopping to pick up some piece of debris and examine it, but simply minding his own business. I knew the patrol would eventually come through and they would stop and harass the boy, or do worse. This was exactly what they'd done. The soldiers stopped their vehicle as soon as they spotted the young black teen sitting on a pile of rubble.

I selected a position about two hundred yards down the street behind the burned-out hulk of some former luxury sedan to wait and could still smell the acrid scent of burnt plastic even after the car had been sitting here in the open for two years. For me, this was a relatively easy shot. At one time I'd regularly shot centers from a thousand yards.

Two soldiers occupied the vehicle. They immediately forced the boy to his knees from his seat on the rubble. I could tell by their body language and facial expressions that they were trying to intimidate him. Their patches of rank were clearly visible on their sleeves. The older soldier was a sergeant and the younger, a private first class. Both also wore a muted red insignia on their sleeves, which denoted their unit.

1

The badge was round, and stitched in tan thread in the middle of the circle was a coiled snake, ready to strike. The reverse stars and stripes patch was on their other shoulder, although it stood for very little in this place. They were regular army. Not a special unit. That would make things easier.

The boy seemed to be in his early teens. He was dark-skinned and seemed thinner and lankier than he should have been, even for that awkward age. His clothes were soiled and well worn. I could see the fear on the boy's face and the sadistic enjoyment on the soldier's. The boy was simply sitting there minding his own business and there was no reason for the soldiers to stop, let alone harass him in this way.

I began to slow my breathing, as I had been trained, so that I could get off the best shot possible. It was best to time the shot at the end of exhaling. It kept the end of the muzzle steadier. I applied just a bit more pressure to the trigger.

I wished that they would get back in the vehicle and drive away but that wasn't likely to happen. This would go bad soon enough. It always did. I wasn't going to let it get there.

The sergeant's head bobbed harder and harder and his face turned a crimson color. He was leaning over the boy and nose to nose with him and I could hear him screaming even at two hundred yards. I couldn't make out the words but the tone clearly carried down to me. The anger in his voice was obvious. Spittle flew from the sergeant's mouth as he yelled in the boy's face.

Both soldiers were clothed in standard U.S. Army MultiCam urban pattern combat uniforms. Over these they wore Interceptor body armor, protecting their torsos. Both wore combat helmets. The Weatherby

Mark V Accumark deer rifle, which I'd been extremely fortunate to find on a shelf in a half burned garage, was as good as most rifles I'd used as a soldier. I was targeting the thigh because the body armor did not cover the leg and a hit there would drop the man instantly. I had no intention of killing them but would not allow them to take the next step in their "interview" of the boy. It was a similar "interview" that had been the spark for the massive riots that began almost two years ago.

Things were quickly moving from bad to worse. It was clear that the soldiers had no intention of simply leaving. It was past that point. The sergeant was way too worked up for that. He raised his pistol to the boy's forehead. I exhaled one last breath, steadied the rifle and slowly and carefully began to apply the final pressure to the trigger. Time slowed to a crawl. My heart pounded in my ears and then began to slowly calm until I could no longer feel it's beat. I took into account the slight breeze and corrected for it. I hoped against hope that the soldier would lower the gun. He didn't. I squeezed a little harder, pulling straight back on the trigger. The report of the rifle was loud and echoed off the ruined buildings. The muzzle flashed and the smoke drifted quickly away. The stock kicked hard against my shoulder. Instantly, the sergeant's thigh exploded in a shower of red. The shock of being shot caused the sergeant to reflexively fire his weapon. The boy fell forward grasping at a wound in his upper right arm. The second soldier wheeled in the direction of the sound of my shot, which arrived a beat after the bullet had. The private was clearly panicked and he began wildly shooting his pistol in my direction. A few of his shots bounced off the building to my left. As soon as I had fired the first shot I immediately aimed on the private, let the air out of my lungs and quickly took the second shot before the soldier could gain his composure and head for shelter. The second shot struck the soldier in the thigh as well, instantly dropping him to the pavement.

I shouldered the rifle and drew my pistols and made my way down the street to the fallen trio. I moved from car to car, picking through the debris littering the street, keeping some cover available in case one of the soldiers regained composure enough to return fire. I never moved my eyes off of them. I needed to move quickly because the helicopter support would be alerted to the soldier's GPS monitoring devices showing them lying prone.

The boy sat up between the two downed soldiers and was now staring at me. I must have been quite a sight. My size is imposing, and had kept me out of more than my share of potential bar fights. My own homemade urban camouflage in shades of gray and black covered my large frame and I carried two black .44 pistols aimed in his general direction. I was moving directly toward him. I had coated my face in soot to further camouflage it. Strands of black sweat soaked hair hung from beneath my black cap.

The boy's face was twisted in pain and terror. His unblinking eyes wide open in fear. Blood had stained the sleeve of his worn sweatshirt and judging by the lack of color and the sweat on his face he was going into shock. I carefully approached the soldiers from behind. Both were still alive and writhing in pain. My hope was that neither of their femoral arteries was severed. They wouldn't last long enough for the copters to get them help. I carefully slid their pistols out of reach with my foot.

"Are you going to shoot me?" the boy whispered.

I simply raised my index finger to my lips to shush the boy. The expressions on the faces of both soldiers asked the same question. I responded by raising my pistols and aiming one at each of the men. I moved in close to the sergeant and knelt down, keeping the barrel of the .44 in his face.

"Tell me why," I whispered as the anger rose in me again. "Tell me why. Why did you have to kill them?" I paused for an answer but got nothing but fearful stares. "One way or another I'll find out. You make sure you tell your commander that I'll find out".

At first the sergeant looked confused then recognition swept across his face. "It's you...you son of a bitch," the sergeant whispered through clenched teeth.

The corner of my mouth rose in a smirk as I picked up the soldier's guns, and placed them in the backpack I was carrying. I turned to the boy and said, "Can you stand?"

"I can try. My legs are okay but my arm hurts like hell."

"I can take care of that but we need to get a move on."

We headed down the street and away from the soldiers as the sound of approaching helicopter blades filled the air.

Chapter 2

Halfway down the next block the boy was laboring and beginning to stagger. I slowed to allow him to catch up, being careful not to fall over the debris in my path as I looked over my shoulder. A few seconds later he dropped to his knees and then collapsed on his side. I strode quickly back to him as the sound of the helicopter blades grew increasingly closer. We had to move now or the chopper would spot us.

I lifted the boy over my shoulders in a fireman's carry as I'd been trained to do so many years ago. He was shockingly light. At first sight the boy was undernourished and well underweight for his height but his baggy sweatshirt hid how truly thin he was. I could feel his ribs on my shoulders as I hoisted him up. How difficult it must be to live in this world for a boy like him, I thought.

The sun was beginning to set over the hills at the west end of the San Fernando Valley, in the northwestern most part of Los Angeles, and the thinning light made the landscape of burned out homes and businesses look even more surreal than it was. Shadows blended with the darkened, charred forms. Blackened hulks of former cars looked like strange creatures lurking all around just waiting for the chance to pounce on me. Burned palm trees looked like spent matchsticks. Even as a kid I had hated this time of day even more than dark. In the dark nothing could play tricks on my eyes. The twilight caused everything to look wrong and out of place. Neither the rods nor the cones in my eyes could decide who was in charge leaving me in a murky world of gray.

The sound of the helicopter was almost overhead so I ducked inside the shell of a house until it passed by. It wouldn't be long before a second would arrive to begin searching for us so I had to move quickly to get back to my safe house. Hiding from the copters would do no good. They were equipped with infrared cameras and with little or no background life to blend with we would be easily located. I checked the boy to make sure he was still breathing and he was. The wound had stopped bleeding but had soaked the sleeve of his sweatshirt. It was likely that the lack of food, the terror of the moment and the loss of blood had caused him to go into shock and pass out. The wound would need stitches when we made it to the house.

The copter passed and I stepped back out to the street with the boy draped over my shoulders. I had grown up here in the Valley and could remember when the west end was still mostly orange groves. I recalled the devastation that the '94 earthquake brought. Whole neighborhoods had been left in ruins. But even that hadn't killed the city. It took people to do that. The devastation left after the riots made the quake look like a picnic. What the looters and rioters hadn't destroyed themselves the fires finished off. In the early days of the riots news trickled in to us that almost a dozen other big metro areas had erupted in the same rage of frustration and wound up with the same fate. The government didn't have the resources to rebuild and had simply blocked the cities off. It had all started here in Los Angeles so it was worse here. Bad cop, angry crowd. Like a match to a powder keg. It had been so bad in California that the whole state was blockaded off. They had given everyone the opportunity to relocate at the beginning, warning everyone else that there would be little or no help after that.   In fact, all they had provided was the military patrols to enforce martial law. Most of the people had fled, trying to find a safe haven. I had stayed. It was my home. My family had been here. We had had hope and I'm a stubborn guy. That was almost two years ago now.

I shut off the thoughts and stuffed them back in the box in my mind where I kept such things and re-focused on my effort to move quickly away from the shooting. I had no time for feelings anymore. With darkness finally closing around us, and the sound of the copter well behind us, I stayed to the clearer part of the street and made my way to the house in no time.

Chapter 3

"Where we at man?" the boy said, waking from almost six hours of sleep.

"At my place," I replied. ""You passed out halfway down the street so I just carried you here."

"Thanks. You saved my ass back there."

I felt an uncomfortable silence fill the room. The boy stood and stretched. He was actually taller than I'd first thought. Now in the glow of the oil lanterns I could see him more clearly. I'm 6'2" and he was only about three inches shorter than me but I had seventy-five pounds of muscle on him. His hair had grown into matted clumps that reminded me of Rastafarian braids. There was life in his eyes though and you could almost see the workings of his mind through them. He was processing very carefully. Intelligent eyes. He looked nervously at his surroundings. His face showed his concern and discomfort. I'd chosen the house because it was relatively intact. The window glass was missing in a few windows and I'd covered those in black plastic to keep the cold out and the light in. At least the walls and roof seemed to be sound. Soiled and stained light blue carpet covered the floor. It smelled faintly of urine and mildew. Through the second story windows I could see tops of the trees. Dark mold was growing in some of the corners of the room. All things considered it was pretty decent lodgings.

"This your house?" he said.

"For now."

"What's your name?" he asked.

"Ryder. Ethan Ryder, and yours?"

"Donte Johnson." There was another long pause while Donte waited for me to ask another question. When it didn't come he asked, "So why were you there? I mean, why were you hangin' around with a rifle at the right time?"

"Just luck I guess."

"Luck my ass. I may be young but I been around long enough to know you don't have someone with a rifle just hangin' around to shoot two assholes. What's your story?"

"No story. Just luck. Leave it at that." I made a face that made it clear that I wanted it left alone. I reversed the roles. "What's your story kid? You have family around here?"

"Naw. My Dad ain't been around since I was little."

I made myself busy with a portable propane camp stove while I waited for the rest of the story. I got the flame going and put on a pot of water I got from a big jug on the far side of the room.

"What about your mom, brothers, sisters?" I asked as I took a box of macaroni from a metal locker in the corner of the room.

"No brothers or sisters." He paused and stared at the floor for a few seconds. "I don't know where my Mom is. She was at work when the riots started. Her job was across town. She left as usual that morning. I kissed her goodbye before I went to school and I haven't seen her since. I waited at home for a couple of weeks hopin' she'd come back. Never did. I took off when the riots started movin' into my neighborhood. Our house is gone. I know she dead but I've been looking for her ever since. Keeps me going ya know?"

"I understand. More than you can know. How old are you?"

"I'm fourteen. Almost fifteen."

"Fourteen, huh? How have you made it this long on your own? You're just a kid."

"I been on my own more or less since I was ten. Mom was workin' all the time so I grew up early, I guess."

I felt the hint of sadness in his words. He was proud of his independence and his ability to survive but it also seemed to me like he felt cheated out of his childhood.

"Still, pretty impressive that you're still around. There are some pretty vicious assholes out there."

The corners of his mouth rose at the compliment, but he looked down at his shoes. It seemed like he hadn't heard many kind words in his short life.

"Yeah like those two pricks today, they was pretty vicious."

I grinned at the comment. "Speaking of that how's your shoulder feel? You had a deep cut where the bullet grazed your arm, but no penetration. I had to put a couple of stitches in it."

He lifted his shirtsleeve and looked at the gauze coving the wound. He touched the bandage and winced. "Hurts, but I guess it coulda been worse, huh? You a doctor?"

"No, but I had some first aid training once. I hope you like macaroni and cheese. It'll be ready in few minutes." I studied Donte's face. He looked so young but the past two years of survival had aged him beyond his years. He was a good-looking kid, far too skinny for his frame. In another time he would've probably been a good athlete. His demeanor seemed wiser than his fifteen years. Just the fact that he had survived this long demonstrated his wisdom.

"Donte, tell me something. Why didn't you run when the soldiers rolled up?"

"Man I wasn't doing nothin'." He answered as if he was being accused of something. "There was no reason to run. I was just out lookin' for stuff to survive on, you know? Those assholes shouldn't have even stopped, let alone wanna kill me."

"Have you seen them do things like that before?"

"I've seen them roust people before, and I seen them shoot people for runnin'. I figured at worst they'd give me some shit and send me packin'. Those two guys were nuts."

"When you get back out there on your own, you need to stay away from the guys with the coiled snake patches on their uniforms. They're no good. It's one company, about sixty or seventy guys, but they're bad news. Stay clear of them. I've seen them do what they did to you before. In fact they would've shot you had I not been there. What did they ask you?"

"They wanted to know why I was out there by myself. They kept tellin' me I needed to stay near the settlements. They said they weren't gonna tolerate anyone living on their own and I better move my ass along. I told them I wasn't doin' nothin' and they should mind they own damn business and I could live wherever I pleased."

I nodded my approval. I admired the kid's toughness. "Is that when the sergeant got so pissed?"

"Yeah, he went ape-shit. Real quick, ya know? He's supposed to be holdin' the peace and he went all crazy. I never been that scared…'cept when you was walkin' up." He smiled weakly at the comment.

"I guess I made quite a sight, huh?"

"Hell yeah, ya did. You was spooky lookin' in all that black and grey cammo stuff and your face all painted black. You're a big dude, too. Course those two big hand cannons you were holding didn't help."

"Well, those guys are the bad guys for sure. If I hadn't seen certain things in the past few months I would guess that they just have too much territory to cover and not enough men. I've counted about seventeen different patrol pairs all from the same unit. There are no other units out here and I've seen them all over this end of the valley. It's a lot of ground to cover. But there is more to this. You're the first guy I've had a chance to talk to that I've seen get rousted."

"They all run off?" he asked.

"A few got away when I fired on the soldiers, but I never got to talk to them. The others...dead. Fourteen people. Just like they were going to do to you. I don't know why but they really want people into the settlements and not out here on their own. Their actions are too violent just to keep the peace and make it easier to patrol. That's kind of why I was there. I've been hoping to catch a glimpse of something more. When I saw them raise the pistol to your head I had to stop them. It's just not right. I'd been watching you for hours just waiting in case they showed up."

"You were there watching me that whole time? Well, I'm glad you were." He paused and seemed lost in thought for a long moment. "You said somethin' earlier about when I get back on my own. Can't I hang with you for a while? You got lots of room here."

"I've been solo for a while and I like it that way. I don't need a kid hanging around with me."

"I ain't no kid and I can take care of myself. You could use my help," Donte said, puffing out his chest for effect.

I didn't mean to but I chuckled at the sight. "Take care of yourself? Like you did today? No, you can stay tonight but you've got to move on tomorrow. I can't do what I need to do with you hanging around. I'm sorry."

Donte's eyes begin to well with hurt and angry tears and he quickly wiped them away with his sleeve. I turned back to the pot of macaroni and pretended not to notice so the boy would not be embarrassed. I felt for him and I felt like an asshole but I just couldn't have him stay. It would just complicate things.

The macaroni was done and we ate in silence. By the way he wolfed down the food it was probably the first time he'd eaten in a few days.

After the meal Donte quickly fell asleep. I took a tour around the perimeter of the house checking the doors and the trip wire warning systems that I had placed in each of the hallways and at the base of the stairs. As always it would be a restless night full of nightmares.

Chapter 4

I woke as the sun began to rise, backlighting the grey overcast morning. It turned the undersides of the high clouds covering the morning sky myriad shades of pink and gold. I stood at the window and enjoyed the brief moment of color before the sun slipped behind the clouds and everything went gray. It had been a decent night's sleep after all. Only a few nightmares. Donte was still sleeping quietly under the extra blankets just a few feet away. Little puffs of steam coming from his nostrils in the cold air of the morning. It was winter, or as much winter as there is in Los Angeles.

I started a pot of water boiling on the portable camp stove. Water was almost easier to get now then when the city was populated. Los Angeles was built in a desert and without bringing water in via the aqueducts from the north and east the city never would've grown as big as it did. Maybe it shouldn't have. There had been too many people in too little a space. Made for too much tension. Might be why things got so explosive. I just collected water out of pools, used a bit of chlorine bleach to sanitize it. Plenty of water. Sometimes you could find a faucet that worked. There was still a little pressure in the city pipes. Food was another issue entirely. Fresh food was out of the question. The few trading posts in the settlements occasionally had fresh vegetables from co-op gardens or on even rarer occasions one could find meat, but it took a pretty hefty barter to gain even the smallest amount of fresh meat. I hadn't had fresh meat since the riots began. Canned stuff was easier to find and much of my time was taken up with sifting through the destroyed or abandoned homes and businesses in search of necessities. I had my ever present list: canned goods, small filled propane tanks, reading materials, weapons and most importantly ammo for the Weatherby and my two .44 magnum revolvers that I carried in holsters under each arm. Maintaining the revolvers was easier than an automatic, although I had a few of those stashed away at the safe house. It meant in a pinch I would need to reload more often but I also knew the pistols would be reliable. Revolvers don't jam. The pistols were my defensive weapons. They were loaded with soft tip ammo. The soft tip would spread on impact and break apart. Nice neat entry, nasty messy exit. But at least the bullet wouldn't keep going and hit someone it wasn't intended for. The Weatherby was a different story. That had become my weapon of offense. It was a fantastic rifle. Best civilian rifle I'd ever owned. The composite stock was durable and lightweight. It was also accurate as hell.

I'd lived a lonely solitary existence for the past two years. The fire of revenge pushed me forward from day to day and kept me from eating the end of one of the pistols.

Next to me Donte began to stir from his deep sleep. He yawned deeply and stretched his long, lean arms out from under the blanket. I made a decision at that point that I would let the boy hang around for a while. The need for some companionship outweighed the need for caution…barely. I missed having a conversation. I might go days at a time without speaking a word. I'd learned to cope with it but after all is said and done we're social creatures and some companionship might not be so bad after all. Truth is I just liked him. He reminded me of my son. I needed to take it slow with him to make sure he was trustworthy. I hadn't trusted anyone in a long time and the thought of it made me very uncomfortable. I'd been burned before.

Donte instinctively flinched when he laid eyes on me as he woke and it seemed to take a second for him to remember the events of the day before.

"Good morning," I said cheerfully. "Forget where you were?"

Donte rubbed the sleep from his face with both hands then sat up on one elbow. "Yeah. I ain't used to waking up with someone else around. Kinda startled me, ya know?"

"Yes. I know." I had some dry cereal poured out in bowls. No milk anymore but the plastic bag and the preservatives kept the cereal fresh still. "Have some breakfast," I offered. I carried the bowl over and set it in front of Donte.

"Thanks man."

The water had boiled and I made coffee. I offered a cup to Donte. He sipped it and made a face.

"Not good?" I asked.

"Naw, just not much of a coffee drinker but it's hot. Thanks"

"So Donte," I took a long pause and thought one more time about what I was about to say. "I've given it some thought and if you'd like to stay I wouldn't mind the company." I held up my hand, as he was about to speak. "You will have to keep up your end of the bargain. Help find food, lug water and so forth. My house, my rules. OK?"

His face told me all I needed to know about the answer but he added, "Hell yeah, I want to stay."

"Very good. Here are the rules. One, you don't tell anyone where you are staying and when you are out you make sure no one follows you back. Too many people out there looking for the easy place to loot and I don't want to have to replace the stockpile I've got. If I even think you've told anyone where you are staying or you are careless about coming in here when people are around you're gone. Two, when you are out with me you must follow my instructions to the letter. If you don't we might get killed and I'm not at all interested in doing that right now. Third, don't ask too many questions about me. If there's something I want you to know or you need to know then I'll tell you. Deal?" I stared at him hard to let him know I was serious about all of this and saw him nodding his head in the affirmative. Then he smiled.

————

His smile reminded me. And it hurt. It had the innocence of youth and it reminded me of my son. He had been a quarter of Donte's age but their smiles were the same. Their faces lit up in the same way. It was infectious. You could sense the pure happiness and it made everyone feel the same way.

I did two tours in Afghanistan. What kept me going through that was my family. I got sent home for all the wrong reasons, but it was ok because my wife and son were here waiting for me. And then after I got home someone took them from me.

We'd made it through the riots. Our house and most of our neighborhood had been left alone. The world was upside down and we thought in those first few months after the riots that things would go back to normal, that everything would be ok. But no matter what happened my family kept me going. We stayed in our home when we were told that we should probably leave because there would be no way to provide services and we'd be on our own for the most part. It was our home and things had to get better. I thought I could take care of everything myself. I thought I could get them through the tough times.

Things weren't really as bad in those first few months as they are now. Many people left the city but there were supplies to be found. The military was trying to bring relief. There was still a chance that things would return some normalcy. There was my family. We had hope. It was our home after all. We really had nowhere else to go anyway.

I've beaten myself up the past two years over that decision. My wife stayed because I wanted to stay. If I just hadn't been so insistent on staying. In many ways it's my fault.

It was a Monday when it happened. I had taken the car to the local high school to pick up the supplies that were to be delivered that day. Mondays were the day that the military brought truckloads of canned goods and basic supplies. Some of us still had cars then. You could siphon gas out of the abandoned vehicles. I never drove more than a few miles so a few gallons would last for weeks.

I'd gone early to get in line. When I left the house, the last thing I saw as I closed the front door was my son waving good-bye in that overly enthusiastic way that only a child can. I was excited when I left the school parking lot because the military had had cereal and canned milk. Frosted Flakes to be exact. They were my son's favorite. I'd waited in an extra line to get them. I'd been there about four hours but I couldn't wait to see how excited he'd be when he saw them.

Driving back I saw the smoke from a mile away and I just knew. I don't know how I knew but deep in the pit of my stomach I just knew. I punched the gas. My fears were confirmed as I turned onto our street. The block was a smoking ruin. I couldn't breathe as I drove the block. Smoldering debris choked the road halfway down the street so I stopped the car, jumped out, and ran the rest of the way. The house was already a charred ruin. A few spot fires still burned but there was little fuel left for the flames to devour. I screamed for my wife and son. I screamed their names until my lungs and throat burned. No one else was on the block but me. My neighbors were gone. There had been five families still living there. My legs were jelly. I couldn't breathe.

I walked up the path towards where the front door had been and noticed spent shell casings shining in the glow of the fires. There were boot prints in the soot. The military had been here. There was a pile of debris smoldering on the porch. As I got closer the smell of something I had only smelled in the horror of war filled my nose. Burning flesh. The pile of debris was my wife and son. They lay on the porch locked in an embrace. His smile was gone, replaced by a grimace of terror. I will never forget that face. It's seared into my mind.

What I did find at the house has driven my life ever since. A velcro patch had been in the debris. Just a simple round patch, muted red background, tan silhouette of a coiled snake ready to strike. A unit patch from a combat uniform.

I buried my wife and son in the front yard, under a tree that we'd all planted when my son was born. I said a prayer and then asked God to forgive me for what I was going to do next. I've been doing that since then. I will never let those soldiers destroy another family again. I still don't know why they did it. Why were they there in the first place? Why did they have to kill them? Those questions eat at me. Finding the answers is what keeps me going. But I know who did it and eventually they will give me my answers.

———————

Over the next few days Donte and I went about sharing the daily chores. Most of our time was spent providing for life. But we'd done two missions as well. Only surveillance. I shared my rules of engagement with him. One: shoot to disable not kill, unless I was threatened myself. Fortunately that hadn't happened yet. I could not reduce myself to their level. And I wanted answers from them. Two: shoot only when sure we have a soldier that's gone bad, like the two that had stopped Donte. Three: be smart.

I shared the story of my family with him. He understood the loss because of his mom. I understood his loss. It gave us a common thread. It was good to have a partner and confidante. I realized then just how much I missed caring about someone.

Chapter 5

Five days after I'd saved Donte, and his turning up saved me, we woke to another gray morning. The clouds looked swollen and bruised. The air smelled like rain. The wind was blowing hard and bending the trees.

"Morning," I said. "How'd you sleep?"

"Morning. Great."

"We need to redress your wound and probably pull the stitches today. Come over here and let me take a look at it." I peeled off the gauze I'd used to patch the wound. It was very red all around the area I'd stitched. I had washed the needle and the injured area with alcohol but it was clearly infected. The first aid kit I'd found in the house had no medicine in it. I gently poked the skin around the wound and Donte reflexively winced and pulled away. "It's closing but it's also infected. We're going to have to get some antibiotic on it. I think we'll have to head to the trading post today. We need a few other things anyway."

We got dressed and packed. I gave Donte a .22 semi-automatic and spent a few minutes going over how to use it. It had a full clip of ten rounds. Not very powerful, but reliable and at short range would do just fine. The kick wouldn't tear his skinny arm out of the socket either. The plan for the day was to make our way to the trading post at Topanga and Vanowen, which was a good four-mile hike from the house. It was set up inside the old Macy's store in the mall. I tried to take a different route each time I made my way over there. It might've been safer to take a known route each time but by going down new streets and searching some houses along the way I always seemed to find something useful. I'd been hoping to find a generator, even a small one, but those were scooped up fast in the early days after the riots.

I tried to avoid the trading post if at all possible. Too many people, too much risk, but a necessary evil. If it wasn't for Donte's arm I would've waited a few days but he needed the antibiotic. There were just certain things so in demand you couldn't scavenge them anymore and often the only place to find them was there. Finding batteries, medicines, and canned meats were like finding hundred dollar bills. They had great trade value. There were also those who had the means to pay off border guards and ran handsome smuggling businesses as well. I really didn't care if the stuff was legit or not. You need what you need. Legal or illegal, it really didn't matter to me anymore.

Donte needed some new clothes as well. I had changed into my "street" clothes. Just some jeans, a dark, long sleeve t-shirt and a zip up hooded sweat jacket. The jacket was a size too big for me so I could hide the bulge of the .44's under my arms. Donte was still wearing the bloody clothes that he had on when our paths first crossed. My clothes fell off him and we hadn't found anything that would fit his frame. We tried one of my extra shirts to wear but he looked like a little kid wearing his dad's shirt.

I packed a couple of day packs with water, some energy bars long past their expiration date but still edible, some space blankets, matches, rope, my field glasses, extra ammo for the guns and two towels. I always brought a towel. I remembered reading *The Hitchhikers Guide to the Galaxy* many years before which shared the idea that a towel was the most important thing a traveler could have. It could be used as a pillow, blanket, jacket, torn into strips to make bandages, a rope, a basket or even just a towel. The book was right. Towels were damn helpful to have around.

The day after I asked Donte to stay I'd shown him my security system. "I need to show you the security measures in the house," I'd said. "If for some reason we get separated come back here but don't forget the trip wires. Some just make noise. There is one wire inside both the front and back doors. The wire will pull down a bucket full of cans. Makes a helluva noise. If someone comes in while we're asleep we'll know. I also set one in the hallway leading to the stairs. That one's wired to a spring-loaded bar with spikes on it. Trip the wire and the bar will swing out about thigh high and drive six-inch spikes into the intruder's legs. Top of the stairs is another that causes a bar to fall about chest high. Same six-inch spikes. The spiked ones get set every night when I come up here. The door ones are monofilament, I just leave them all the time. You just need to know where they are."

Donte's face had been twisted in confusion. "Who the hell are you, man?" He'd shaken his head in disbelief.

"I've learned a few things about staying alive over the years."

"Ya think," he'd said sarcastically. It was hard to believe that we had met only five days before. Donte and I had become old friends very quickly. I enjoyed his dark sense of humor and I think he enjoyed having an older man to teach him things. One of those things was my love for magic.

In those short five days I had begun to teach him some of the slight of hand tricks I had learned over the years. Ever since I was a small child I had a fascination with magic and specifically slight of hand. I liked the big stage tricks but found the close up stuff amazing. I think I took a liking to the slight of hand magic because it took dedication and patience. It built those skills. I had taught myself quite a bit over the years and was now enjoying having someone to teach it to. Donte proved to be a good student. He had nimble fingers, which made performing many of the tricks easier. Sharing the magic helped to pass the time and to build our bond. I had made him take the magician's oath not to share the secrets with anyone and that seemed to create a special bond between us.

In the gray morning we made sure the security measures were set on the way out the door and we headed down the street toward the trading post.

Chapter 6

We'd been on the side street about an hour, picking our way from house to house looking for supplies and making progress towards the trading post. We came to a block I'd never been down before. The first house on the right was a typical two story and looked to be in good condition. The door had a big red "X" spray-painted on it. Donte and I looked at each other knowing that there had been one or more bodies found in there right after the riots.

"I ain't goin' in that one," Donte said.

"This may sound kind of crappy but those houses are likely to have more leftovers in them. Most people won't go in those. Makes them uncomfortable, just like you. The owners don't need it anymore either." I was trying to calm Donte's unease about going in the house with some gallows humor. Donte looked genuinely appalled at my lack of sympathy. "Sorry, that was kind of morose," I said with a shrug of my shoulders.

"All right. If you say so, man. But if we see a ghost in there I'm gonna kick your ass." Donte raised his fists in mock combat. The sight of the skinny kid just made me laugh.

The front door was closed but not locked. It was funny, before the riots almost every door you came to was locked. Now it was just the opposite. The house was still intact but didn't look like anyone had squatted there. I still had a code of ethics and didn't want to take from anyone who was still using the stuff. If the house was truly unoccupied then all's fair but only take what you need, leave some for the next guy. I called out, "Anyone here" several times but got no answer.

26

We checked the kitchen and came away with some canned goods. No swelling in the cans. I found two disposable lighters in a drawer. There was a door off the kitchen that led into the garage. As we entered the garage we heard the sound of a vehicle turn the corner onto the street. The sound told me it was moving slowly. I had a bad feeling that it was going to stop and it did. We ran to the front of the house and carefully peered out a front window. At the curb two soldiers were climbing out of a Humvee. They were grunts. We quietly watched as they walked down the middle of the street, one on each curb, M-4 Carbines at the ready.

"Standard security sweep. Usually done two by two. They must be short-handed. They're going to start checking these houses. I don't want to be here when they do. We're going out the back. There's an alley behind the house. Should be a gate out there. We'll go out and go opposite the direction they're walking in," I whispered. I slid open the patio door and we dashed across the yard to the back gate. I drew one of my pistols and cocked it. The latch for the gate was near the top and I quietly reached up and slid the catch open. It made a small grinding sound that made me wince. I waited ten seconds, not breathing, hoping no one was on the other side of the fence to hear the sound. I opened the gate just enough to see both directions into the alley. It was clear. We moved through the gate and turned right. I wanted to get out of there as quickly as possible. Being in the alley was dangerous. If a soldier suddenly stepped into the opening at the end our only option would be to shoot our way out. The soldier's Carbines would seriously outmatch our pistols.

I breathed a sigh of relief when we came to the intersection of the street. I carefully checked both directions and didn't see either of the men. We moved to the corner of the house and I looked back up the street the direction the soldiers had gone. They were coming back a few houses down from the parked Hummer facing our way.

"They're down the street a bit. If they get back in the truck we're okay. If they go past we could be in trouble. There's no cover here," I whispered right in Donte's ear. "Pull your pistol and take the safety off. Don't do anything unless I tell you to but be ready, okay?"

He shook his head nervously. I could hear the crunch of the soldiers' boots on the pavement. I resisted the urge to peek out, afraid that any slight movement might alert them to us. I heard them stop, the click and creak of the doors opening and the engine start. I let out a breath, waited to hear the wheels make the tell tale sounds of movement before I glanced out to make sure that it was clear. It was.

"I think I crapped myself," said Donte and he gave a nervous chuckle.

"You and me both. That was too close. Let's get moving."

We walked a few minutes listening for the sound of the Hummer but it was gone. The neighborhood we were in was typical for the Valley; long bisecting streets running parallel with shorter streets every block. By the third block down we were at ease, making good time. Maybe it was the letdown from the tense moment but we got sloppy and walked right into the intersection without noticing the Humvee parked two houses down.

I was alerted to it being there by the sound of the doors opening.

"Freeze you two," came the shout from one of the soldiers. I looked over and saw they had left the Carbines in the Hummer.

"Run!" I shouted, and we started sprinting down the street. "When we get to the next block split. You go left, I'll go right. I'll meet you at the car wash behind the old Shell station at the corner of Vanowen and Topanga, opposite the trading post. Stick to backyards for a few blocks, run some more then duck to backyards again. Keep that up until you get to the meeting spot. Listen for the trucks. Be careful." I heard the Hummer start up and the tires squeal right as we got to the corner. "Go!" I yelled, and we split.

Chapter 7

I made it to the Shell station without encountering the soldiers, hoping that Donte had beaten me there. I was surprised that I hadn't heard the helicopter. My guess was that the two grunts hadn't figured out who we were, and just assumed we were the typical garden-variety scroungers who didn't want to be hassled. At least that's what I hoped. It was likely that even if they did recognize us they wouldn't want to get blamed for losing us so it was just better to forget the whole thing. They'd keep their eyes out but once we split I guessed neither one of the soldiers had the desire to run after us on foot alone. Of course, they might've both gone after Donte.

The gas station itself had been stripped clean long ago. Behind it was a shed that housed the automatic car wash that you could pay for when you bought your gas. I drew a pistol and peered into the tunnel to see if there was anyone else in there. It was empty, which meant that Donte hadn't made it yet. It smelled of urine and old motor oil. The giant arch covered in brushes stood in the end of the tunnel. There were several blue barrels that used to hold the soaps and waxes, now long dried up, lining the far wall. I carefully swept through to the far side to make sure it was clear. From that end I had a clear view of the approach to the trading post. It was set up just inside the north entrance to Macy's. The mall had been one of the first places the looters and rioters had cleaned out when they had rolled through this end of the valley but they hadn't burned it.

I pulled the field glasses from my pack and scanned the parking lot and entrance. I saw no sign of military patrols out front and they rarely went inside. It posed too much of a strategic disadvantage. No military vehicles were parked in the lot either. It would be a bit dicey covering the distance across the open parking lot from the station to the door. We'd be exposed with little cover for several hundred yards. A few discarded cars littered the lot but they were spaced far too far apart to be useful cover. Trees were set in diamond shaped planters every ten spaces but they weren't much thicker than saplings and most were broken and dead. Hip high dried weeds filled the remainder of the planters, but not thick enough to provide any cover. They wouldn't even hide Donte. I was amused at the thought of the rail-thin kid trying to hide behind one of those trees and almost be able to. I returned my thoughts to the parking lot. In our favor, you could hear a vehicle coming for miles since there was no traffic so we'd have plenty of warning to start running. I just didn't want to call attention to ourselves by doing so. "Where was Donte?" I wondered again.

The sky had turned a nasty grey color. The thick clouds had boiled in from offshore and a cold wind had come with them. The air smelled wet, like the rain was just behind the wind. The rain would help hide us if it came but would make for a lousy hike home. The soldiers tended to stop patrolling in the rain. I checked my watch and it was a few minutes after noon, already three hours after we'd left the safe house just four miles away.

I was worried about Donte. I'd been sitting there for twenty minutes. He should've arrived by now. I shook my head. It had been a long time since I'd worried about anyone. It was an odd feeling. I'd been alone for so long I had almost let myself forget what it was like to care enough to worry. I found myself both happy and sad at the concern. I knew that worrying about someone would probably lead to more hurt but at the same time that part of me that was still human needed to care. I soaked in the feeling and I began to really worry. At that moment I heard footsteps outside the shed. They were heading for the far end. I drew my pistol and aimed at the floor just inside the far end. I could bring the barrel up quickly and drop the intruder. Donte came around the corner and I relaxed. I breathed a sigh of relief. I holstered the pistol and motioned for him to join me at the other end. His face lit up when he saw me. When he reached me we hugged. No thought or hesitation, we just did. Like a father greeting a son he hadn't seen in years. It was nice. Donte and I had shared an event that day, which created a deeper bond between us. We knew we could trust and count on each other. It was something we both desperately needed. It was something we realized we both craved after years of solitude. We said nothing for a long moment. Finally I said, "You okay?"

"Never better," he replied.

Chapter 8

Heavy rain had begun to fall in big, fat drops   I was glad for the rain, which would likely keep the patrols off the street. The drawback was that it would be harder to hear a vehicle approach, and we were starting to get cold. An icy wind had come with the rain.

"You ready?" I asked Donte.

"You think we should still go in the trading post?"

"Here's what I think. If those two had really wanted to find us they would've called in the copters. My guess is they felt it was safer to give a look around hoping we'd blunder back into their sight but they didn't want to explain how they lost us in the first place. Besides you need those antibiotics." I patted his shoulder trying to calm Donte down and trying to convince myself at the same time.

"If you say so. I'm still shaky though."

"Me too. If we get moving and refocus we'll be fine. We'll stick to the buildings along this side of Topanga. Hug close to the walls, duck in and out of the recesses until we're directly across from the entrance to the trading post. That way we spend less time out in the open parking lot. We can cross next to the parking structure. It's not much cover but it's better than the open lot on the north. Wait for me to vacate one recess and move to another then you move up and fill the one I just left. Understand?"

He nodded his head and we moved out. It was only about a quarter of mile down the street to the spot where we would cross but it seemed like it was ten miles. I was concerned that I couldn't hear anything

33

over the pounding rain. The rain sounded like vehicle engines.

Donte made a good soldier and followed directions perfectly so neither of us was exposed for more than a few seconds at a time. I motioned Donte up to join me in the recess I was standing in. There was one lone guy approaching the entrance to the trading post from the opposite side of the parking lot and one couple walking north toward the high school across the street from the mall. I waved for Donte and we quickly crossed the lot against the wall of the parking structure to the entrance. The curtain of rain soaked us but also helped shield us from view.

As we entered the trading post I felt a weight of sadness fall over me. I was glad we had made it and the warmth was welcomed but entering the old Macy's department store and seeing the sorry state it had become and the hopeless mass of people milling about like ghosts was a lot to handle. Entering someplace that I used to frequent before the riots made me sad, especially a place that I used to go with my wife and son. It made me miss the old world.

We paused just inside the entrance to scan the crowd, make sure it was safe to stay and to let the rain drain off our clothes. My jacket was soaked through and I could feel the rain running off of my head and down my back.

It was warm inside. Several dozen "merchants" had set up shop on the first floor using the old display tables or counters as their shops. Everything was sold on trade and I'd brought several items in my pack that I felt might fetch us the supplies we needed. I searched the merchants for the one guy everyone called "the pharmacist." I don't know if he really had been a pharmacist but he was the one guy who seemed to have medicine. I'd cut my hand half a year ago and he'd had some topical anti-septic, which took care of the infection that had set in. I'd used that up but hoped he still had more.

Sometimes the soldiers would set up outside, in the parking lot, and distribute some basic supplies. For several months after the riots this had been a regular occurrence but now it was pretty rare. They passed the stuff out every now and then just to keep the peace. Fortunately today they weren't there.

Less people were milling about than usual, maybe two hundred or so. There was usually twice that. The mall had become home to many people who needed the comfort of others to get them through. A few of the faces were familiar to me as regulars. The place smelled of humanity. Being on my own for so long I sometimes forget how much people stink, especially when they don't shower often. Water still ran in some places but hot water was a luxury long forgotten.

I glanced over to Donte and he looked stunned. "You okay?" I asked.

"Yeah," he whispered. "I just haven't seen this many people in a long time. Makes me nervous now."

"You haven't been in here?" I asked.

"Naw, never needed nothin' from here. Seemed unnecessary."

"All right. Let's get what we need and get back. Number one priority is the antiseptic. Number two priority is the small propane canisters that fit the camp stove. I just can't get used to eating cold things that should be hot. I guess I'll need to someday but until then it's worth the effort to trade for them. I'd also like to find you some boots. Those sneakers have seen better days. Plus if you step on a nail I doubt I we could find penicillin to fight off an infection. The topical will take care of that surface wound you've got but it won't do much for a puncture. I'd like to find you something with a hard sole. What size do you wear?" He shrugged his shoulders. "That's OK. Chances are we won't find anything but if we do we'll just try them on. Next we need clothes for you. Batteries are the last item on the list."

As we began to make our way through the trading post I started to feel a sense of unease. I'd had it before. Maybe the experience of combat brings out that sense in people. The shopkeepers kept their eyes on us for too long. They paid us more attention than the other shoppers.

I found the "pharmacist" about two thirds of the way down the first aisle. He was an odd looking Asian man, remarkably small even by Asian standards. He had wild salt and pepper hair that stuck out all over his head like little wires that made him look like Albert Einstein. He moved like a little rodent, sort of hunched over and in quick choppy movements. It was a strange ballet to watch. He finished helping the woman at the counter and came to us next, looked up, started to say something, hesitated for just a second and looked nervously around the store.

Finally he returned his gaze and asked in a hoarse, shaky voice, "What you want?"

"Antiseptic. My friend has a cut that's infected."

He looked around the store again, straining to see over the tops of the counters to look at the far side of the store. I leaned my 6"2" frame over him and looked down and asked, "Is there a problem?"

36

His eyes moved quickly up and down, then he moved with his choppy little walk over to a stack of boxes. He rooted around and came back with a tube of Neosporin.

"What do you want for it?" I asked.

"You just take. I don't want no trouble."

"Why do you think I would give you trouble?"

"You just take. Okay? No trouble. Okay?" he said almost in a panic.

"All right, If you insist." His behavior had me worried. I wanted to leave right then and looked around for Donte so we could go.

Donte was standing at the tables at the next "shop" and as I turned to head over to him I felt a hand on my left shoulder. I reached into the pocket of my jacket and wrapped my hand around the grip of the .44 and put my index finger on the outside of the trigger guard.

"You don't need the gun for me. I'm a friend. You need to get out...now," the voice said in a non-threatening tone.

I slowly turned to face the voice, which belonged to a man about sixty. I looked to his free hand to make sure he wasn't armed and his hand was empty. He showed me his palm to prove it. I then looked up at his face. He had kind eyes, the kind of eyes that seem to be laughing even when he wasn't. Perhaps it was the deep crow's feet that gave him that appearance. He was big but not fat, just kind of thick. Perched at the base of his forehead were a pair of bushy grey eyebrows that went in a hundred different directions. They looked like two old caterpillars parked there. Along his jaw line was a closely cut salt and pepper beard. If he had let the beard grow out he would've made an excellent

Santa Claus. He had on a U.S.M.C. hat and a heavy navy pea jacket.

"Two soldiers dressed in plain clothes walking around in here. Have been all morning. Looking for you two. They're up by the front now. Follow me. I'll take you out the back. They passed these out this morning to all the merchants and they posted them on the entrance. I'm surprised you didn't see it when you came in."

He held out a reward poster. There was a grainy picture of me from the shooting yesterday, obviously taken from the camera on the Hummer. My face wasn't clear. Next to my picture was a clearer picture of Donte. Below the images was a caption in large bold lettering: *Wanted for Attempted Murder. Reward for information leading to capture. Contact any US Army personnel to report.* There were brief descriptions of both Donte and I following the caption.

"Name's Alan Nash," he said as he held out a big meaty hand to shake.

I shook his hand but didn't reply with my name. I was still sizing him up. "Pleasure. How do you know they're soldiers?"

"I was one myself. I know." I gave him a questioning look. "Okay. Okay. Hair's too short, clothes too nice, but mostly the combat boots."

I nodded at the last comment. I was also impressed by his observational skills.

"We've got to move now. They see a white dude with a black kid they'll stop you for sure. You are this guy, right?"

"Not necessarily, " I answered quickly, "but I don't really feel like being hassled so show us the way. By the way, I'm still holding the gun if you're trying to pull some shit with us."

He ignored the comment, leading me to believe he was legit, started off and waved for me to follow. I tapped Donte on the back as I went by and motioned for him to follow as well. He looked puzzled.

Alan picked through the crowd like a man half his size and half his age. He moved with a confidence that only comes from surviving combat. I liked him immediately.

We snaked our way through the back of the ruined department store. I could clearly see the destruction that both the rioters and then the squatters had brought to the store. We entered the mall on the second floor. We paused just outside the Macy's entrance and I filled Donte in on what was happening. Even though we'd come out on the first floor of Macy's we were on the second floor of the mall. The first floor shops were below ground. As we made our way down the frozen escalator I could see into many of the former stores at this end. Each had become housing for multiple people. Blankets littered the floors. Small fires burned in metal barrels. The smell of smoke, rotting trash and too many people filled my nose and almost made me gag. I looked back over my shoulder to see what Donte's reaction was and over his shoulder, stepping out of Macy's, were two men. I knew immediately that these were the two soldiers that Alan had seen.

"Alan," I called quietly. "Bogeys at 2:00. Are those the guys?"

"Yes. Let's not panic. Let's see how they play this."

"That them?" Donte asked.

"Yep, soldiers'" I replied. "Pull your hood over your head." I whispered. I knew I was fairly unrecognizable.

39

My face had been very blurred on the wanted poster. They might not see Donte's face from this distance but they would be very curious about a big white guy moving with a tall, skinny black kid. I was hoping that they wouldn't put two and two together. They did almost immediately.

A deep authoritative voice boomed across the large open space of the mall, "You three hold it, military authority!"

We quickly glanced at each other and without saying a word took off running. The sound of our shoes pounding the marble echoed off the walls. Alan led the way and was surprisingly fast for his age. I was next in our little parade and Donte followed. I could hear the footsteps of the soldiers clanging down the escalator and knew we only had a few seconds to change course. The mall was shaped like a figure eight. Two parallel sections ran the length of the big building. They were joined at the ends and the middle by perpendicular corridors. We reached the intersection of the middle corridor and turned left. The corner was square, not angled off like corner stores sometimes are and I knew the soldiers wouldn't want to tear around that blind angle. They would approach slowly and cautiously. I took a position across the hallway and down one storefront. I was in a shooter's position, down on one knee, just inside the entrance to a former shoe store. Donte and Alan continued running down the corridor.

"Go, I'll meet up with you two where we met up earlier today," I yelled to Donte. I knew he would know to find his way to the car wash again.

I could hear Donte and Alan's footsteps receding as I kept my attention on the corner I thought the soldiers would approach. My heart was pounding. I drew one

of the .44's and leveled it chest high at the corner. I
listened for the pair approaching but they didn't come.
I sat motionless, waiting for the two soldiers to peek
around the corner. They should've been there by now.
I waited one more minute until I heard gunfire behind
me. The huge plate glass window on the other side of
the doorway shattered into a thousand tiny pieces. I
instinctively dropped, rolled and returned fire. A
second shot came from across the hall two doorways
down. I was pinned. There was nowhere to go
forward so I retreated into the store hoping the soldier
would follow and put himself in a vulnerable position.
Then I heard gunfire coming from somewhere farther
away in the mall. A distant popping sound. The
unmistakable sound of a gun battle. The soldiers had
doubled back and split up. The gunshots continued in
the distance. Faint screams drifted down to me. I
hoped it was the noncombatants fearing for their lives
and not Donte and Alan.

I backed into the storeroom at the far end of the
store. I assumed there was a rear exit for deliveries or
employees to use. The storeroom was small, only about
fifteen by fifteen feet. Shredded shoeboxes were
everywhere. All the shoes were gone. Empty shelves
lined the walls.

I heard the sound of crunching glass. I found the
rear door, tried the knob and found it unlocked. If I
went into the access hall outside the exit door it might
be five or six feet wide at best with no cover and I
could never make it to the end of the hall before the
soldier joined me there. I would be a sitting duck. I
needed to solve this problem here. The room was
small and I needed to draw the soldier into the room if
I was going to get out. Otherwise he would wait me

out, call for help and I would be trapped. I quickly looked around. There were storage shelves just inside the door on the side it opened on. It would be the last place the soldier's eyes would scan to. I opened the rear door, swung it all the way open. I ran for the shelf and climbed onto it, laid flat, brought my pistol to bear, as the automatic closer swung the door. I watched it swing slowly, heard my heart pounding in my ears and heard it make a bang and a click as it closed. The soldier began running, assuming I had gone out the back and made the classic mistake of not clearing the room before entering.

I yelled, "freeze" as he got to the door. He stopped for a moment then swung around and began to raise his gun. I doubt he even knew what hit him. The sound of the .44 was deafening in the small room. My shot hit the soldier square in the chest leaving a nice clean entry wound. The soldier's insides exploded out his back in a spray of tissue, bone and blood showering the door and wall. He dropped in slow motion, dead long before he hit the floor. Smoke from the pistol hung head high and the room smelled of cordite and gore. He wasn't the first man I've had to kill but I still felt a twinge of guilt. Bottom line was: it was him or me, and I chose me. I picked up his radio and his M9 Beretta, slipped them in my backpack and went out the front.

I slid out into the mall corridor listening for sounds of conflict, footsteps, shots, or even screaming with my .44 leading the way. It was quiet. Too quiet. I worked my way from entryway to entryway, in the direction that Donte and Alan had gone, stopping at each to listen. I got to the next intersection and carefully looked around the corner in the direction I had heard the shots earlier. Someone was whimpering farther down the corridor. I moved rapidly down the hallway crisscrossing from side to side and checking in each window. The second floor overhang concerned me and I scanned it as I moved from side to side. The center section of the upper floor was open to allow the light from the skylights to the bottom and from the cantilevered walkways above you could look down and see most of the lower floor that I was on. Fortunately, the front rails of the upper walkways were glass so I could see if someone moved against them to look down or fire down on me. As I got toward the end I could smell the distinct odor of gunfire. A faint haze of smoke still hung in the air. Glass was shattered in several of the large windows. Behind one of them a woman was seated on the floor, crying and cradling a man in her arms. His shirt was filled with blood. It was clearly not Donte or Alan.

One store down, lying in the opening to a Gap store was the backpack Donte had been carrying. For the first time I felt real concern. I knew he wouldn't have left the backpack without good cause. I looked into the store cautiously, wondering if the soldier had lain the backpack there as a trap. It was dark inside. The natural light from the skylights didn't reach very far into the store. I paused behind a pile of discarded boxes to let my eyes adjust to the dim light. I held my breath and listened carefully. I heard the faintest rustling sound coming from the counter at the back of the store. It might've been nothing. I waited a minute more straining to hear. Then it came again. There was definitely someone there. I decided to wait them out. If they were setting a trap they would get impatient first. It only took about ten minutes when I heard shuffling. My eyes had adjusted well and between the boxes I could see the outline of someone glancing over

43

the counter. He began to step toward the opening at the far side. Finally he stood and slowly maneuvered toward the opening. I could've dropped him right then but I wanted to make sure he wasn't a friendly or non-combatant. If it was the soldier I wanted him alive. I needed to find out what happened to Donte. I held my breath and stayed perfectly still. I was in a position to leap as he passed by but I would only have a brief moment of surprise. I needed to time my assault perfectly.

At the precise moment I sprang from behind the boxes and in one action wrapped my left arm around his neck and crashed my right arm down on his right arm. He yelped. We went down in a heap with me on top. He let out a grunt as he hit the floor. He was stunned for a moment and I rolled him over to see his face and secure my position on top of him. I lined up a right hook just to seal the deal and stopped the punch inches from Alan's jaw. He let out a gasp and whispered, "Stop."

I helped him to his feet. He was clearly shaken and the adrenaline was still coursing through my veins.

"Are you okay?" I asked.

"Yeah I think so but my ribs are going to hurt like hell tomorrow. I'd hate to see what would've happened if you hadn't stopped that punch."

"I'm sorry. I thought they were lying in wait for us. What happened? Where's Donte?"

"We had a gun battle with one of the soldiers. He came up behind us. He must've doubled back."

"My guy did that too."

"What happened to him?" he asked.

"You don't want to know. Needless to say we don't need to worry about him anymore. So, go on. What happened on this end?"

"We got split up when the soldier came up behind us. I dove in here and the boy ran into the store across the way. I dove behind the counter and just listened. His name is Donte?"

"Yes," I replied.

"By the way you still haven't told me your name."

I figured after what we just went through it was safe enough to share with him. "Ethan Ryder. Pleased to meet you." I reached out and we shook hands. "So what happened to Donte?"

"Donte fired off a few shots but never hit the soldier. The soldier left me and went in after him. I heard one more shot. Then there was the sound of a scuffle, stuff getting banged around, knocked over, you know? Then it was quiet. I waited ten minutes or so until I didn't hear anything, or so I thought, and decided to see if it was clear. Then you tackled me."

"I need to go see if anyone is still in there. Do you have a gun?"

"No, I wish I had. We'd have two dead soldiers now," he said.

I swung the pack off my back and pulled out the Beretta I'd taken off the other soldier, popped out the magazine, checked how many bullets were left, re-racked the cartridge and handed the gun to Alan. "Back me up."

I checked the corridor in both directions and saw it was clear. I motioned for Alan to go to the right and I went to the left. We ran across and flattened against the windows of the stores on either side of the one Donte had gone into. I slid around the edge of the door opening. This store was brighter than the Gap store across the way. The sunlight from the skylights managed to penetrate most of the way into the store. This store was almost clear of debris. There was trash littering the floor but no racks or movable shelves to use for cover. The cashier counter ran the length of the store and it was clear that no one was behind it. I was getting a very bad feeling about this and I knew I wasn't going to like the way this was going. There were three ways this could end up and two were bad; either Donte was fine, hurt or dead. I pulled the flashlight out of my pack and flipped on the switch. I swung open the door to the storeroom, moved the beam of light around the room and quickly realized there was a fourth option. The room was empty. No Donte, no soldier.

"Alan it's clear. Come on." I continued to swing the beam of light around the room hoping to find some clue. I saw it just as Alan entered the room. "They've got him," I said quietly. I moved across the room and checked the service hallway, but I already knew there was no one there.

"How do you know?" Alan asked.

"No blood on the floor, and if he'd been shot the soldier would still be here waiting for backup. And obviously he's not here and there is no dead soldier." I swung the light into the corner and the .22 I'd given Donte was lying on the floor. I walked over and picked it up, pulled the clip and confirmed that most of the bullets were still there. "If Donte had run he would've taken the backpack. I'm sure of it. It's still sitting out front. And he certainly wouldn't have left the gun. They've got him. They'll be back for me. We need to get out of here. Now"

"We can go to my place. It's not too far. Then we can figure out our next move"

"Our?"

"Hell yes, a Marine never walks away from a fight."

Chapter 9

We made it out of the mall, across the south parking lot and up the street to the gas station carwash without incident. It was unlikely that Donte would show but I had told him that was where we would meet if we got separated. The evidence was fairly clear that the soldiers had captured him. We waited for over an hour. I made the decision to leave before it was too late and the area was crawling with soldiers. We snaked our way down about a mile of side streets on the way to Alan's house. It rained on and off and by the time we came to Alan's street we were both soaked and shivering.

Alan's house was halfway down the side street on the west side. The front yard was walled off at the sidewalk by a thick juniper hedge, twenty feet tall, so thick you couldn't see through it. Set in the middle of the wall of bushes was a wrought iron gate. Attached to the middle of the gate was a hand lettered sign warning potential intruders of an electrified fence. Alan approached the gate and placed a key into a metal box set into a recess in the junipers. He turned the key.

"That shuts off the electricity," he said.

"I thought the sign was for effect. You really have an electrified fence?"

"Hell yes. Nobody's coming in here without a fight. I'll show you when we get in the yard."

He unlocked the lock in the gate and we stepped into complete order and neatness. The yard was immaculate. Every bush was trimmed into either a perfect cube or perfect sphere. There wasn't a leaf on the ground or a weed in a planter. The lawn was perfect. Nothing I'd seen since the riots looked like this. My first thought was how he was able to water it.

Before I could ask, my eyes made it to the backside of the juniper hedges. A fifteen-foot chain link fence surrounded the entire property. It ran the length of the front yard and down both sides. I had to assume it went all the way around the back. The top was ringed in razor wire.

"Is this whole fence actually electrified?" I was stunned. I thought my security was great. This was a fortification.

"Yep. There are deep cell marine batteries wired into the electrification system every 25 feet around the perimeter. It can be turned on and off at the gate and inside. The batteries are recharged by solar panels and two wind generators in the back. I built those from scratch. I have another dozen batteries in the back of the house that are wired into a converter and patched into the house wiring. I can run lights and small appliances with no trouble. I also have a 6500-watt generator in the back for special occasions. I can use my air conditioner in the summer." He grinned at that last statement.

"Holy shit. You did all this work yourself?" I was amazed.

"Yeah. There are chain link fences all over the city and they simply bolt together. I just disassembled the parts and brought them back here and built the perimeter fence. I had installed the battery system, solar panels and wind generators before the riots because I was sick of the sons o' bitches at the DWP ripping me off. I wanted to be self-sufficient."

We went inside and Alan used the key to turn the fence back on again. The inside of the house was as immaculate as the outside. Alan obviously kept himself busy.

"You want something to drink," he offered.

"Coffee would be great if you have it."

He wandered off to another room and left me in the living room. I looked around like I was on a social call. Alan had pictures of himself as a young man in his Marine combat uniform posing at this place and that place somewhere in Southeast Asia. By his age I guessed he'd served in Vietnam. He had several frames with various medals and ribbons.

He wandered back into the den with two cups of coffee and saw me admiring the pictures. "Two tours in 'Nam. Marine. Hoo rah. Spent the last four months in a gook prison camp. You're military but not Marine. I can always tell a fellow Marine. Like it changes you. Army right?"

"Special Forces." At that moment something dawned on me. Why was this guy helping me? He was military all the way. I slipped my hand into my pocket and wrapped my hand around the grip of the .44. "Alan. I have a couple of questions and I hope I'm going to like the answers. Why are you helping me? You've got a lot to lose here. You're military all the way and you're helping someone accused by the army of attempted murder. I need to know why."

"First, I don't have as much to lose as you think. Fences work both ways. They keep people out but they also keep me in most of the time. For a guy who spent four months in a prison camp in Nam being inside a fence is not the ideal place to be. Second, those assholes riding around in those uniforms are not military. We had a code of honor, as you did. These guys are thieves and murderers. Anyone who still lives in this area knows it. Third, your reputation is becoming legendary."

50

I was shocked by this news. "Legendary?"

"Yes. People see you as a defender and an avenger. Hell, it makes sense that you are Special Forces. The Special Forces motto is 'De oppresso liber", to free the oppressed. Isn't that what you're doing?"

"Not really. I wish I was that noble." I sat down on the sofa and Alan took a seat in a big armchair on the other side of the coffee table. I shared the story of what happened to my family with him. I watched his reactions carefully. I was looking for any sign that he wasn't what he said. When I was done with the story he looked down at the floor for a minute, slowly shaking his head. We didn't speak for a few minutes.

He raised his head slowly, looked me straight in the eye and said, "You've got this Marine on your side. Let's bring them a war."

"First things first. I need to find out if Donte got away or if they took him. Tonight I want to go to my safe house and see if he's there. I figure if he got to the carwash after we left he'd go back there. It's a risk because if they did capture him they might get him to compromise the location of the house. I want to approach carefully and see who's there. I also need to get some of my supplies. That's the first step."

"I'm going with you," he said emphatically.

"No you're not. This is a one-man operation. You need to stay here so we have a place to come back to. I have to be able to move quickly and quietly."

"Can't blame me for trying."

"No I can't."

It was four hours until nightfall. Alan cooked a late lunch of canned chili on his electric stove. I was amazed by his ingenuity. We ate lunch quietly. Near the end of the meal Alan asked about my service time.

I'd never really told the whole story to anyone. My wife lived the story with me so there'd been no need to tell her the whole thing, and honestly I don't think I wanted to share all the details with her. She didn't need to share the nightmares.

I'd enlisted in the Army right out of high school and she was my high school sweetheart. We got married right before I left for boot camp. I was just a smart-ass teenager who thought I was invincible. I joined the Army because my parents had been pacifists and I knew joining the Army would really piss them off. Alan laughed at that. I completed basic training and I turned out to be a good soldier with a knack for shooting long range. I'd received an expert badge in rifle during basic and I was recommended for Q course, the Special Forces training program and I was shipped out to Fort Bragg, North Carolina. I actually breezed through the first phase, Individual Skills. Because of my ability with the rifle my second phase of training, MOS Training as a Weapons Specialist went easily as well and I eventually became our group's Weapons Sergeant. Collective training went well too. The fourth phase, Language Training was a bitch. They wanted me to learn Arabic, for obvious reasons, and my brain just didn't work that way. That was how I became friends with James Stark. He was in our group. Smartest guy I'd met in the army, maybe too smart. He helped me through the language part. Tutored me. He struggled some with the soldiering stuff. He was physically smaller than most of the guys, just 5'8", so I helped him as much as I could with that. He was tough as nails though. I think he tried harder than everyone else because of his size. He saved my ass in the language portion. If it weren't for him I would never have passed. We had a good partnership.

The final phase of Survival and Evasion was a breeze. I came out near the top in my class, would've been tops if not for the language part.

My Operational Detachment was also tops for our course so we were immediately sent to Afghanistan. My wife and son moved in with her mom here in the valley when I shipped out. My OD was a great group of guys. A twelve-man team. We were brothers. Things were good; as good as they could be in Afghanistan. Because of the stressful nature of our assignments we rotated out every three months for R&R. I'd get to spend a week with my wife every three months. It was rough on her but my wife understood. Or at least she was good at pretending. It was on leave at the end of my first tour that my wife became pregnant.

My OD was the team that was called to do the tough jobs and we always came through. We were the guys in our company who were asked to dig a tick out. Recon would find a Taliban group hunkered down inside a civilian population or some well fortified location and we'd be the guys sent to get them out. We were good, too. We'd had twenty-seven serious incursions and had only one loss and one injury. Our group was fearless and smart. Stark was good at figuring out approaches. He had been designated as our group's 18F, Assistant Operations and Intelligence Sergeant. He had a knack for finding the best point of attack against our target. I guess that's why the guys tolerated him because when it came to execution of the plan he seemed to shrink back when we had direct confrontation. He would find a safe spot and make little effort to move forward. It wasn't really an overt thing. He just didn't seem to have the balls we had. It rubbed some of the guys the wrong way. That and Stark had become increasingly arrogant about his smarts. He just had a way of getting under people's skin. He hadn't known it at the time but I saved him from a beating on more than one occasion. It was right around the start of my second tour when things started to really go bad.

The grandfather clock in Alan's hallway chimed us back to the present and told us it was 6:00. The rest of the story would have to wait until I got back. I refilled my water and put my pack on my back. Alan turned off the electricity to the fence and walked me to the gate.

"Good luck. I'll see you soon," he said.

"Thanks. I'll be back before sunup. I appreciate all your help and hospitality." It felt like a goodbye rather than a see-you-later. We shook hands. Alan still had the grip of a man half his age.

"Good, you've still got to finish your story. You make sure you get back here to tell me."

I nodded to him and walked out the gate. I had no idea if I'd ever see him again. I sure hoped so.

Chapter 10

People who live in the city forget how dark the night really is when there are no electric lights burning. It was dark enough that you couldn't see your hand on the end of an extended arm. There wasn't even a moon out to give a hint of light. It was almost palpable. This kind of dark panics most people but I was very comfortable in it. It was my element.

One of the challenges given to every Special Forces candidate at Q-Course is a nighttime drop and return test. They took us out to an unknown and unfamiliar location in the back of a truck with no windows and dropped us separately. We were given no special equipment either. No flashlights, no night vision goggles, not even an old fashioned compass. We were tagged in case we got lost but that was for search and rescue, not us. Then we had to find our way home before morning. We were given all night to return to base from 5 miles away. I was back to base in an hour and a half and was asleep in my bunk before anyone else in my team made it back. The CO even had me patted down to make sure I hadn't cheated and brought a GPS with me. I got my nickname that night. The guys all called me Batman after that. It seemed kind of cool at the time. Stark had been the second guy back. The guys called him Robin after that because we always hung around together, and it was also kind of a backhanded insult to his size. He never seemed to mind though. At least I thought so at the time.

Tonight, I only had to make it about three miles from Alan's to my safe house and the roads and sidewalks were much easier to navigate than the forest so I made great time, and was at my street in under an hour. Getting to the house from this point was going to take some time. If the soldiers were waiting they certainly had night vision goggles working in their favor. I had thought this through when I was securing the house and knew that anyone watching the house would have the front and rear approaches covered. I had created a pathway through the side yards of the four houses in a row adjacent to the side of mine. I could enter one yard from the side, work my way around the backyards and go through an opening at the base of each fence until I reached the safe house. I built it as an escape route but tonight it would be a mode of entry. Unless they posted a sentry in the side yard or they were in the house I could get in and out without alerting anyone. It was likely that they would only post watch on the alley out back and the street out front. As dark as it was I would have to almost walk up on them to find out they were there and I preferred not do that. I didn't even know if they would be there. I had no idea if Donte would crack but I had to assume he would. I knew what these guys could do to get information. I hoped that he had given up the information easily and had not tried to be a hero. It would save him a lot of pain. They would get the information they wanted no matter what. No one was that tough.

I was going to have to move very slowly and cautiously. Sound was my ally and my enemy. The soldiers would be less concerned about sound since they could see with the night vision goggles. It was just human nature. We're visually oriented and will rely on that sense if it's available. We'll ignore the others.

They would be noisy even when they were trying to be quiet. A cough, a sneeze, a sniffle, a whisper, a rustling of clothing, or a click of boots on a stone would all give them away and they wouldn't even think about those sounds. They wouldn't talk of course because they were trying to be quiet. Without my eyes to rely on I would have to rely on my ears to guide me. In order to do that I'd have to stop every few steps and listen for any sounds out of the ordinary. I stayed low to the ground and felt my way along. I didn't want to trip over anything.

I made it through the fence, around the backyard and out the fence between the first and second houses without any incidents or making any significant noise. When I'd worked my way around the second house and made it to the fence between the second and third houses an idea came to me. It was a little risky but if it worked I'd know for sure if there were anyone out there and where they were.

I felt around the planter box that lined the fence and found what I was looking for, a nice size rock, about five pounds. I reached back and heaved the rock across the street then dropped down flat against the fence and waited to hear the result. The rock hit something solid, perhaps the side of the house then bounced off and hit something metal. In the dead quiet of the night it sounded like a hand grenade going off. I immediately heard someone say, "What the fuck was that?" There was a response in a different voice, "I don't know, let's check it out." Two out front. I heard their footsteps, heavy on the pavement running and then slowing down. I could see flashlights playing over the front of the house as the soldiers tried to figure out the source of the noise. I was relieved to know where they were, but knowing they were there answered another question as well. I now knew for sure that they had Donte and he'd broken. I thought for a moment about turning around and heading back to Alan's but there were several items hidden in the house that I needed.

I scurried through the hole in the fence and moved quickly around the back of the house. I stopped at the corner and listened. I heard the men out front walking back to their position and nervously whispering to one another. I waited a few minutes and moved quietly to the fence between the last house and the safe house. I dropped to the ground and paused another five minutes to make sure there wasn't anyone in the side yard. There were no sounds of movement. I drew one of the .44's and slid through the opening in the fence. There was a side door that had a large dog flap in it. The dog flap had given me the idea for the side entry in the first place. No need to open a door and risk a hinge creaking or a lock clicking. I crawled through the opening and knew to slide to my right and into the laundry room. I waited again. I crawled back into the hallway and worked my way to the staircase.

At the base of the stairs my hand touched something wet and sticky. I brought my hand to my nose and smelled the unmistakable coppery smell of blood. I reached up and felt the spiked bar in it's sprung position. The tines were sticky with already drying blood. I grinned a bit knowing that I'd gotten at least one of them. I wondered if the spikes at the top of the stairs had gotten a second.

I crawled the length of the stairs and got my answer. The carpet at the top was sticky with blood as well. I knew the guys outside were going to be extra pissed off if I had to confront them. They would want revenge. I crawled under the spiked bar and stopped before entering the upstairs hallway. I listened. I waited. I heard someone clear his throat. The sound came from the room I'd been staying in. I moved to the doorframe and felt that the door was closed. I holstered the .44 and drew the fighting knife from the sheath on my leg. I stood up next to the door on the side it opened. I gave one sharp rap on the door and listened. One set of steps coming at the door. The door swung open and I swung the knife on a perfect arc right into the center of the man's chest. I hit him with the knife as hard as I could. The knife glanced off the body armor and flew from my hand but the force of the blow and the shock of the attack knocked the man off his feet. As he fell I heard his gun skitter across the floor. I dove for the sound of the thump and landed on top of him. My weight hitting his chest forced out an audible "oomph". I threw a right hook with everything I had and felt the man's jaw shatter. He went limp. I checked for a pulse. There was none. I checked his neck and his wrist. No pulse. The force of the blow had killed him. I shut the door and immediately moved into the corner of the room directly behind where the door would open. It would give me a few extra seconds of cover if someone should enter the room. I sat there with one of the .44's pointed at the door and waited a few minutes. No one came.

I crawled the length of the wall to the corner. Behind a large stuffed armchair I had cut a piece of the drywall down near the baseboard. The cut piece fit back over the opening and inside the wall I placed the Weatherby and the ammo for it. There were several other pistols and all the ammo stuffed in there also. I loaded it all in my backpack. I slung the rifle over my shoulder. In the adjacent bathroom I'd strapped a get-away bag with clothes to the sink pipes under the basin. There was one other valuable item under there as well. This was the second reason I had risked coming back. Finding Donte had been the first. At that moment I realized that Donte was really the reason I'd risked coming back. Originally, I thought I had been more motivated by retrieving this small photo album. It was the only thing I'd found in the burned house that my family had been killed in. It was amazing that it was intact. I don't know how it survived but it did. There were ten pages in it, twenty pictures of my wife and son in all, one per side. It was all I had left of my family. I placed the get-away bag and the album in my pack and decided I'd been there long enough.

I made my way down the stairs being mindful of the increased weight and equipment on my back. At the base of the stairs I turned right, crawled below the windows in the living room and into the kitchen. I had stored most of the propane tanks that I'd found in backyards in the kitchen. There were 14 of them in all; some filled more than others but all containing some propane. I'd found a case of Duraflame logs, which burn very hot, a few weeks back, and those were in the kitchen as well. There were 12 logs in the case, more than enough to do the job. I surrounded the box of logs with the propane tanks and placed three tanks on top of the box as well. Then I pulled a lighter out of my pocket and set the whole box on fire. The kitchen was in the back of the house so it would be a few minutes before the soldiers saw the glow of the flames or smoke rising out of the pyre. I hurried on through the kitchen as the fire began to lick its way through the box and ignite the logs.

I poked my head out of the dog door, listened for a moment, moved quickly across the ten-foot wide side yard and vanished through the hole. As I arrived at the second house I heard the panicked voices of the soldiers altered to the fire. I snaked through the hole in the fence between the second and third houses when I heard the first of the propane tanks explode. In the relative quiet it was a massive sound. I also heard the screams of someone who'd been way too close to the blast.

I broke into a run and made it to the final hole in the fence at the fourth house when all hell broke loose. The propane tanks started going off like a string of giant firecrackers. I stopped to look back and saw that the house was now fully engulfed. The brightness of the flames cut through the darkness and lighted the street. I stuck to the shadows as much as possible until I was able to make the corner. I started into a jog and made it back to Alan's neighborhood in less time than it had taken me to get to safe house. I could see the helicopter circling in the distance. The flames were still clearly visible against the night sky.

Chapter 11

I stopped at the corner of Alan's street and buried myself in a group of bushes leaving a good view of the approach I'd just taken. I wanted to make absolutely certain that no one had picked up my trail. The worst thing I could do was to bring this fight to Alan's front door. After waiting about ten minutes it was clear that I had not been followed.

I approached Alan's front gate and whistled. A few moments later I saw the door swing open and Alan walked down the steps with a shotgun in his arms.

"Who's there," he yelled, racking a round in the shotgun with a loud click-clack sound.

"It's me," I yelled back. "How about those Packers?" It was a code we'd worked out. Alan had told me he was originally from Wisconsin and once-upon-a-time had been a die-hard Packer fan. He came to the gate. He checked to my left and right just to be sure no one was standing there holding a weapon on me, then lowered the shotgun.

"One second," he said and trotted back into the entry. I heard the light hum of the electricity click off and he trotted back to the gate, unlocked it and let me in. As soon as I stepped in he gave me a big bear hug and actually picked me up off my feet.

"Damn, you're pretty strong for an old man, " I said and chuckled.

"No Donte?" he asked.

"No, and since there was a welcoming party I can assume they have him and got him to talk."

"When I heard the explosions I figured you had company. Come on. Let's get inside. It sounded like you started a war out there."

"I did," I replied.

He relocked the gate and we stepped inside. I had to squint while my eyes adjusted to the lights in the house. It was such a strong contrast to the absolute blackness that I had just waded through. Alan turned the key and reactivated the electricity to the fence. As we walked down the hallway I noticed it was 9:30 on the grandfather clock. Three and a half hours to get there, take care of business, and get back. Not too bad. But I realized then that I was hungry.

"I'm starving," I told Alan.

"Yes, of course you are. Let's go in the kitchen and you can fill me in."

I sat down, actually collapsed, into the chair. I was exhausted. My muscles were beginning to ache from both the physical activity and the adrenaline hangover.

Alan heated some soup and put the bowl in front of me with a sleeve of saltines. I thanked him and then wolfed it down without talking and felt a little revived when I was done. I told Alan all about the trip to the house. He listened with the intensity of a small child hearing a bedtime story for the first time. And like the little child he interrupted right at the end.

"What was the explosion, what did you do?" he asked excitedly.

I described the propane tanks in detail. He grinned when I told him it sounded like I got at least one with the blast.

"Good mission then," he said matter-of-factly. "What goodies did you bring back?" He saw the Weatherby. "That's a helluva good deer rifle. I guess that's what you've been using to create the 'legend'," he said making quotation marks in the air with his fingers.

"I suppose," I said, feeling awkward about the comment. I emptied the contents of the pack on the kitchen table and took inventory. There was the Weatherby, four boxes of ammo for it, the two M-9's I'd taken off the soldiers when I'd first met Donte, two boxes of 9mm ammo, four extra clips I'd gotten from another solider I'd taken down. I heaved his pistol into the rubble of a burned house and thought about the danger of that after the fact. There were three boxes of .44 ammo for my pistols. Actually only two and a half since I'd used about half of one box here and there. There was a KA-Bar assault knife in a sheath, two large Maglite flashlights, the bag of clothes and the photo album.

"Nice arsenal." He scanned the table again and I saw his eyes stop at the album. "May I?" he asked.

"Sure," I replied. I looked over his shoulder as he flipped through the pages. On the fourth page was the picture of my son in the nursery at the hospital right after he'd been born. I thought back to that day and back to Stark.

———————

Nine months into my second tour in Afghanistan I got word that my wife had delivered our son. I hated that I hadn't been there for his birth but fortunately R&R leave was coming up and I would get to see him just home from the hospital. Out of the blue Stark asked if he could come with me. It seemed a bit odd since he'd never even hinted about joining me on leave before. In fact, I found it peculiar that I had no idea where he usually went on his leave. The squad would all get together when we got back from R&R and swap stories. The married guys would live vicariously through the single guys and their stories of conquest and debauchery. Some of it may have been bullshit but knowing these guys I would guess that most of it was not. Then the four of us that were married would bore the rest of the guys with tales of changing diapers and shopping at the grocery store. All the single guys would fake falling asleep and we would all laugh. We had the same routine every time. Except for Stark. Stark just sat and listened. I asked him about it once and he just sort of shrugged it off. I'd asked why he didn't share a tale or two just to be a part of the group and he'd been annoyed. He said he was just shy about his personal life. Some of the guys were beginning to think he might be gay. He blew me off for the next few days. I eventually apologized and told him it was none of my business and promised I wouldn't give him grief about it. It got me wondering though. What did he do? Where did he go?

Because of all that I thought it might be good idea after all to have him come home with me. Maybe away from the military environment he would relax some and we could talk about getting him to fit in better. It was becoming an issue within the unit. Away from Stark his aloofness had been a frequent topic of discussion. Some of the guys flat out didn't trust him and in a Special Forces group you'd better be able to trust your teammates or people die.

It was an emotional visit. Seeing my son for the first time was amazing. My wife and I shared hours just holding each other and our son, not saying a word, just enjoying being together. Stark left us alone during those times. He and I shared a few beers in the garage but I never found the opportunity to bring up his detachment from the group and he certainly didn't offer anything up on his own. He was polite and respectful but when it came time to leave, my wife pulled me aside and said, "Don't trust him." I gave her a puzzled look and she replied, "You know me Ethan, you know I get feelings about people and I'm rarely wrong. I don't trust him."

———————

Alan's voice brought me back to the present in his kitchen. "Hello. Ethan. Where are you?"

"Sorry, Alan. The photos just took me to another place and time."

"Where'd you go?" he asked.

"Just a place I don't really want to go to again."

"Fair enough," he said respectfully. "Bigger question is, what's next?"

"I've got to do something about Donte. They have him, or at least did have him. There is no other way those soldiers knew to be there at my house. They were waiting for me. It wasn't random. The only place they could've got that information was from Donte. The scary part is I know he wouldn't have compromised me willingly."

"How can you be so sure," he asked. "What is your relationship to him?"

"Actually just met him a week or so ago, but time doesn't really make any difference. I just know that he must've been coerced into giving the information." At least I thought so. Alan's comment had allowed a little doubt to slip through the cracks and into my thoughts. What did I really know about the kid? I'd never been to where he was living. Had he ever given me any clue or reason to doubt or was my subconscious just playing games with me? I thought through the past week. The initial confrontation, the time spent together, the conversations we'd had, the trip to the trading post and the subsequent fight in the mall. For that matter what did I know about Alan? He had approached me at the trading post. He'd led us down the mall into the ambush. He was with Donte when he'd disappeared. He'd taken me to a place that by all rights shouldn't exist with all its electricity. This was why I'd stayed a loner the past two years. It was just easier. Ultimately relationships all come down to faith and trust. There was no way to be certain that Donte wasn't a plant or hadn't turned on me because he'd been given a reward or a better deal by the soldiers. There was no reason to believe that Alan wasn't working for the military, put in place to gather information. He certainly had the skills as a former Marine. I weighed what little evidence I had but it really came down to my gut. My gut had been right every time but one. That one had cost me dearly though.

"He's a good kid," I said to Alan, more to reassure myself than him. "There's just something that's just…" I paused searching for the correct word, "kosher about him," I finished.

"Ok, then what are we going to do next?"

"Again, no 'we'. I can't put you at risk. This is my fight. I need to go get him if he's still alive or pay back the guys that killed him. Either way it's my fight."

He stood quiet for a moment then looked me squarely in the eye, a cold hard stare, and said, "Son, you're asking a Marine to back down from a fight. To back away from doing what's right? No sir. Not going to happen. The last article in the Marine Corps Code requires me to fight for freedom, and be dedicated to the principles that made our country free. These guys are not U.S. soldiers anymore. They are enemies of the United States and all it stands for. I can no more opt out of this fight than I can choose to stop breathing. I know you understand this. You chose a tough road to become Special Forces, so I know you get this. Don't waste your time or mine trying to convince me to stay out of this. It would be much more productive to figure out what you need me to do. Got it?"

I slowly nodded my head. "Yes sir, I've got it." I knew then my gut was right about Alan, no doubt about it.

My wife had been right about people every time. It was shortly after I met my son the first time that I found out she was right about Stark. We'd been sent out on a search and clear mission in the Kandahar commercial area of Kabul Darwaza. The block we were sent to clear was full of small shops specializing in antiques and war relics. We'd gotten information that a Taliban cell, which had been wreaking havoc on supply convoys were headquartered in this neighborhood. We were going in and out of each shop, two by two, one man guarding the front, while the other cleared the back. The shops were small, usually no more than twenty by twenty feet. Most had a front room that took up about three quarters of the space with a smaller back room for storage or office. The buildings were older. The neighborhood was on the edge of the old town of Kandahar. Stark and I were working the right side of the crowded street and two other members of our group were working the left. We were trying to stay on pace so that we were moving from store to store in a side-by-side fashion. It meant that help was right across the narrow street if it was needed. Stark and I started to drop behind so I yelled for him to hurry up. He was taking several minutes in the back room of each store. It seemed odd but I thought he might've just been checking closets or under furniture just to be thorough, looking for any signs of Taliban activity. He yelled back, "Yeah, yeah I'm coming," but he didn't. I left my post at the door and slowly walked to the opening in the back to tell him we needed to pick up the pace. As I got to the opening I could see Stark placing something into his pack. It was clearly not a U.S. army approved item. I was stunned. Theft from civilians was a court martial offense. I decided I would wait until we returned to base to confront him but it would need to be done. I didn't want to be drawn into any punishment if he got caught. I quickly returned to the front door and reached the opening just as Stark came out of the back.

"What's your rush?" he asked.

"The other team is two doors down. Let's go."

We kept up the pace the rest of the day and met the transport at the end of the block. When we returned to base and Stark and I were alone I asked him about the incident in town.

"Stark, I need to ask you something."

"What's up," he said.

"When we were in town, when I was trying to get you to hustle along, I walked to the back where you were and I saw you putting something in your pack. I hope I didn't see what I thought I did."

His demeanor changed. He stepped back and crossed his arms across his chest. His eyes narrowed.

"What exactly do you think you saw?" He'd put the accusation back on me.

I couldn't think of an easy way to say it so I just decided to go the direct route. "It looked like you were putting something that didn't belong to you in your pack." I expected him to deny it and was hoping he had a good explanation.

"So what?"

"So? I can think of a million 'what's'. Let's start with a court martial for one thing."

"I'd have to get caught first, wouldn't I? And right now the only way I get caught is if you rat me out. And you're not going to do that." It was a statement, not a question, which really pissed me off.

"That's a hell of an assumption you're making. Why shouldn't I? You get caught and I probably burn with you. Not to mention the fact that you're putting all of us at risk. You should know that we're dependent on information we get from the locals to help us do our job. If they won't trust us and see us as the bad guys not only will they stop feeding us info but might even turn us out or set us up. What prize could be worth the risk in this shit hole?"

"There's plenty. Antiques, jewelry, war treasures, weapons, even some cash," he said in tone that almost seemed like he was proud. He was actually beginning to brag.

"You mean you've done this more than once?"

"Hell yeah. I've got a nice side business. Where do you think I go on leave? I can't store everything here can I? I've got a nice retirement beginning to build and you'd better not even think about burning me. I'll tell them you were in on it. They'll buy it. You're my partner. You were in all those buildings with me." He turned and just walked away with me standing there. He was right. The MP's would bury both of us. He might even get a lighter sentence if he rolled over on me. Military justice doesn't hold to the same standards as civilian courts. They don't need warrants and the accused doesn't get the same standards of due process. All I could hear was my wife's words resonating in my head; "Don't trust him." She was never wrong but I sure had been.

———————

Alan and I spent the rest of the evening discussing Donte and what our next step was going to be and no matter what direction the conversation took we came to the same conclusion; that we simply didn't have enough information to go on. There were several problems. First, we really didn't know if Donte was alive or not. Knowing that might affect our approach. We could be more reckless in our plan if there were no friendlies to worry about. Second, we had no real idea where he'd been taken. The assumption was that he'd been taken to the base, wherever that was. Third, neither of us knew the exact location of that base. I had an idea, but it was only in terms of direction or area. It was something I had searched for but had been unable to find. There was too much area and too little of me. Fourth, no matter what, our "army" was just the two of us, and unless we were very lucky we'd need some more soldiers on our side. Bottom line was we needed information. The question was where were going to get it? We decided that a few hours of sleep might clear our heads and get us headed in right direction in the morning.

Alan showed me to the guest bedroom. I took a hot shower and slept in a real bed for the first time in two years. I fell asleep immediately.

Chapter 12

I woke as the sun was rising. No matter how tired I'd been the night before, that internal alarm clock I'd developed during my Army days still went off every morning right on schedule. Outside the bedroom window I could see the clouds that had been over the city for the past week had finally given up and moved on. It was still cold outside. The chill was working it's way through the insulation and making the inside wall icy. I lay in the bed for a few minutes until the smell of breakfast wafted into the room. It was another first in two years, the odor of bacon cooking. It was a glorious smell. I floated down the hall after the source of the smell. Alan was just taking the bacon off the electric stove. He'd set the table with homemade bread, canned fruit cocktail and the bacon. It was a meal fit for a king.

"Good morning. Another early riser I see. Just can't seem to shake the 0500 wake up in my brain. Marines drilled it into me," Alan said cheerfully.

"I just had the same thought. Of course four hours in that bed is better than eight hours on the floor. Bacon, huh? Where in the hell did you get bacon?"

"I've got a whole deep freezer full of goodies out there. You know before the riots everyone thought I was the neighborhood nut job. Crazy old man. Walled off his house with bushes, big security lights. The neighbors even tried to get me to cut down the Junipers because they thought the trees were an eyesore. They complained the bushes lowered the property value. Guess who had the last laugh? I've always been a boy scout. I was prepared for anything. I guess I saw the worst in 'Nam and wasn't going to get caught there again."

"I get it. I think I went the other way when I got sent home. I had seen so much horror that I just wanted everything to be normal. I guess I sort of stuck my head in the sand. It cost me a lot."

He nodded slowly as I spoke. "I get it, too. Anyway, I had lots of supplies stockpiled and when everything went haywire I stored even more. I got to thinking about our problem this morning and when I went to get the bacon I had a thought. At one time I'd needed a part for the freezer and everyone told me to see this guy over in the mall. He's the sort of guy who seems to know everything. Where to get things, where to find things, how to do things. They call him Mr. Google, like the old search engine," he paused to let the humor of the name set in. "He knew exactly where to find the part. I'm thinking he might have some of the information we need. Problem is we'll need to go back to the mall. He trades information for books."

"Might be worth the risk. The only person there who saw me clearly is dead. I can disguise myself. Getting you in might be a bigger problem though. You're a regular there, right? Also, the soldier who chased you got away and I assume got a decent look at you. It would make identifying you much easier. On top of that there's a bigger problem potentially. Does anyone at the mall know where you live? If so we may have soldiers all over this place very shortly. It won't take them long to put it together that you helped us out."

"No, I've never and would never bring anyone back here. You were the first and only. I am a regular over there though. I go by once or twice a week. Just to have a conversation or two, you know?"

"Yeah, I know."

"It might create the same problem you and Donte had. By yourselves you would've blended in, together you were an obvious match. Perhaps, if we both disguise ourselves and leave some distance between us, we might be okay. I'm thinking we stay a few hundred feet apart as we make our way to Mr. Google, and we should avoid being together inside the mall until we get to his place. I think we'll be fine. We can assess the risk better when we get in."

"Next question. How well do you know this guy? Would he sell us out? I'm sure the reward is getting to be pretty irresistible," I said.

"Not all that well. I only met him the one time. Unless he has a radio with him and the soldiers have already got him on the payroll as an informant then it should be safe. Most people hate the soldiers. Many of the mall dwellers were forced out of their homes by the soldiers and forced into the settlements. If one of them were an informant I doubt they would do well living right in the mall. They wouldn't have much business or a very long life. My gut tells me it's the best option we have."

"All right we go. Time is moving against us. I have an idea of the general location of the base because of troop movement but not enough of an idea to go searching for it. Plus stumbling around in broad daylight looking for it would be foolish. Let's hope Mr. Google has the answer. If Donte is still alive there isn't much time left for him. When they realize he can't help them get to me he'll either be dead from them extracting the information or they'll just be tired of messing with him. They might also take out their anger because of my activity last night."

We both changed clothes. I put on some "ordinary citizen clothes" from my get away bag. I pulled a watch cap down tight over my ears to cover my hair. I figured I'd hunch over a bit to hide my height. It was serviceable. The disguise would never fool someone that knew me well but I was banking on the fact that I've really not been seen, at least not by anyone who's still alive and can I.D. me. All Alan had to do was shave his beard and put away his Marine cap and he looked like a totally different person. It was striking. I was surprised that he was almost completely bald without the cap. Shaving off the beard made him look like he was ten years younger. Even people who knew him would have a tough time recognizing him. Looking at the two of us in the mirror reminded me of the last time I'd worn a disguise.

One of the last missions I went on as a Special Forces member was undercover. Few people know that one of the basic functions of the Special Forces is to fight insurgents by assimilating with the native freedom fighters. This mission was to be just one of those cases. We were scheduled to join with a local group who knew of a Taliban stronghold in the area and serve as support for them during a raid. They were to do the heavy lifting. We wore the traditional clothing of the region. We were each given a set of shalwar kameez, which consists of pajama like pants and a tunic that comes down to about mid thigh. Most of us had grown beards since being in Afghanistan because it was traditional among the men and it was good politics to conform as much as possible to local custom. The great thing about the shirt, the kameeze, part of the outfit is it's loose fitting so you can wear the body armor underneath without alerting the casual observer to it being there. We wrapped our helmets in a keffiyeh, the traditional and very practical scarf worn throughout the Middle East. It could also be wrapped around the mouth to cover the face and further conceal us.

Stark and I were checking each other out and making sure that nothing was out of place that might give us away. His smaller size was more convincing as a local. My height was rare in the local population so I would have to hunch down some as I walked. We looked the part.

That night we were headed to a goat farm on the outskirts of Khandahar. We'd been given hand drawn maps and a few photographs made by the locals who had worked with us on the plan, but when push came to shove they were a rag tag group of insurgents and we were well-trained soldiers. It was hard to take the support role but in a politically sensitive area it was more than necessary. The farm had two main buildings and three smaller out buildings. The two main buildings were one story, built of stone and mud in traditional Afghan style. Two of the outbuildings were made from old metal storage bins about forty feet long and ten feet wide. Crude windows had been cut into the sides with a blow-torch. Scorch marks scarred the paint around the cuts. The third out building was made of plywood sheathing and the roof was covered with a canvas tarp. Surrounding the compound was a low stone and mud wall. It was a crude installation. Our job was to secure the out buildings while the locals took the main buildings. The approach was the tricky part. The farm was on a rocky outcropping surrounded on three sides by low, flat, arid land. The fourth side was against a sheer cliff of a larger hill. We would have to approach from the front. Our team was assigned to take the two metal storage buildings while another unit took the wood and canvas building and covered the flanks. The insurgents would take a straight frontal assault on the two main buildings.

We chose a night with only a sliver of a moon. Going on a night with no moon was dangerous even though it would be much darker. It was dangerous because the enemy knew that would be a likely night for an attack and were more on guard. We planned the attack for 0300, when most of the enemy would be asleep.

The intel was that the enemy force was about forty strong. We had twenty-four Special Forces soldiers and thirty insurgents. We would have had them outnumbered if it was just our guys. I would've liked information on where and how they were defending the compound but considering our force and training I was confident we would take care of business fairly easily. We had the element of surprise on our side as well.

We met our local group at the edge of town and moved to the outlying area without incident. Night vision goggles allowed us to see that the compound was lightly guarded. Stark and I were assigned to the metal shed farthest away from the main building. We were with four other guys from our unit.

We zigzagged our way one at a time across the open approach until all six of us were in place against the low wall. I could just make out the freedom fighters approaching the front of the house as my watch ticked to three. Our team leader motioned to us and we began to go over the wall one by one. Stark and I were set to go last. I went over the wall and after a few steps I looked back and Stark hadn't come.

It was at that moment that all hell broke loose. Shuttered windows on the two main buildings suddenly swung open and heavy machine gun fire let loose on the approaching freedom fighters. There was nowhere for them to go. I watched as they heroically continued their death charge and in short work they were all cut down. The first guy over the wall, our assistant detachment commander, Anderson, turned and signaled for us to cut and run when the window covering on the shed we were approaching dropped open. We were fifty feet from it and fifty feet from the wall. Stark was still nowhere to be seen. I hit the deck as soon as I saw the window open. The other four had been turning when it opened and had their backs to it. I called out to them to hit the deck when I heard the tell tale thud-thud of a heavy machine gun open fire. Shots were hitting the dirt all around me. I could hear the guys behind me screaming as they got hit. I turned and crawled back toward them. The first three guys had fatal wounds and were already gone. Anderson, who had been the closest, had been hit in the leg. He was already in shock and out of it with pain. I did the only thing I could do. I picked him up, threw him over my shoulders and took off on a dead run for the wall. As I dove I felt a burning in my side. I fell over the wall.

I awoke in the base hospital the next morning. My head hurt like hell and so did my side just above my hip. There was a corpsman there and I called him over.

"Hey, good morning," he said cheerfully. "How do you feel?"

"Like shit. What happened? How did I get here?" I asked through a fog.

"The story is all over the base. One of the guys in your unit, Stork or Stark, ran out against the machine gun fire twice and drug you and Anderson over there out." He pointed to the bed next to me as he said the latter. "The extraction team came in and blew the hell out of the whole compound and got you guys out. You had a flesh wound in your side and were unconscious. You also have a nasty contusion on your head and a concussion"

I took a minute to recall the story he's just told me. I was fuzzy about everything after going over the wall but I was sure I'd pulled myself, and Anderson out of harm's way. "Is there any way you can get Stark here? I want to thank him." I really just wanted to find out what the hell was going on.

"I'll see what I can do for you."

About ten minutes later Stark strolled in. He had a big grin on his face. "I guess you owe me big time now."

"What the hell are talking about? You didn't even follow us out when you were supposed to. Now I hear you saved both me and Anderson over there." I hooked a thumb towards his bed. Stark raised his chin and glanced at Anderson's bed.

"That's not how I remember it. That bump on your head must've screwed up your memory of things. You went down out in the yard and I made two trips out against enemy fire. I drug both you and Anderson back to safety. You both had wounds and I tended to them until the extraction team got us out."

"You prick. You are so full of shit. I remember very clearly dragging Anderson over the wall then going down. I saw you cowering there next to the wall as I came over."

"CO's already bought my story. Besides if you have a different story I'd keep it to myself if I were you. That stolen contraband in your footlocker will not do much to your credibility. I understand you'll be in here for a week or so. Too bad your wound isn't bad enough to send you home. Anderson there is done. Femur is shattered. They're just waiting for him to be stable enough to transport him to Germany for surgery. It'll take him a year just to walk again. No more Special Forces for him."

His smug attitude had my blood boiling and all I could think about was jamming a KA-Bar between his eyes. Problem was he had me by the balls. I was in this bed and he had access to everyone's ear and my footlocker. I was fucked unless I played along.

He stood to walk away and stopped. He turned and looked back at me over his shoulder. "By the way I hear through the grapevine that I'm being recommended for the Silver Star. Get better pal." As he walked out I rolled to the side of the bed and puked on the floor. I heard the corpsman mutter "Dammit."

Chapter 13

Alan and I made our way back to the entrance of the
mall. Less than twenty-four hours ago we'd fought our
way out. The mall stretched almost a half-mile along
Topanga Canyon Boulevard. With just a few disabled
cars left in the parking lot it looked sad. The colors had
faded some over two years leaving the whole thing
looking bleached. All of the plastic covers and light
bulbs in the big electric signs on the outside that
denoted the big anchor stores were shattered long ago
either in the riots or simply by people who were bored
and had made sport of breaking them. The planter
boxes throughout the parking lot and around the
exterior of the buildings were overgrown and unruly.
Many of the small trees in the lot were dead, snapped at
the trunks and looked like skeletons standing watch.

Alan led us along the south side of the building to
the adjacent parking structure that lined the length of
the east wall. It was four stories high. I figured that
from the top floor you could've had a great view of the
whole valley. We scanned the lower level for military
vehicles and seeing none we climbed the ramp to the
second floor of the structure. We checked the area for
military vehicles and again it was clear. The second
floor had become something of a tent city. All along
the building were camping tents, lean-tos, cardboard
box homes, and shacks made of used plywood. It
looked like a third world country. Several dozen people
sat around the tents. Their eyes were lifeless and
hopeless. Only a few even bothered to turn their heads
to look at us. The smell of urine and human waste was

almost overwhelming. I could never figure out how people who were of sound mind could ever give up like this. Even after the death of my family I'd found something to keep me going.

"You go in first and lead the way. I'll follow behind in a minute," I said. "If you see anything that leads you to believe we need to bug out then stop and tie your shoe. We'll go back out the way we came and rendezvous behind the old Crate & Barrel across the street."

"Sounds good."

Alan disappeared into the mall and I slowly counted to sixty and then entered myself. On the left of the short entry corridor was an old sushi restaurant. I peered inside as I walked by. Same as all the other stores I'd seen the day before. Blankets, mattresses and pillows covered the floor. There were a few dead eyed people sitting around. They had the same detached look as the people outside. They just had a better address. I figured twenty to thirty people called that place home. I did some quick mental math guessing at how many stores there were in the mall plus the parking structure and the mall must've been home to more than two thousand.

I rounded the corner and saw Alan about a hundred feet down. Despite the number of people that I saw in each of the stores there were very few moving up and down in the walkways in front of them. I tried to avoid eye contact with the few that I did pass. I could hear voices speaking softly in each store as I walked by. The sounds of children laughing and of children crying drifted in and out. A few bronchial coughs drifted through the building. Occasionally I could smell food cooking. The sense of hopelessness in there was concrete. You could actually feel it. It was instantly depressing.

Alan turned down a side hall on the west side. I waited thirty seconds and followed him down just as he entered the former Neiman-Marcus store, which had been the anchor store on that side of the mall. I let him get inside and followed him in thirty seconds later. Light from the floor to ceiling windows on the far side lit the space well. I stopped a few feet in and watched as he crossed the store. The inside was a shambles. Racks were tossed this way and that. Trash littered the floor. Some areas had smoke damage from squatter's fires. There were a few isolated groups of people who called the store home. I wondered why this area was so sparsely populated while the people in the smaller stores were right on top of each other. Perhaps it was simply the idea that there was safety in numbers. Maybe being jammed together in the smaller stores would bring some sense of belonging. I was too much of a loner to connect. Anywhere in the mall would be the last place I would choose to live. Of course the soldiers hadn't given many of these people a choice. They were forced into these conditions. I crossed the store on the same route that Alan had taken and got to the bottom of the escalator just as Alan stepped off at the top. I stopped there and looked back to see if anyone else had entered the store behind us. It was clear.

I climbed the dead escalator and was shocked by the order and scene I found on the third floor of the store. Someone had taken time and care to remove all of the debris, broken shelving, and fixtures and piled them against the far side of the room. I turned in a circle and surveyed the space. The entire third floor was one giant loft apartment. Furniture was arranged in separate areas, representing various rooms. There was a living room, several bedrooms, a kitchen and a den. One entire corner of the space was a giant library. Neatly arranged shelves held rows and rows of books. In the center of the space were three lush armchairs. One was occupied. I could see an arm on the armrest of the chair that was facing away from us.

Alan was standing about fifteen feet away speaking with a mountain of a man. He made me look small. He was 6'6" and almost as wide at the shoulders. He looked to be chiseled out of rock. He stood over Alan, his massive arms crossed over his chest. He wore jeans and a t-shirt that was about two sizes too small. He and Alan were discussing something. Alan waved me over.

"Ethan, this is Steve. Steve is Mr. Google's, er, ah, Mr. Feldstein's, personal assistant."

More like bodyguard, I thought to myself. I reached out my hand and Steve grabbed my hand roughly. I readied my hand for the inevitable crushing. Instead he gently shook my hand. It was almost dainty.

"Likewise," he said in a surprising high-pitched voice. This man was a complete contradiction. On the outside he appeared rough but the shake and voice were completely opposite to the exterior. Two thoughts occurred to me then. First, steroids had created much of the muscle mass on Steve, hence the voice, and secondly, for no real reason other than a hunch, he was probably more than just a bodyguard for Mr. Feldstein. "What business do you have with Mr. Feldstein? And it is Mr. Feldstein. He does not care for the nickname he's been given." he squeaked.

"We are hoping he might have some information that would be of great help to us."

"What information is it you need?"

I glanced at Alan and he gave me a nod of affirmation.

"We're looking for the location of the military base for the gentlemen that patrol this neck of the woods."

"Why would you be in need of that information?"

"I'm not sure that's really an answer we need to give you."

He took a small step forward and dropped his arms. He pushed his chest out. He expected me to step back. I'm sure most people would, but I'm not most people. I took a step forward instead. He stopped short of the step he was taking and retreated his foot. I stared into his eyes and dropped my arms and puffed my chest. It was like two gorillas meeting in the jungle. We were sizing each other up. It was a pure testosterone moment. Bottom line was I knew size didn't mean shit. Big wasn't always better when it came to a fight. Big guys tended to be slower. I'd seen many of my Special Forces buddies kick the crap out of some big, dumb ass grunt, who was fifty pounds heavier, in a bar fight. It was more about what you knew. And I knew I knew more. He figured it out as well.

"Wait here," he said as he backed down and strode off towards the library area. He looked back over his shoulder once on his way across the space.

Alan let out an audible breath. "Shit, I thought for sure you two were going to go at it."

"Naw, big guys like that are generally pussies. They never really have to fight. Most people are so intimidated by their size they never have to throw a punch. If you don't back down, or better yet, posture in an aggressive manner, they usually back down."

Steve had reached the library and was leaning over the occupied chair and I saw the top half of a man's head peer over the back of the chair. Steve hung a moment longer then straightened up and waved a big paw for us to approach. As we started over he headed back to his post. We passed in the middle and he tried to hard stare me, but he'd clearly lost the intimidation battle. He was just trying to salvage his own ego at that point.

The library area looked like how a library in a mansion should, without the walls, of course. The floor was covered in large oriental rugs. The big overstuffed armchairs were covered in maroon crushed velvet. The oak bookshelves took up forty feet of wall space in both directions radiating from the corner. The shelves were lined with books. Hardcover, soft cover, tabletop, magazines. Hundreds of them. To one side of the sitting area was a giant roll top oak desk and on the other was a large conference table with six matching high back chairs.

Seated in the chair was a blob of a man. He had to weigh 400 pounds. It was hard to tell his height without him standing but I guessed he was about 5'6" to 5'8". He wore glasses on his round head. The top of his head had a sparse grove of white, wiry hair sticking up in all directions. I guessed him to be about fifty. He was wearing slacks and a huge cashmere sweater vest over a white t-shirt. He had slippers on his feet. He certainly didn't look like he moved very often. If Steve really was more than a bodyguard then what an odd pair they made. Polar opposites. But, as the old saying goes, opposites attract.

"Good morning gentlemen. Please, have a seat." He waved his hand at the two empty chairs." We sat. "Let me begin by saying that if you have come to do me harm I would advise you that your mission would be a suicide mission. As we speak there are two guns trained on each of you. I wish you no harm either. We are here to make an exchange. But, sadly, we live in a very dangerous world and there are those who would like to get into my castle here. You might call me the king of the mall. I'm a fair man but I control most of the trade that goes on here. I'm careful about who I deal with. Information is my ally, which is, I would guess, why you are here."

I was impressed again. Three surprises in such a short time. Didn't happen very often.

"By the way Mr. Ryder, I am a fan of your work. I've paid far too much 'protection' to those that you hunt," he said with a confidence that came from power.

I was stunned by the use of my name. Before I could say anything, Mr. Feldstein said, "Pick your chin off the floor. I told you information is my ally. As soon as the wanted posters went up I made it my business to find out who you are. Don't worry; I haven't sold the information to the soldiers just yet. I'm more curious about your proposal first. What information do you desire?"

"Well, I'm impressed. You do your homework. What I need should be a snap. Where is the military holed up? Where is their base of operation?"

He laughed. It was a cackle, like a chicken clucking. "That's such basic information. I would think a man of your accomplishments could find that information without too much trouble or coming to see me."

"Given time I would find them. I just don't have the time," I responded.

"All right. Fair enough. Why the urgency?"

We came to the tricky part. Asking him about where they were located was a simple matter. Having to tell him why, that gave him valuable information and there was really no reason for him not to turn around and make a profit off both ends of this. Payment from me, and payment from them, with him sitting pretty in the middle. I weighed the options. I decided to volley back, "why do you need to know?"

"We haven't discussed a price yet. I need to know why you need the information to gauge its value to you. For example, in the old days you could've asked me where the nearest hospital is. You might need to know that because you are visiting a sick friend or because a rattlesnake has just bitten you. In the first case you'd pay very little for the information, in the second you'd give everything you own. Everything has a price and the market sets the price. So I ask again, why do you need this so urgently?"

I looked at Alan and he gave me no help. He just tilted his head to one side as if to say, "I have no idea". I decided to roll the dice. If Mr. Feldstein went to the soldiers and sold off the information we could still get the job done. It would just make it a lot harder. He had no advance warning that we were coming today so he couldn't have been setting us up for a trap then and there. "A friend of mine was captured by them yesterday."

"Ahh yes, the young black gentleman."

"Yes. I need to get him back."

"What makes you think he's still alive? And before you ask, that is one piece of information I do not possess."

"I have no idea if he's alive," I answered. "But I have a duty to bring my soldiers back or get the sons-o-bitches who killed them."

"Your soldiers? You see this as a war?"

"Absolutely," I answered without hesitation.

"I have the information you are seeking. Let's talk price. I've heard of your exploits. I know about your war with these men." He paused. He seemed to be searching for the next set of words very carefully. "Some people may see me as an opportunistic pig. And perhaps I am. But I'm fair and I've never hurt anyone who wasn't trying to hurt me. I believe you live by that same set of values. Those soldiers do not." He paused again. Looked down at his knee and picked away some imagined lint. "What do you intend to do with the information?"

"My first objective is to find my friend and get him out. My second objective is to fuck them up...badly." I leaned forward in the chair as I said the last word.

"For you, today, the information you need is no charge. Just make me one promise."

"If I can."

"Get their leader. Cut off the head of that snake. Literally. Deal?"

"Deal," I said as I extended my hand. We shook in agreement.

"They are using an old elementary school as a base. It's just south of Vanowen and just east of Platt."

I had been near that neighborhood dozens of times but never wandered into that area. In fact, Donte and I had passed it on our way to the trading post just yesterday.

Alan and I stood. We shook Mr. Feldstein's hand and we headed for the escalator.

90

"Good luck," he hollered at our backs.

Outside the mall I turned to Alan and said, "Whaddya say we go to school?"

Chapter 14

We headed back to Alan's and picked up the supplies we needed for a stakeout. We packed some food, water, field glasses, coats in case we needed to stay after dark, some basic tools, wire cutters and our weapons with extra ammo. I had the two .44's in my shoulder holsters, and packed the two M-9's in the pack along with ammo for all of them. Alan had a few weapons of his own. He had a Colt Commander semi-automatic holstered on his right hip and a Browning Hi-Power semi-automatic, strapped to his other hip. He told me how he'd won the Browning off an Australian officer during a poker game. The soldier had pleaded for it back but, as Alan said, fair is fair. They were both reliable, accurate, service pistols. He had maintained them in pristine condition. Slung over his shoulder was the real surprise: a PPSh-41 Submachine gun. This had been one of the most mass produced weapons during WWII. The soviets had sold truckloads of them to all of the communist countries in Southeast Asia. The gun used a drum magazine that held 71 rounds or a box magazine that held 35 rounds and fired close to 900 rounds per minute. The drums were difficult to load and tended to jam. The box magazine had solved this problem. With the box magazine it was reliable and very low maintenance.

"Nice," I said pointing to the PPSh.

"War memento," Alan replied. He slipped a loose fitting jacket over the gun, which made him look a bit like a hunchback but served to hide it. When he put the pack on his back you could only see the bulge if you were looking for it. We were both dressed in raggedy, dark clothing. We smeared some soot from Alan's fireplace on our faces and arms. We looked like a pair of scavengers. The only thing that might give us away was our combat boots. But people rarely look at another person's shoes. It was worth the risk with the hike we needed to take.

Alan had an old copy of the Thomas Guide, which was a highly detailed map usually of one or two counties and bound in a wire binding. Each page covered about sixteen square miles. Before GPS navigation systems no one in Los Angeles drove without one. We turned to the page that contained the school. It was almost dead center in a one-mile square residential block. The square was bordered on all four sides by major streets. Approaching the school through all those blocks of homes would be extremely dangerous. If I were commanding that unit I would post lookouts in some of the houses on the approaches to the camp. There could also be remote sensors placed randomly as well. It would depend on how paranoid the commander was. As we examined the map trying to figure out what the safest approach would be I noticed a small unlabeled blue line running just one block west from the school. "What's this," I said as I pointed to the line.

"Flood control channel. If it's not labeled then it's probably one of the smaller ones. They tended to give the bigger ones cute names that ended in creek and stream. Most of them eventually run into the Los Angeles River, which is just a bigger concrete flood control channel," Alan said.

"That might just be our answer. We could move up the channel then climb out when we're parallel to the school. The ditch won't provide much cover but if we act like scavengers they probably won't pay us any attention even if we are spotted. We can find an unoccupied house across the street and take watch from there."

"Sounds like a good plan. Let's bring some trash bags and we can fill them as we go. We can put the packs in them. If we do get stopped all they'll do is look inside the bags. They won't want to dig through them."

"Nice touch."

Our little army of two worked our way without incident the two miles down Victory Blvd. to where the flood control channel ran under the road. We were fortunate. First, there was no security where the road and the wash met. Second, this particular wash had sloped sides. Some of the ones in the system had vertical sides, which would've made escape almost impossible. With the slope we could get out anywhere we needed to. We climbed over the railing. On either side of the wash were apartment buildings. The one on the right was three stories. Black smoke marks showed around every window frame. The wooden railings of the balconies were burned away. The building was a shell. There would be no one watching us from that building. The apartment on the left had been two stories. Only the back wall was evidence of this. The rest was a collapsed and charred pile of twisted rebar and concrete. That building had backed up to a shopping center, which had been totally destroyed and burned by looters in the early days of the riots. The flames had likely made their way to the apartment building.

We hopped the low chain link fence that was supposed to keep people out of the wash and made our way to the bottom. There was still a steady steam of water, three feet wide, running in the center of the channel. Runoff from the recent rains. We walked along slowly, scanning the top of the wash. The rim was about ten feet above the base. On either side of the top were access paths about five feet wide. On the right side of the channel, behind the pathway were the back fences of the homes along the street that ran parallel. On the other side was the back wall of the burned out shopping center. We were mindful of any openings in the fences on our right, looking for signs of movement or sentries. The plan was to travel about a half-mile down the wash and come up on the path, find a good backyard to enter and begin our surveillance of the school. I had made so many marches in my life I could sense distance with great accuracy. The guys in my unit used to test me against their G.P.S. units. We'd bet on my accuracy. I rarely lost.

Alan and I stopped every now and then to pick up some piece of garbage. That also gave us the opportunity to listen to our surroundings as well. At just about the halfway point we rounded a bend in the wash and came upon a small encampment. There were four or five tents set up on the edge of the wash closest to the houses. As we approached, five men, who had been sitting on the edge, stood and stared at us as we moved by. Four of the five were fairly scrawny. The fifth was as big as me. Individually they were no threat. As a group the five of them posed a mild threat. They appeared to be unarmed. They looked unhealthy and I made the assumption that they were not soldiers. We kept our eyes down and walked by. As we passed I heard the group scrabble down the slope. We continued to walk without looking back. I heard one of the men yell "Hey!" at our backs. We kept walking. He yelled again, and I guessed it was big guy doing the talking, "I'm talking to you." They weren't going to go away. They were bored and somehow we'd offended them.

I looked over and saw Alan begin to slide the Colt out of his holster. I slowly shook my head "no" to him. "Too much noise if we have to use them," I whispered. We stopped and turned. The men had fanned out across the bottom of the wash. Two scrawny guys and the big guy were on our side of the stream, the other two scrawny guys on the other side. They stood with their arms crossed or hands on their hips trying to take an aggressive posture.

"You think you can just come through here without paying the toll?" the big guy asked.

"Yes," I replied.

"Then you're wrong," he said and took a step towards us. As if on command all four of the other guys took a step forward.

"We're just passing through. You don't want to go through this, do you?" I asked, giving him one last chance.

He laughed. He slowly counted each of his men and himself and held up his palm to us to show five fingers. Then he pointed at each of us and held up two fingers.

"Not very fair, is it?" although I meant we had them outnumbered. "We're going to start walking that way," I said, as I pointed in the direction we'd been traveling in. "And you are going to back up there and sit your asses down, got it?"

The smirk dropped instantly from the big guy's face and was replaced by rage. It was exactly the response I'd hoped for. The big guy came at me on a dead run. As he reached me I sidestepped him, stuck out my right leg and gave him a shove to the back as he tripped and flew headfirst into the cement. Before he could recover I walked over and kicked him in the ribs. I felt one or two of his ribs break.

One other brave guy decided to try his luck and moved toward me. A second guy stepped up and moved toward Alan. The other two moved forward but didn't really look like they had any interest in engaging us. My guy got to me first. He looked like he had no idea what to do now that he was in front of me. He swung a wild right haymaker that seemed to move in slow motion. I easily stepped aside to my right as his fist passed in front of me. I countered with a right hook to his jaw and he dropped like a sack of flour. A moment later Alan's guy got to him. He stopped in front of Alan who had moved into a boxing stance. The guy stood square to Alan waiting for a response. Alan waved his right fist just above his ear. I saw the man's eyes follow the fist and I knew immediately he'd made a fatal error. Alan swung his right foot, toe pointed, straight into the man's groin, lifting him off the ground about six inches. He dropped to the ground howling in pain and grabbing his crotch.

I looked up at the others and said, "Anyone else want some of this?" The two of them held up their hands as if to say no thank you. Then they just turned and walked away. We watched them as they started up the slope, then we turned and moved on.

"Do you think they'll make trouble for us?" Alan asked.

"No. They won't admit they got beat down by two guys."

Chapter 15

It took us about thirty minutes to make the half mile. Without the fight we would've made it in twenty. We climbed the slope out of the wash and onto the access path. Alan pretended he was examining some trash while I peeked through the fence. The last family that occupied the house must've had young kids. There were two plastic playhouses designed for toddlers and a kiddie pool sitting in the yard. The grass had gone to weeds. I could see the back sliding patio door and had a clear view into the house. I watched for a few minutes and saw no movement. We heard no sounds. There were two fences back to back. On our side was chain link, no doubt put there by the city when the channel had been built. The homeowners had built an equally high wood plank fence on the inside for privacy and esthetics. It was good for us. The chain link provided a ladder for us to climb; the wood fence gave us cover.

I went over first, dropped quietly on the balls of my feet, rolled to my left and lay flat in the tall weeds. I waited a minute to see if we had alerted anyone. Again I saw no movement. I quietly whistled and a moment later Alan came over the top of the fence. He was remarkably agile for a man pushing sixty. He dropped and rolled in one motion, giving out a grunt when he landed.

"Shit, that didn't used to hurt so damn much," he whispered.

"I haven't seen any movement. Let's stay along the fence and check the windows on this side. We need an entry point and we can also check for sentries. It's not a likely position but we need to check things carefully."

We belly crawled until we reached the corner of the house, keeping our heads below the tops of the weeds. There were three windows along the side of the house. The side yard dead-ended with a wood fence identical to the one across the back. The fence between the houses was pink cinder block. All the fences were about six feet high. I wouldn't want to get pinned down in there so I left Alan at the corner with the Colt in his right hand. I pulled one of the .44's and held it in front of me as I made my way from window to window. The first window looked into the same room I'd seen through the patio doors. It was still clear. I ducked down and moved to the second window. This one looked into the dining room. Through the room I could see into the hallway. I watched for a minute and again saw no one. I guessed the last window would overlook the kitchen sink. The drain clean out was on the wall about three feet below the bottom of the window. I peered in and my guess was correct. Beyond the kitchen was a den, which overlooked the front yard of the house. The front or back rooms would be the likely place for a sentry. All three windows had shown the house was still mostly untouched. Most of the furniture was still in place, nothing looked broken. The house seemed clear and I checked to see if any of the windows were unlocked as I made my way back to the rear of the house. None of the windows were unlocked. I wanted to avoid breaking a window to get in. The noise might alert someone if they were in the house or close by.

We snaked back around the corner and tried the patio door and were pleasantly surprised when the door slid open with a slight squeal. We retreated at the sound to the corner of the house both figuring that if someone were in the house they would come to investigate the noise. I moved to the first side window, watched and waited. No one came. We returned to the door, slid it open far enough to get in and closed it behind us. Leaving it open might give us an extra second for escape, but closed the squeal would make it far better as an alarm in case someone came in from the outside.

We moved through the house, clearing every room. We checked every closed closet, under the beds and in the showers. The attached garage was empty as well. Even though the house was furnished there were no personal items left. There were no pictures on the walls, knick-knacks on the tops of tables, no clothes in the closets and no personal effects in the bathrooms. Whoever had owned this house had moved in a hurry, or had given up hope of finding a moving company. I guessed the owners had waited until the warning came that if you stayed you were on your own. By then, if you could find a moving company, they were charging far more than most people could pay. Most simply left California at that time in their cars loaded with what they could fit and got out.

The big picture window in the living room provided a clear view of the school across the street. There was a three-foot tall picket fence across the front lawn against the sidewalk. I was somewhat surprised at how close we were to the school. I had known we would come out across the street but it just seemed so close. It was a bit uncomfortable.

The school appeared to be like most elementary schools in the Valley. The school was surrounded by ten-foot high chain link fence. Its original purpose was to keep kids from wandering off campus and into the street. It was also there to keep people from easily wandering onto campus from the outside and vandals from sneaking in at night. The only addition to the fence was the coils of razor wire that had been attached to the top of the fence. We were looking at the west side of the school. All of the buildings we could see were single story. Everything was painted a dull tan color. To our left we could see the back of one of those low buildings that was set in the corner of the campus. The length of the building ran parallel to the fence and about twenty feet behind it. It appeared to be the administration building. To the right of that building were two other buildings, perpendicular to the administration building. The short sides were facing us and were windowless. These appeared to be classrooms. There were two classrooms in each building. Children's drawings were still taped to the windows. In between the first two classroom buildings was a playground that seemed designed for younger children. To the right of those two buildings were two more set closer together. There was no play area between them. There was about ten feet between the right most building and the corner of the fence. Farther east of those buildings we could see another row of low buildings that mirrored the ones closest to us. Most of the windows were covered with wire mesh grates, which were bolted to the walls. The only windows that faced us were the three on the back of the administration building and they too were covered with grates.

I could see very little activity on first glance. A few soldiers were moving between buildings in the interior of the campus. The only building I could see into was the administration building and there was no activity at the moment.

"What do you think?" asked Alan.

"Pretty quiet. We're eventually going to need to see one of the other sides of the campus so we can have a clear idea of what we're up against. But for now I want to watch here for a while to see what kind of security they have set up." In answer to my statement a lone soldier came around the corner from our right. He had an M4 slung over his shoulder. His hands were in his pockets. A cigarette hung from his mouth. He looked like a guy on an afternoon stroll. He was not a soldier at the ready or worried about an assault. I'd been there before and it was tough to stay alert. We watched as he sauntered the length of the fence, made it to the corner, turned and followed the fence line away from us out of view.

"It looks like there are just two sentries walking a post. One is walking the west and south sides and the other the north and east. I want to see how long it takes for him to come back and then time him on this side. If he comes back in about the same time we can be assured he's just walking the two sides. He's very relaxed. They aren't on alert. That's good for us. They aren't expecting trouble. I doubt anyone even comes near here, unless they blunder into this neighborhood by accident. We might as well get comfortable. I think we should stay here for a while before we move to another side."

"Agreed," said Alan.

We pulled cushions off the sofa and placed them in front of the window to sit on so that just the tops of our heads might be visible. We sat back a few feet from the glass making it more difficult to see us inside. The glare from the outside would make the windows a bit like a mirror. As long as it was as dark or darker inside than outside it would be tough to see us unless you walked right up to the window. I pulled out the field glasses and sat down on the cushion and started to scan the school.

————

I recalled another recon mission just like this one where we'd been camped out for several days, just outside of Kandahar, to gather information we needed. That mission took place just two weeks after the disaster at the goat farm. I was given medical clearance for duty just two days before. We were still looking for the Taliban cell that we'd been trying to take down at the goat farm. Our informants told us that the cell had pulled up stakes and relocated by the next morning. Our sources gave us reliable information that they had moved back into town so that any attack would surely cause some collateral damage, most likely to civilians. We needed the most reliable information possible to avoid hurting or killing anyone unnecessarily.

The intel came from informants that we had cultivated from the locals. We took months to build up trust with them before they began to see us as the good guys. We used a number of techniques to build that trust. We provided food, water, medical care, and education. We helped with building projects and infrastructure repair. All of these things served to build up a rapport with the locals. In turn we began to get information on the location of Taliban strongholds and spies. They saw us as a better option than what they had. And we were. Some of our best information came from the kids. Kids could move freely and were largely ignored by the adults. We never recruited them but if they brought us info we always followed up on it. The information on this particular location had come from a ten-year old named Tariq.

He claimed to have seen about thirty men file into an apartment building in the southwest part of the city. They had arrived 0600 the morning after the raid on the goat farm. So, we quietly moved into a home across the street from the front entrance and another across from the rear entrance to that apartment to set up our surveillance. We were working in shifts of two at a time in each location. Each shift was eight hours to give around the clock coverage.

I was assigned as usual with Stark and we were into our third shift. We were scheduled for the 0800 to 1600 shift. Nothing significant happened in the first two days. Our job was to photograph everyone that came and went, log the times that they left or arrived and the method of departure or return. We were also required to note anything unusual. Our unit was there over two days and the same eight people came and went and nothing unusual had taken place.

At 1000 our communications sergeant arrived at the house and relieved Stark. He told him to report immediately to our CO. Stark asked what it was all about but the CS had no answer for him. Stark looked to me for an answer and I just shrugged my shoulders. I had no idea. It was highly irregular to pull someone out. The more we came and went the more likely we were to blow our cover. After the incident at the goat farm, and Stark's subsequent behavior, I was hoping to myself that somehow the CO had learned the truth and was going to bust him.

About two hours later the first unusual thing we had seen during our surveillance took place. A medium sized delivery truck pulled up in front of the apartment. Two men jumped out and proceeded to unload fourteen boxes. All were labeled as different types of food. I jokingly mentioned that it was enough food to feed an army. Other than that the day was uneventful.

I was excited when I returned to our base. It was the first interesting thing that had happened and I wanted to share. My excitement quickly disappeared when Stark shared his news first. Because of his "heroism" at the goat farm the week before, he was being promoted to Assistant Detachment Commander of our group and being given a pay grade increase from Sergeant First Class to First Sergeant. The ADC was second in command of our group. It was a position of high responsibility. He was getting a two-step promotion, bypassing Master Sergeant and the ADC position was almost always given to at least a Warrant Officer One. Both things were unheard of, not to mention the fact that it was completely unmerited. He'd done none of things that his promotions were being given for. In fact, he had been cowering in a corner like a little bitch. He knew I was pissed. But I was also worried. He was now in a position of authority. He now had all the lives of our group within his hands. We all knew it but no one else had the weapon to bury him except me.

As I turned and began to walk out of the room he called to me, "Ryder." I stopped and turned. "What," I snapped.

"What, what?" He drew out the second 'what ' to emphasize that I'd left something out.

"What?" My anger began to boil. I started to think of all the ways I could dispatch him.

"That should be 'What, Master Sergeant," he said in the most arrogant tone possible.

I began to take a step towards him and caught myself. "No, no," he said as he wagged a finger at me. "Remember, I burn, you burn brighter. Besides I'm a war hero. Who will they believe?"

I knew I needed to find a way to burn him without scorching myself. I wasn't sure how to do it but I was going to find a way. I had to.

———————

Chapter 16

Alan and I had been at the window about an hour and nothing had changed on the school campus. We had no idea what we were waiting for or what we were watching for. We just hoped to gain some information to make our rescue of Donte possible and successful.

During that hour we saw no change in the security. The same lone sentry would make his way up and then down the west fence, turn the corner and head along the south fence, disappear from view for about two and a half minutes and then reappear to do the slow dance all over again. Only occasionally did he pause to flex his knees or light another cigarette.

Alan and I had said little and were both beginning to yawn more and more often. "We'd better start talking or I'm going to nod off," he said yawning for emphasis.

"I'm getting drowsy, too."

"You never finished your story about your service time. I recall you left off after telling me about meeting this Stark guy. You were just about to tell me about your second tour when you had to take off for your house. We've got some time."

"Sure." I filled him in on Stark's visit to my home and my wife's warning. I went through the story of catching him stealing and his attitude about it. I revisited the goat farm disaster with him and shared how Stark had taken the credit for saving both me and Anderson, and how he had received the Silver Star, the rank promotion and the bump in leadership within our group. I shared with him my concern of going down

with him if I turned him in. He said little as I
recounted these episodes.

"What a douche bag. Unfortunately the military is
filled with them."

"Not like this guy. It gets better," I said sarcastically.

"Better, huh?" he said. "Terrific."

"Yup. Let me tell you how much better."

———————

Our guys, who were watching the back of the
apartment building in Kandahar, ended up tailing the
truck that had delivered all the food back to a
warehouse. We immediately set up a surveillance team
there as well. We weren't sure if the two delivery guys
were involved with the Taliban cell or were simply
delivery boys. We decided to wait the remainder of the
day and see what went on with the warehouse. See who
came and went, what went in and out. If by the end of
the day we hadn't seen anything to merit going into the
warehouse we were going to pick up the two guys for
questioning. At the very least they might be able to
give us some insight into who was inside the apartment,
where they were located and so forth. It could prove
useful if we needed to storm the apartments.

As the day wore on it became clear that nothing was
happening at the warehouse. Stark and I were sent
back by our CO to assist the team that was already
there on surveillance to pick up the guys when they
came out. Our orders were clear: affect an orderly
arrest of the two men and bring them to base for
questioning. Our CO made it very clear that he didn't
want the men harmed in case they were simply
deliverymen. It all came down to building relationships
with the locals. If we started looking or acting like

thugs then we were no better in their eyes than the Taliban. We were not to try and enter the building either. We had no idea what was waiting for us inside.

We parked the Humvee down the block and were watching the front of the warehouse. The first two guys from our unit, Blake and Richardson, that followed the truck to the warehouse, had already determined that there was only the rollup door, which was closed, and the standard entry door to it's right, also closed. At 1800 the door opened and the two deliverymen came out. They were laughing as they began to walk down the length of the warehouse. They seemed like two U.S. blue-collar guys who'd just punched a time clock at the factory and were headed to the local bar for a beer. They wore standard work shirts with the sleeves rolled up, blue jeans and work boots. I felt no threat but you could never be too careful. They were still laughing and carrying on as we approached them quietly from behind. They never heard or saw us coming until we were about ten feet behind them. Blake, Richardson and I all had our hands on side arms but they were still holstered. Stark on the other hand had drawn his gun and was pointing it at the men.

When the two finally sensed they were being followed they whirled around and immediately threw their hands up. Stark, seeing the men whirling fired one round from his service pistol. The round whizzed by one man's head and whacked into the side of the warehouse. The men's faces showed total terror. They began begging for mercy in Pashto, the language spoken most commonly in Kandahar. Ironically this was the language Stark had helped me learn at Q-course. We held our hands up and I told them we

meant them no harm. They stopped begging and I
turned to Stark and said, "What the fuck is wrong with
you?"

"I thought I saw a gun."

"Bullshit," I screamed at him. "Why did you have
your gun drawn in the first place? I thought we agreed
to keep them holstered, you dumb fuck." I was hot.
Not only could he have killed one of our witnesses
without provocation but also he could have started a
major incident. Fortunately we were in a fairly isolated
area. There were a few onlookers but as we scanned
the crowd most just wanted to slink away and not be
noticed.

Stark was beginning to regain his swagger. "Listen,
I'm the ranking guy here. You can't speak to me this
way. I'm telling you guys this incident goes no further
than right here. That's an order."

I glared at him, walked up to him and leaned down
until my nose was inches from him. "Fuck you," I
whispered, "I don't give a shit what rank you have.
You're a pussy and have no business in Special Forces.
For that matter why are you here? No more, Stark. No
more of your bullshit. You better straighten up or I will
take care of you. Mark my words." I walked away
leaving him speechless.

Blake and Richardson followed right behind me with
our two witnesses and called out to me as they glared at
Stark, "We got your back."

After we returned to base and made the witnesses
comfortable I returned to my bunk. Stark was waiting
for me. He looked anxious.

"What do you want," I snapped.

"Ryder, you're right. I've got a good thing. Maybe I
got the promotion for the wrong reason but that

doesn't mean I don't appreciate it. I'll clean up my act. I'll fix it," he said it with an air of sincerity.

"Fine. But you'd better toe the line or I will make sure you don't make it out of here. There are ten other men in this unit who are done with you as well. You need to fix that. You need to figure out how to get genuine with them again. We do the nasty jobs. All we have is each other. You screw your brothers they're going to screw you…big time. Someone's going to get killed because of you and I won't put my head in the sand anymore."

"I will Ryder, I will." He held out his hand to make peace and we shook. I watched my back though. I just kept hearing my wife's voice saying, "Don't trust him."

By the time I'd caught Alan up on my military life we'd spent a good two hours watching the same sentry do his slow walk around two sides of the school. The whole waltz took about five minutes each time start to finish. It was early afternoon and the shadows were getting longer. The sun would be gone in just a few more hours and the cluster of buildings along this side blocked our view of the rest of the campus. To get a better look at the rest of the school we were going to need to move to either the south or the north side. Based on the location of the administration building the front of the school would likely be on the north side. The largest building we could see was also on that side. It was probably the auditorium. Those were almost always at the front of the school. They usually had an entrance that opened to the sidewalk so that parents and guests arriving for school plays and orchestra recitals and PTA meetings could enter from the outside.

That big building would block a good portion of the front view into campus so I decided we should move to a position on the south. Either way we would have to cross the street in broad daylight, not something I was excited about doing.

"We need to get another view and I think the south side will offer the best angle," I said.

"I agree. Getting there is the tricky part. We were lucky with the wash. I suggest we go back the way we came about eight or ten houses so we can take a straight shot across the street. As long as the sentry we've been watching is away from the corner and there are no vehicles I think we can cross with reasonable safely."

"My thought exactly." We returned to the wash, checking carefully that it was clear before entering, moved down the row of houses counting ten fences as we went, found another double fence with the chain link on the outside and quietly dropped down into another weed-choked lawn. We checked the side windows to see if the house was occupied and again found it empty. Unlike the one we'd just left, this one had been ransacked.

The next forty yards was going to be the danger zone. Alan seemed to sense the same thing because for the first time he readied the submachine gun for action. I hoped we wouldn't have to use it this soon.

The side gate was about five feet tall so I was able to peer over it. Unfortunately, the house we picked offered a poor view of the street. On the right side of the driveway was a stand of Italian Cypresses stretching thirty feet into the air. These types of plants are usually manicured into tall thin columns but these had become overgrown and parts were leaning over on their neighbor forming a solid screen. On the left side the owners had left their motor home. It had since been trashed. The door hung open on one hinge. The tires had gone flat. Weeds had grown up through cracks in the driveway and were trying to climb inside through the bottom and the door. Spider-webs were spun all along the bottom edge of the camper to the driveway. The webs gave the appearance that they had trapped the RV in its place. We were blind to anyone or anything approaching from both directions. The good news was that we had guessed correctly and the house faced the entrance to the side street we needed to go down, which was one block south of the school. Lining each side were the same type of houses we'd seen throughout the neighborhood. Like so many areas in the valley this whole neighborhood had been developed as a tract by one developer who used four or five designs and flipped the floor plans to give eight to ten different looks. By adding subtle differences to trim and color the developer could disguise the fact that in reality everyone's home was really just like their neighbors for the most part.

We would have to take a chance and go out almost to the sidewalk to see if it was clear. Based on our observations from the first house it seemed to be a fairly low risk proposition. If we did see someone we could retreat to the rear of the house or even the wash if need be.

The gate was latched on the inside and the hinges were galvanized so there was little rust on them, but most likely the gate hadn't been opened in years. The latch opened without a sound but the gate made a scraping noise that seemed as loud as a jet engine in the relative quiet. I'm sure it wasn't that loud but to two

guys trying not to get killed it was plenty loud. We had
decided I would go left to the RV and Alan would go
right to the cypresses. When it was clear he would cross
first to a low hedge in the yard of the house directly
across the street and provide cover and I would cross
second to a low wall in the yard directly across from
me. We moved from the gate to the driveway at the
same time, quickly reaching our agreed positions at the
sidewalk. I was able to look south on the street and he
was able to clear north. He watched until the sentry
made the turn and started along the south side of the
school. We knew we had about two and half minutes
until he returned. I gave Alan the thumbs up sign. My
view was clear. He moved his fingers like they were
walking to indicate the sentry was still visible. About
thirty seconds later he gave the thumbs up. I double
checked the south approach and gave him the thumbs
up. He sprinted like an Olympic runner across the
street, jumped the hedge and dropped down quietly. He
popped back up a few seconds later and scanned both
directions. He gave me a thumbs-up. I figured I had
about a minute and a half left before the sentry
returned to the corner. I began my run across the street
and looked to my left just as I stepped off the curb.
For the first time all afternoon the sentry had changed
his pattern and was at the corner. He was looking
down the street and I could almost feel his eyes on me.
Either I was the unluckiest bastard or Alan had tripped
a sensor crossing the street. Rather than run I began
the slow walk of a scavenger. I kept my head down
glancing out of the corner of my eye as I went. The
sentry reached for his lapel mic and I could see him
talking into it. Alan was looking at me like I'd lost my
mind. I continued unhurried across the street and out

of the sentry's view. I waved for Alan to cross north to me and he did so quickly.

As Alan trotted up to me I said, "You must've tripped a sensor. The sentry appeared at the corner right as I stepped out and he was already looking in this direction. I played it like I was just a scavenger. I don't know if they'll send a patrol out or not but I don't want to be standing here if they do. We ran down about five houses, opened a side gate and ran into the backyard, closing the gate behind us but ignoring the previous caution of checking windows. There was a plastic shed in the back corner of the yard. We moved over and found that there was a small space between it and the back wall. We slid inside the space and waited, listening carefully for a response to our being spotted.

Off in the distance an engine fired up. Over the next minute the sound of the engine got closer, moving in our direction. It turned down the street we were on. The vehicle moved slowly, perhaps just rolling on idle. My heart was hammering. We were in a terrible location. I had no idea how many sensors were out here. If the patrol knew we were in this yard we would be trapped between them and the base on the other side. I kept imagining soldiers coming over the wall behind us. The space was too narrow to even pull a pistol out. The vehicle reached the house. We could hear the big eight-cylinder V8 engine rumbling in the street. It felt like time had stopped.

"Keep going dammit," I whispered to Alan.

The engine idled out front for another moment and then shut off.

"They've stopped. We're screwed," Alan said.

I risked stepping out from behind the shed long enough to draw my pistol and then quickly retreated.

Two doors slammed out in the street. I turned my head to look at Alan and he'd done the same. We were in deep trouble. Next door I heard the gate crash inward and bang on the cinder block wall separating that yard with this one.

"Hey you motherfuckers. You better show yourselves. If we have to pull you out of some hiding place you will not be happy campers. Just come out and we'll escort you out of the area," one of the men called out.

I looked back at Alan and shook my head. "Wait 'em out," I whispered.

A minute later we heard the gate to our yard crash in. My heart was racing. I tried not to breath for fear that the men might hear me. We stood stone still. I had the pistol pointed ready to fire if one of the me looked around the edge of the shed. Footsteps through the weeds in the yard came close. The shed vibrated as the men tried the doors. It had been locked. The next moment seemed to last for hours as we both waited for the men to come around and look behind the shed.

Then we heard the footsteps retreating. We both breathed. We still waited until the truck's engine fired up and slowly the vehicle moved down the street. We waited behind the shed while we heard the truck move down the next block south.

"That was way too damn close," Alan said as we moved out from behind the shed.

We listened as driver accelerated the big vehicle as it reached the corner of the base. A few minutes later the engine turned off.

For the first time in ten minutes we breathed easily.

"I guess they just figured I was a scavenger, took a cursory look and moved on. They probably got rousted out of a good poker game and didn't want to come looking for some smelly guys to ride out of here anyway. If they really saw me as a threat they would've done a more thorough search and gone house to house or sent more guys."

"Unsettling just the same. We would've been between a rock and a hard place, literally. So what now?"

"Let's check this house," I said hooking my thumb toward the house directly over the wall. "We need to know more about the layout of the school and I hope we can get some idea of where they might be holding Donte."

"We're in this far what's one more yard?"

Chapter 17

We made it over the wall and went through the routine of checking the windows on both sides. The house appeared to be clear. We weren't as lucky here as we were at the first house though. All the windows and doors were locked. There was a side door on the right side of the house that had an inexpensive looking locking knob. There was no deadbolt. I slid the KA-Bar from its sheath, slid the tip of the blade in between the door and the jamb and leaned hard on the handle of the knife. It was made of hardened steel and easily beat the wood in the door. The door splintered opened with crack and a pop.

We entered, cleared the house from room to room, pistols leading the way. We confirmed that the house was unoccupied. Again we found a picture window in the front of the house with an unobstructed view of the school looking north across the campus.

There was a new soldier on watch but he was doing the same back and forth dance we'd watched from the other side. From this side we could now see the layout of the campus. The school was divided in half. The left side held all the buildings and the right side was all playground. Between the rows of buildings we'd seen from our first location was another row of buildings. Four portable bungalows had been added as classrooms to the right of those. Right down the middle of the school was a covered walkway that allowed us to see all the way from the back to the front.

The playground had been turned into a helipad and motor pool. Two UH60 Blackhawk helicopters were parked on the grass portion of the yard. These were the replacements for the Hueys that Alan had flown in Nam. The blacktop part of the yard was a parking lot for a number of Humvees, trucks, and light armored vehicles. Between those and the buildings were a truck mounted water tank, a refueling truck and two massive electric generators, one of which was noisily clunking away.

I could now see the matching sentry walking the east and north fences. There were only two guards for four hundred yards of fence. Even if they doubled this at night, which I doubted they did, it was still not much security for such a large area. They had gotten complacent. That was good for us. It meant they probably weren't running drills. They would be caught off guard by any sort of attack. Still, I would prefer to run a stealth mission, but we would have to have some idea of where Donte might be held. I counted about thirty classrooms, a number of rooms in the main building, the cafeteria and the auditorium. There was no way we could go in and pull off a blind search.

I pulled my field glasses and scanned the school. Attached to the auditorium on the north side was a covered patio with lunch tables. I assumed the lower part of the building attached to the auditorium was the cafeteria. On the roof of the auditorium was a lookout post. One guard was stationed there as well. That made a total of three guards. They were all focused on the fence line and the streets outside. I watched for a while and saw no sentries patrolling the inside. There were a few soldiers milling around taking care of various duties. Two soldiers were playing basketball on one of the courts down by the parked Humvees.

Alan broke the silence. "So, what do you think?"

"I think we need more information. There are too many rooms to do a blind search. If we could narrow it down we might have a chance to sneak in and sneak out. The security is weak. They don't expect any trouble."

"Do you see any rooms being guarded?"

"No, there doesn't appear to be any interior security at all. They're minimally concerned about the perimeter but nothing at all inside," I answered.

"Let me take a look with the glasses."

I handed the glasses over to Alan. He spent a few minutes scanning the school. "I think I know where he is." He handed the glasses back to me.

"How?"

"Watch the center corridor. You should see two soldiers coming back from that classroom building right in the center of the complex. They're pushing a cart."

Sure enough a minute later two soldiers, pushing a serving cart appeared from the building and turned away from us. I followed them through the glasses until they entered the cafeteria area. "Ok, what am I missing?" I asked.

"They just brought trays of food on that cart."

"Yeah, so?"

"When was the last time you got room service on a military base?"

"Never," I said.

"Who gets room service on a military base?"

"Nobody. Even the officers go to the officer's club if they don't eat in the mess. Noncoms always eat in the mess. I would guess they are using the auditorium as a mess. Those usually have fold-down tables built into the walls for rainy days. Or they are just feeding them at the tables under the patio outside. I would make no sense to take food across the campus."

"Exactly," he said.

Then it finally sank in. "Prisoners."

The thought of "prisoners" took me back to Afghanistan. We had brought our two witnesses back to base, the two guys we'd followed to the warehouse. I kept referring to them as witnesses. Stark kept referring to them as prisoners. I saw them as two working class stiffs, just working for a day's wages. Stark saw them and every other Afghani; as inferior, as terrorists. Witness. Prisoner. Terrorist. It was all a matter of perspective. To many of the Afghans we were the terrorists. Just perspective.

We put our two witnesses in two separate rooms and were questioning them about their knowledge of the apartment building, Who were they were delivering to, what they were delivering? I was questioning one guy; Blake was talking to the other. Our goal was to ask the same questions then compare notes and see if their stories matched. I guessed that they would. I asked a series of pre-arranged questions, made notes and when I was done, politely asked the man to wait a moment while I went outside. Blake joined me shortly afterward. We compared notes while Stark listened over our shoulders. The guy's stories were spot on. They were assigned to deliver groceries to the apartment building. No, they didn't know the men. Yes, it seemed like a lot of food for two apartments but a sale was a sale. Their boss gave them the instructions. Their boss was the father-in-law of the man I was interrogating and the other man was his brother-in-law.

There was no reason to go further. Anyone could see they were telling the truth and were not involved in any way. They had been forthright and cooperative. They had provided us identical directions to the two apartments on the second floor. We should've thanked them for their cooperation and driven them home.

Stark would have nothing to do with it. He saw them as terrorists and prisoners. It was just that simple to him. He insisted we continue questioning them. We switched guys. Blake interviewed the guy I had interviewed and I got his. We asked the same questions in a different way and got the same answers. It was a waste of time to talk to them any more. When we came out the second time and told Stark that the stories were exactly the same he came unglued. He ran into the first room and began screaming at the guy. When he got nothing but fear and apologies from the man Stark began to punch him in the face, over and over in a fit of rage. I burst into the room and grabbed Stark and drug him from the room.

"I'm taking these guys home and when I get back I'm going to the Captain. You're done. You've lost your mind and you're a danger to this unit." If he had said one word then I would've smashed his face in but he just stood and stared, slack jawed and spent from beating the witnesses.

I went to the men and apologized. I lied to them told them Stark had lost a good friend to the Taliban and that he was crazed in his effort to avenge his death. They understood this. It wouldn't make the swollen eye and bruised face go away but they could understand why a man could go into a rage over it. They accepted my offer for a ride home.

When I returned all hell had broken loose. Our surveillance guys had verified that the Taliban cell was in the apartment and were getting ready to move. We needed to move and move fast or we would lose them. Stark would have to wait until after we dealt with these guys.

———

Chapter 18

Over the next eight hours Alan and I went over and over our plan to infiltrate the school and extract Donte. We ate and took turns napping. It would be important to be fresh and fed for our mission. Our goal was a simple one. Get in, get Donte, and get out, without being detected. It was simple on paper but my experience told me no mission was ever simple. It was the unknown factor that always mucked up some aspect of a mission. Our intel was weak at best. It was logical and it seemed right but there could be many other reasons why food was being delivered to a room. For all we knew a few guys were working on something vital in those rooms and couldn't stop down for lunch. But it didn't feel that way. My feeling had generally been good when it came to combat. Our explanation made sense and was the only reason we'd ever seen for room service on a military installation. But these were not normal times or normal circumstances. This was more like an occupation. This unit was the occupying force in a hostile environment. Their mistake was forgetting that. They saw themselves as U.S. soldiers on U.S. soil. That would work to our advantage.

We were going in at 0300, which was a half-hour away. Most people would be asleep at that time. We checked our weapons, stowed extra ammo in our pockets. It was likely that we may have to try and shoot our way out.

"No shame in backing out now," I said to Alan.

"Nope. I'm in all the way."

"You and I both know this has a high probability of being a suicide mission," I said.

"Listen, I've lived like a prisoner sentenced to solitary confinement myself for the past two years. I haven't felt anywhere near as alive as I have the last two days. You've given me purpose. So there is no option here. I can't go back to locking myself in alone, no more than you can give up your fight. No sir, I'm ready."

"Let's do this then."

The soldiers had strung light poles at each of the four corners of the school. The big metal halide spotlights were pointed out at the street directly away from the corners, which kept the centers of the fence relatively dark. The interior of the compound was poorly lit as well. There was no exterior lighting, no lights on the outsides of the buildings, no sconces, no light posts. The only light came leaking out through windows and the glow from the four spotlights at the corners. No new patrols had been added at night so we were facing the same security. We put our coats on. Mine was the black hooded sweatshirt I'd been wearing when I first met Alan and he had on the same black pea coat. I pulled the hood over my head and he wore a black watch cap. Our pants were black. The fireplace still held some soot, which we rubbed onto our faces, necks and hands. If we were going into pitch-blackness we would've been virtually invisible. In the dusky conditions on the campus we still would be hard to pick out in the shadows. Nothing would help if we got into the light. We checked and rechecked our weapons. It was time.

Our plan was to enter the school directly across from the house. Fortunately for us there was a gate in the middle of the fence almost directly across the street. If we'd had to cut through the fence it would've been impossible to hide the hole. The gate was locked in place by a chain wrapped around the two poles and secured with a padlock. One of the small tools I had brought was a set of ratcheting bolt cutters. They were a nice design. About the size of large pliers they had a ratcheting mechanism that gave them almost the same power as a pair of long handled bolt cutters. Those could be used to cut a link in the chain, remove it and enter, then rewrap the chain to look like it was locked. Unless someone physically checked it they would not be able to detect that it had been breeched. From there we would have to freelance based on circumstances. Our first step was just to get inside unnoticed.

We looked at each other wondering if we should say anything else. Alan and I had developed a bond in a short time, as soldiers in battle often do. I started to say something and he held up a hand and said, "Save it for later when we get back."

"Agreed. Let's go."

We slipped out the side door that we'd entered, out through the side gate and stopped at the sidewalk behind a low round bush. We waited for the sentry to make the corner and turn north. We quickly scanned the campus and saw no movement. We looked left and right on the street and seeing it clear we dashed across. The adrenaline began to pump. My fingers went cold quickly as my body removed blood from my extremities and brought it to vital organs in response to the hormone racing through my veins. Alan watched the corners with his submachine gun at the ready. We were as vulnerable as two people could be. Dark forms in a lighted area far from cover and trying to break into a military installation. My numb hands were making it difficult to use the cutters. I finally got the link seated in the jaws and began ratcheting. It felt like we'd been standing there for hours. Alan whispered, "One minute."

"One minute out or until he comes back."

"Out," he replied.

We had a minute and a half to get in, reset the chain and find cover before he came around the corner, that is, if he didn't pick up his pace, or turn early or if we tripped a sensor coming across the street or going through the fence. I realized then that this was hopeless. It would take more luck than we could possibly have to pull this off. There was so much we didn't know about the facility. We were trying to extract a prisoner that might not be alive. We were certainly outmanned. We had no backup, no plan of retreat because we didn't have and couldn't have a specific plan of attack. Everything I'd been taught to do, and everything I'd been taught to think about in planning a mission I was ignoring. But I forged ahead anyway. Saving Donte was a way to save my family. I had to continue.

"One fifteen," Alan announced as the cutters bit through the link. The broken link fell and I instinctively reached down for it and caught it inches before it hit the concrete of the sidewalk. We looked at each other and mouthed "Whew" at the same time. I carefully unwrapped the chain from the fence.

"One thirty," Alan counted.

I slid the latch up and slowly swung the gate open, praying it wouldn't squeal. First bit of luck, the gate opened noiselessly. I opened it just wide enough for us to slip through, closed it and began to wrap the chain around.

"One forty-five", Alan said.

I got the chain around the gate and it looked almost like it had before we entered. The sentry would never notice. Twenty feet away was the first row of classrooms. The doors and windows were shielded from the street by a four-foot tall wooden partition. We moved quickly towards it, and slid behind. I checked the windows. The rooms were dark. It was likely that the rooms on the outside were unused by the soldiers. They would be too vulnerable to an attack from the outside of the fence. A drive by, a lobbed Molotov cocktail, or a sniper could do reasonable damage to these rooms without ever entering the campus.

"Two," Alan said as we settled in back to back to watch as much of the approach to us as possible.

"We wait for him to pass, return and head up the side again before we move, okay," I said.

"Roger."

We heard the soft click-click of boots on the asphalt. It got louder and louder then receded as the sentry moved to the end of the fence. I could hear faint voices in the distance and the hum of the generator. Occasionally we could hear someone cough. There were no sounds of hurried activity, which was good. It made me think we hadn't tripped any alarms. The base commander here was not a smart guy, or he was too smart and confident. The alarms were fine down the street but his perimeter defense was woefully inadequate. Either he needed more manpower on the fence line or he needed to alarm it or both. He was prepared for a large force to move on him. I imagine he had sensors on all the approach roads at one hundred yard intervals, which would give them time to be ready for an invading force, or a roving riot. Perhaps the security had been there as long as the beginning, when the martial law had been established and this unit had been assigned there. The threat had been large groups at the time. Now that those were gone and they had the firepower they perceived little threat. Stupid and sloppy leadership lead to death. Experience had taught me that.

———

My final mission as a member of the Special Forces had been one of those missions. Stupid and sloppy leadership. While I was returning our witnesses to their homes, Stark informed the squad that our guys working surveillance had verified the Taliban group was in the apartment, and looked like they were ready to move.

Our CO had been recalled to a rear headquarter for a strategy session, leaving Stark in charge. I knew from the get-go we were in trouble, and I sensed from the other guys in our unit that they felt the same way. But we wanted these bastards; we wanted them bad. And we were Special Forces after all. No one, but no one could beat us, least of all these amateurs.

We rolled up in two transports, parked two blocks away and approached our surveillance location from the rear. We were in full combat gear, ACU's with complete Interceptor Body Armor. It made you feel invincible. I sometimes wondered if that was more it's purpose than actually protecting us. It definitely made us feel bolder.

Stark's plan was simple. We knew the location of the apartments from the two witnesses. The apartments were on the backside of the building, away from the street, side by side on the second floor. We knew there were stairs on either side of the building. We would split into two teams, one going up one stair and one going up the other. We would enter the hall, pincer the two apartments and storm them simultaneously. Those going in first knew the risks but volunteered for the duty.

I was assigned to go around to the far side, climb to the roof of the building across the street and set up for sniper fire. We would coordinate the attack through integrated communication in our helmets. I would give the signal and both groups would surprise the enemy simultaneously. My job was to fire behind on anyone who I saw draw first as our guys entered.

I made my way around to the building and climbed to the roof. I came out to the bright sun, waited for my eyes to adjust and moved low to a concealed position behind the parapet. I sighted in on the two apartments. There were four apartments on this side of the building, each having two windows. The two we were concerned with were the two in the middle. I scanned from window to window. Several men were going about their business. I radioed everything I saw to the rest of the group. I heard Stark give the order to move into the building. There was a minute of quiet. I looked to the windows again. The men were out of sight. I radioed this information to my squad. I heard cross traffic asking for go or no go. I heard Stark order for them to continue.

I looked back to the window. Two men in each apartment were just standing. Something wasn't right about it. The two scenes in two different apartments were mirror image of each other. Two men in each apartment, standing, facing each other. One in each of the four windows. Just standing there. It was too symmetrical. I radioed my concern. I heard each team member call for go or no go. Both added they were in position in the hallway, ready to go. Stark came back with the go command. I heard "go-go-go" reverberating in my headset. I saw both doors crash open. I saw our guys spilling into the rooms. The first guy in went right, the next left, and so on. I could see them yelling for the standing guys to get down. Then I saw each man open the front of his shirt. I heard the call of "bomb-bomb" and then the flash and multiple booms. I hit the deck as debris rained down on me and searing heat and smoke rolled across the roof. I heard the screams of my unit in my headset. Seconds later I heard small arms fire and more screams. I called names starting with Stark, no answer. I called to the team leaders, no answer. I called each name in my unit, no answer. I stood and saw the smoking ruin that had been the second floor of the apartment. There was no movement.

I was shaken but I needed to get over to the apartment and see if anyone was alive. I turned to head to the door and two of the men I'd seen in the apartment when we first arrived were coming onto the roof. I fired my carbine from the hip. The first guy was cut in half and dropped immediately. The second ducked back inside. I charged for the door just as the man turned the corner. I bounded down the stairs after him. He was heading for the next flight of stairs. I no longer cared about my safety. I just needed to catch him. He paused at the top of the stairs and raised his pistol. I fired from the hip as I ran. The stream of bullets walked up the wall and into his torso. He fell and I heard him thump down the stairs. I ran down the final flight and hurdled over the dead body.

I hit the exit door, ran the width of the apartment and stopped at the corner. I did one more roll call into my mic. Nobody answered, including Stark. Where was Stark? He'd been coordinating things from the surveillance house. He should've been safe. The front of the apartment appeared to be clear. I heard the sound of sirens rolling toward the burning apartment. Several civilians were wandering out of the apartment and around the parking lot in front. Some were injured, holding bloody towels to their faces and arms. Two men were lying on the ground with severe injuries to their torsos. The women next to them were wailing. There were no members of my team in sight. People screamed at me. They blamed me. They called me a killer. I ran into the building, climbed what was left of the stairs and turned into the hallway. There was a smoking hole where the interior wall of the two apartments was. Two of my guys were lying in the hallway. Both were missing limbs and parts of their faces. They were dead but I checked for vitals anyway. I moved forward toward the hole. Spot fires still burned. There was little left in the apartments. A huge hole was left in the floor. I could see piles of burning debris and human remains in the apartment below. Through the missing outside wall I could see across to the rooftop I'd just left. A crowd had gathered there. Plaster had fallen in from the roof, which was still burning in several places. The walls were littered with pieces of humanity. I puked. I felt light headed. I backed out of the hallway.

When I returned to the parking lot a huge crowd had gathered, fire trucks and emergency response teams were arriving. I pushed through the angry and stunned crowd and headed for the surveillance house.

It was empty. Stark was gone. There was no sign of a struggle or fight. I thought he'd been jumped like I had. A thousand questions were swirling through my head all at once. I couldn't focus on any of it. I was dazed.

I stumbled back to the chaos. People were running in every direction. Smoke was drifting across the street. Other units from our base were arriving. They began securing the perimeter immediately. The medical response team arrived and they led me to the ambulance to check me out. I was in a fog. I had minor cuts and bruises, and my ears were ringing from the blast.

As the medics finished their evaluation of me two M.P.s approached. They stopped in front of me. One was taller than me, the other shorter.

"Ryder?" the shorter MP asked as a question.

"Yes," I responded as I looked down at my name patch just to make sure.

"You'll need to come with us," the taller one stated.

"You guys debriefing?" I asked. It was unusual for MPs to pick up someone after a mission. My head was still swimming. I felt like the solid ground beneath my feet had turned to Jell-O.

"No, you're under arrest," the shorter one said.

I let his words sink in. I wasn't really sure he'd actually said that. "Arrest?"

"Yes. For violating the Uniform Code of Military Justice section 892.92, failure to obey an order. But by the end of the day we may be adding ten counts of 918.118…murder."

As Alan and I watched the sentry move past again I refocused on the present. We left our hiding place and started slowly into the interior of the school. The building we thought might be Donte's cell was two down from where we were. It was about fifty feet away but it looked like a mile. There was little to hide behind. A few overgrown bushes in planter boxes dotted the walkway. We could hear the occasional voice. They were soft and muted coming from inside the various buildings. I guessed they were using these classrooms as barracks. Once we heard a door pop open at the end of one of the buildings to our right. We waited for someone to head our direction but no one came. We finally reached the corner of the building we were working toward. There was no one visible in the space outside the classrooms.

I still had no idea how we would get into the room even if we did find Donte. We moved, pressed against the side of the building and came to the first door. I leaned to my left and peered into the room. It was filled with valuables. There was silver, paintings, statues, furs, piles and piles of jewelry boxes, with jewelry spilling out, beautiful antique furniture. There were boxes and stacks of the things. None of it had any earthly business being on a military base. It was a room full of plunder. It looked like a pirate cave. In that moment I had clarity. I knew why they were clearing everyone out and forcing everyone into the settlements. They wanted to make it easy to clear houses out. That was what the two soldiers were planning the day they chased Donte and I. The whole unit had to be in on it. This stuff was in plain sight. It was unheard of. I looked over my shoulder to Alan.

He mouthed "What the hell." I shrugged my shoulders in response. We moved on to the next room. I had my fingers crossed. If Donte wasn't in this one we'd have to start a blind search and that would make our chances of success almost zero. Stumbling around in a military base when you are the enemy would not end well. I leaned around and peered in the window. The room was empty. I looked over my shoulder and shook my head no. Alan looked down at his shoes.

We moved on to the end of the building. There was a roll up trash bin at the end. We huddled down next to it.

"What now?" Alan whispered.

"Two choices. We give up and get out while we can. Or we split up and start canvassing room by room. We meet back here in thirty minutes. If you find him don't try to get him out yourself. Come back and we'll figure out the best course of action."

"Okay. I vote for option 'B'." he said without hesitation.

I smiled. "I knew you would. I won't try to talk you into leaving because I already know the answer."

"Yes you do," he said.

"You take this side and the bungalows and I'll take the row on the west side and the front office building. I doubt he's in the auditorium. We'll leave that for last if we don't find him. If all hell breaks loose get out any way you can and we'll rendezvous at your place."

He reached in his pocket and pulled out a key ring. He spun a key off the ring. "Here's an extra key to the fence. The same key opens the door as well."

"Thank you. Thirty minutes. Watch your ass. Be safe," I warned.

"Yes sir," he said with a wink and snapped off a salute. I returned it and we went off in opposite directions. I watched over my shoulder as he disappeared into the dark. I had the distinct feeling I'd never see him again.

I decided the quickest and safest way to check my buildings were to start at the south fence and work my way forward. The closer I got to the front the more likely to run into guards and personnel at work. I worked a serpentine pattern up and down the rows, checking in the windows of each as I went.

On the street side I had to be very mindful of the sentry that was patrolling the perimeter. At one point he passed by me, no more than ten feet away, as I crouched against the building. I held my breath until he passed. Within ten minutes I had checked the first three buildings. That left the two rooms on the north side of the little kid playground and the office.

I moved across the playground quickly. Pausing behind the big play structure in the middle. The rooms were dark. I was hoping I could see in without having to go right up to them but that was not going to happen. I slipped across the last thirty feet. The rooms were barracks. Rows of cots had replaced the rows of desks in these rooms. There were about ten cots in each of the rooms. Most were occupied with sleeping soldiers. But no Donte. I would have to search the office. I recalled the rows of windows along the street side of the administration building. We had stared into them for several hours that afternoon. *That afternoon.* It seemed like it was days ago.

I slipped around the west end of the barracks and crawled down the side of the building. I looked for the sentry. He was on the south fence. I had at most a minute to look then I would have to get back in the shadows. I looked into the first window. The room was dark. I could make out several large shapes against the walls. They were big and boxy. Copiers. There was a door on the far wall that opened to the outside. On the floor was a softer shape. I pressed closer to the window. It was a body. I cupped my hands against the sides of my face and strained. It was Donte. He was there. He was chained to one of the massive copiers. I had to get him out. Then. I couldn't go back for Alan. There wasn't time. I just sensed that getting Donte out was a now or never proposition. I realized then I'd been standing there far too long. I turned slowly to see the guard halfway up the fence and coming my way. I couldn't run and I wouldn't have time to make it to cover. I slowly lowered myself flat in the long grass. I had to hope he wouldn't see me. He would pass by me less than six feet away. I pulled my knife out of my sheath. If I had to kill him I doubted it would be long before someone noticed he was missing. My face was flat against the ground looking directly at the guard. He came closer, passed by me and continued on the last fifty feet to the northwest corner. Once he'd passed I could no longer see him. He could come up behind me and I wouldn't know it. My heart was racing. I knew if I lifted my head he would see the movement. It took every ounce of control to lay still. I finally heard the soft stepping of the rubber boots shuffling along in rhythm. Within a moment I saw his feet. He continued on. I waited until he was about one hundred feet away, his back to me as he walked to the south fence, and I stood. I now had about two minutes until he would be back. I moved on to the next window. I went through the same drill to see in. This had been the nurse's office. Again on the floor was a body. This one was much smaller, much more delicate. It had to be a woman. They had a woman prisoner, too.

The next window looked in on what had been the principal's office. A cot had been added to it. A man was sleeping on it with his back to the window. An officers dress uniform hung on a rack by the door. This was the CO. My heart sank. I was going to have to go into the center of the beehive.

I needed to know what else was in the office. The next window was the outer office. It was unoccupied. Behind the final window was a storage room. No staff was inside. If I could get inside I had only the officer to avoid. The big question was how to get in. I glanced at my watch. I was twenty-five minutes into my thirty minutes. I was going to have to go in by myself. There was not enough time to get back to Alan, work our way back and get Donte out. That would be more risk than reward.

The front of the office faced the cafeteria. That would be the one place where there would be significant activity at this time of night. Cooks would be preparing breakfast for the unit. Hopefully they would be too busy to notice me.

I moved around to the corner. There was no movement anywhere in my angle of vision. The area between the office and cafeteria had more lighting than anywhere else I'd seen on the campus. Light from the kitchen and overhead halide lights in the patio seating area were washing out across the open space and illuminating the front of the office in orange light. There was no sentry in front. If I could catch a break and find an unlocked door I might have a chance. I moved to the first door. This was the door I'd seen in

Donte's room. It was locked. I moved to the next door. I had seen this door through the window in the inner door to the nurse's office. It was locked as well. I moved on. I knew from looking into the CO's room that he had a door that opened into the front office. The size of his office and the door to the nurse's office told me there was an interior hall that went from the front office past the nurse's office and ended at Donte's. There had to be a door at the end of that hallway that opened into Donte's room. It would be the only way to access that room from the inside.

I came to the last door, the last chance. This door opened into the front office. I tried the knob, and it turned. I opened the door and slipped inside. The light from outside leaked into the office through the front windows and gave enough light that I could see where I was going. I started down the hall, and peered in the nurse's office as I went by. I could see the woman's face faintly in the orange light. It might have been the wrong time to have the thought but my first take was that she was attractive.

I got to the door at the end of the hall and tried the knob. I didn't expect it to open since there was a prisoner inside but it wasn't. My luck was holding. I slowly opened the door entered the room and closed the door behind me. I went over to Donte and knelt down. His lips were swollen and his right eye was nearly closed. He'd taken a bad beating. I touched his face and softly whispered his name. He began to stir. "Donte, it's Ethan. Can you hear me?" He moaned softly and opened his eyes. He instinctively flinched away when he saw someone right in his face. "Donte, it's me, its Ethan," I whispered again.

"Ethan?" he asked, confused because I was there.

"Yes, I'm going to get you out."

I took the bolt cutters out of my pack and snipped through the chain on his wrist. I felt around his ankle and cut through the chain there. He was left with a bracelet and anklet set. "Can you stand?" I whispered.

"Yes, I think so. He only hit my face."

"Who?" I asked.

"The boss dude. He's pretty pissed at you." He looked down. "I'm sorry," he whispered.

"For what?"

"For telling him where the house was. I thought for sure they'd killed you. I heard explosions last night, not too long after they made me tell."

"I'm not pissed. I'm here aren't I? I figured they'd make you talk. You're not a soldier. Nothing to worry about. We need to go now." I helped Donte to his feet. "You okay on your own?"

"Yes. I'll be fine," he answered.

We moved into the hall. I was in front, Donte behind. As we passed the woman's cell Donte pulled on my sleeve. "Man, we gotta get her out too. He's doin' some bad stuff to her. I could hear it through the wall." He was practically begging.

"Donte, we've got enough to worry about." He looked at me. His innocence and age made him impervious to the danger that was all around us. But the look in his eyes was pleading. I tried the door and it was unlocked. This is the sloppiest operation I've ever seen, I thought. We went in and I gently woke the woman. She was blonde and just a little younger than me; late twenties I would guess. Her face was pretty, even through the bruising. She stirred a bit, her eyes fluttered and she flinched and let out a gasp just like Donte did. Only my face was not one she'd ever seen.

She tried to shrink away and rattled the chain and bed. The noise seemed very loud in the small space. "I'm here to help you. Don't be afraid. I'm going to cut you loose and then we're going to get out. Okay?"

She nodded her heed in agreement. I cut her loose. "Can you stand?" I whispered to her. She nodded again. I helped her to her feet. Just as we began to file into the hallway I heard the door to the CO's office open. I pointed to the room Donte had been in and we took off for it, made the room and quietly closed the door as the lights snapped on. I tried the back door in Donte's room. I don't know why I didn't the first time. Just carelessness. It didn't matter because this one was locked from the inside as well as the outside. We were trapped in the room. We just had to pray that the CO went back to bed without checking on his guests.

We waited breathlessly. I had drawn both pistols and was pointing them at the door. If someone came through I would cut him in two. After a minute the light disappeared from under the door and I heard the click of the door shut. We waited another minute then I slowly opened our door. There was no one in the hall. We cautiously advanced. When we reached the end of the hall I held up my palm to indicate I wanted them to stop then held up one finger telling them to wait. I walked to the door, reached for the knob and the light snapped on. I'd made the one mistake you should never make: clear the room before you cross it. I spun around quickly with the pistol aimed chest high.

I'm sure the expression on my face matched the expression on the CO's face. It was Stark.

Chapter 19

Stark. My mind flew thousands of miles and two years ago to Afghanistan. The end of my military career flashed through my mind in the instant I stood there facing him.

———————

The MP's had taken me back to base after the disaster at the apartment and brought me into a room with a table and two chairs, one on each side. They sat me down in one of the chairs and handcuffed me to the frame. The shorter MP sat in the chair opposite me while the other leaned against the wall in the corner.

"You guys want to tell me what this is all about?"

"You disobeyed an order," said the tall guy.

"Your acting CO, Stark, says you went to the apartment against orders. He claims you stirred everyone on your team into action," said the smaller guy.

"What are you talking about? He was there. He was orchestrating the whole thing," I pleaded.

"And your proof is what?" said the short guy.

"Talk to my guys. They'll tell you."

The tall guy walked to the edge of the table, leaned over and put his hands on both corners. He leaned in and said, "Now that would be a neat trick. Everyone in your unit is dead. Their blood is on you. Stark says you're a maverick. That you do whatever you feel like. Know what else he told us."

I shook my head "no". My world was so upside down I had no idea what was real and what wasn't. Who were the good guys and who were not?

"He told us to check your footlocker. And guess what we found?"

I didn't answer but I knew. It was the contraband that Stark had put there. Stark had seen his opportunity to get rid of me. He knew I was going to the CO when he returned. He knew his time was short unless he did something. He bailed on us just to bring a charge against me. He hadn't killed our unit; the Taliban bombers had done that.

"You'll fry for this Ryder," the short guy said.

I was shipped back to the states and was set for court-martial and assigned an attorney from JAG Corps. He was a good guy and he seemed to believe my story. He and my wife were about the only ones who did. They were charging me with everything: disobeying a direct order, ten counts of involuntary manslaughter, releasing a prisoner without proper authority, for taking home the two guys Stark had beaten. They decided my reckless disobedience of the alleged order not to go to the apartment was not intended to kill the men in our unit but rather a consequence of my ignoring the order, hence the manslaughter charge. They also charged me with theft from occupied persons. This was considered worse than stealing from another soldier because it had the potential for additional problems. Those were the same problems I'd presented to Stark.

I'd spent two months in Leavenworth awaiting the court martial. The day before my trial was to begin my attorney came to me and said the government had offered to drop all charges if I agreed to waive the trial and sign to a General Discharge. General discharges are given to a service member whose performance is good but is marked by a considerable departure in duty performance and conduct expected of military members. It was a dramatic plea deal. My attorney was amazed. He hadn't even been given consideration for a plea and all of a sudden the prosecution offered the deal out of the blue. It would mean the end of my career and it might look bad on my record. I would lose all veteran benefits but I wouldn't spend the next fifty years in a federal penitentiary. I took the deal. I went home. I never knew what happened to Stark.

Now I did. We stood staring, with guns pointed at each other, in a stalemate.

He broke the silence first, "Ryder," he said nodding his head in recognition. "So you're my shooter. I should've figured as much. Put the gun down, now."

My anger burned. I had thought so many times about what I would do if I were ever alone with him. How I would repay him not only for what he did to me but also for his cowardice at running and leaving us to be butchered.

"Stark," I replied with an icy calm. Out of the corner of my eye I could see Donte and the woman back down the hall out of view. Just Stark and I stood in the outer office, no more than ten feet apart. It was now a matter of who would flinch first.

"You have more lives than a cat my old friend," he sneered. "I've tried to get rid of you four times now and you just keep coming back from the dead."

Get rid of me, four times, I questioned in my head. What was he talking about?

"It's amazing," he continued. "But not this time. You're in my office with a red laser dot painted on your chest, and shortly this camp will all awaken for morning duty. The first guy that sees us in this stalemate will call a general alarm and a sniper, just like you were, will pick you off. You'll get to feel what your handiwork felt like. If you were here by yourself, just to get me I would be worried that you might try suicide and pull the trigger on me, which you know would cause me to involuntarily pull my trigger and kill you. But you're here for him, aren't you. He rolled over on you so quick. What a little pussy."

"Figures you'd let someone else shoot me. You don't have the balls for it. Never did. You're the real coward and pussy here. He's not a soldier. Of course neither are you. You said you tried to get rid of me four times. What are you babbling about?" I was hoping to get him to react to the insults, to lose his focus for just a second. But he didn't flinch.

"You still haven't figured it out? First time was the goat farm. You should've been cut to pieces then. Why do you think I stayed behind the wall? I knew what was going to happen because I made sure of it. It was just dumb luck that you sweetened things by being a hero and then knocking yourself out so I could take the credit," he paused to let that sink in. "The second time was the apartment building. Those two goons I sent up there were just too incompetent. My mistake. Third time shows how quick I can think. When I heard you on the radio I knew you had dispatched the assassins I sent for you so I hightailed it to base, and filed a complaint with the base CO. They bought it hook, line and sinker. I was a decorated hero after all. They sent you away, I looked like a golden boy and got

146

to keep on with my, oh so profitable, arrangement with my Taliban friends. They like to fund their operation with heroin sales. What better way to bring their product to market than on a US Military Transport plane? No customs, no luggage check, no airport scanners. Twenty percent of the cut went to me. I'm a friggin' millionaire but fat lot of good it does now. So now I just collect things to sell on the black market. I'm sure you saw my stash while you were poking around. Not as profitable as the dope but it brings nice things on trade. You were just trying to rescue one of those. Too bad. You and the boy will go out in the garbage. She'll return right there to her room. I have to say I have enjoyed her company."

I felt like I'd been kicked in the gut. I hadn't seen how really evil Stark was. I just thought he was a thief and a lousy solider. He was far worse than that. He was a traitor, a rapist and a serial murderer. My rage was boiling but I needed to know why he'd do these things. No one could be that selfish and demented. I wanted to dive across the counter and rip his throat out. I paused. He'd said four. When was the fourth? "You said four times. What was the fourth? "

"Ahh yes. Well if you were pissed at me before you really will be now. After you were sent away the MP's started snooping around and had some hint that I might not be such a sweetheart. Not enough to convict mind you but enough to sour them to me. So I got transferred out of Special Forces and sent here to play policeman in hell. Got a promotion. Captain now. Ironically I got sent right to the place where your home was. I knew they thought perhaps you weren't such a bad boy after all. They couldn't just let you off Scot-free but they let you out and made you a free man. You can thank me later. Or not. So I remembered that your home was in the area and decided to pay you a visit and finish what I'd been unable to do in Afghanistan. I just wasn't comfortable with you around. Sadly, your wife told me you weren't home, so while we waited for you I had my boys kill your neighbors and burn down the block. It kept them busy while your wife and I became very close, if you know what I mean. After that, well, you know the after that. No need to remind you."

I bolted for him and dove headlong into him. I could see the look of fear on his face as I was flying toward him in a murderous rage. He fired but only grazed my arm. In the state I was in I didn't even feel it. I came at him like a missile. We fell hard with me on top and I heard the wind rush out of him. He still had the gun and I had his wrist. We were locked in an arm wrestle to the death. I was in an awkward position with my left hand on the floor holding up my weight. I couldn't lift it or I would roll off him.

We fought like that for what seemed like minutes but was in fact only seconds. He would gain some ground trying to move the gun up high enough to hit me and I was pushing against both his arms to smack his hand on the floor. I heard our breath raspy and desperate. I could smell fear and hatred in our sweat. Then, I heard in the distance the familiar rat-tat of machine gun fire. Seconds later I was thrown from Stark as the wall blew in. Heat, smoke, debris, brilliant orange light ripped through the room. It took a second to regain my composure. Across the yard I could see a huge billowing column of black smoke and orange fire roaring a hundred feet in the air from where the fuel truck had stood. It was a twisted pile of wreckage.

Stark was running down the hall away from us toward the storeroom, Donte and the girl came running out of the hallway at the same time. I heard the rat-tat of the machine gun again. This time it came from a different spot. A few seconds later there was another explosion as one of the two parked helicopters erupted into flame. Everything had an orange glow to it. Men began spilling out of the barracks, their excited screams filling the air. I had seconds to make a decision. Stay and finish Stark, and likely die myself or save Donte as I had set out to do. And now there was another human life in the balance with the woman. I paused only a fraction of a second. Stark would have to wait.

"Let's go," I grabbed the woman's hand and led her out the hole in the wall. Donte followed. We sprinted down the long corridor past a few confused soldiers. They had been awakened from a deep sleep by an explosion and still had no idea what was going on. Most stood in their underwear, gawking at the flames. They gave us confused looks as we went by, more concerned with the explosions than us. Only once did I hear one soldier yell for us to stop but he made no effort to do so.

We made it to the gate. The woman was winded and was beginning to hyperventilate. "You okay?" I asked them.

"Can't breath," she whispered.

"I'm okay," said Donte. "Thank you.'

"Don't thank me yet. We aren't safe yet."

"Thank you for coming. That's all that matters."

I shook my head. I knew what he meant. I unwrapped the chain, swung the gate open, scooped up the woman and threw her over my shoulders in a fireman's carry and we took off down the street.

The trip back to Alan's was uneventful. Stark's guys must've been too busy with the fires to expend much energy looking for us. We heard a few Humvees off in the distance but none ever came near us.

It was close to 0500 when we made it back. The eastern sky was beginning to glow with the first light of day. A cool breeze was blowing from the north. I set the woman down on the sidewalk and she began to stir. I disarmed the fence. I reached a hand down to help her up and couldn't ignore the fact that she was beautiful. The faint light of morning hid the bruises on her face and I could clearly see the beauty that was hidden beneath. She was about 5'5", almost a foot shorter than me. She had shoulder length strawberry blonde hair. She was petite but there was an air of strength about her. Her most striking feature was her eyes. They were the bluest of blues, almost clear. I thought I could see to her soul through those eyes. She smiled as she stood and straightened her dress out of habit. I smiled back.

"Hi, I'm Amy Thalia."

I felt like a schoolboy. I almost forgot to reciprocate with my name. I regained my composure, "Ethan Ryder." I offered my hand again and we shook. I caught Donte out of the corner of my eye. He had picked up on my interest in the woman and was smiling and shaking his head at me. I shrugged my shoulders. We went into the house and I reset the fence. We kept the lights off to avoid bringing attention to the house. I tended to my arm. The bullet had created a flesh wound and had bled little as the hot bullet self-cauterized the wound. I washed it and taped some gauze over it.

By the time I came out of the bathroom Amy had fixed a breakfast of some of the homemade bread, canned fruit salad and was cooking some spam on the stove. We were just getting ready to dig in when we heard the door. I grabbed one of the .44's and moved into the hallway. It swung open and Alan stepped in. He had a huge smile. "Damn did you see that fire ball? Wow. That was interesting. What next?"

That was a good question: "What next?"

"A person often meets his destiny on the road
he took to avoid it" –
Jean de La Fontaine, 17th century French Poet

PART II – On The Road

Chapter 20

What next? We'd just blown apart an army installation and I'd come face to face with the guy I'd dreamed of dispatching with extreme prejudice for the past two years. But we were safe. Beyond some cuts, scrapes, bumps and bruises we'd pulled off the almost impossible. But Stark was still alive.

"Here's what I'm going to do. I'm going back to get their commander."

Alan looked puzzled, Donte and Amy looked horrified.

"Why in the hell would you want to do that?" asked Alan.

"Because I have to." I retold the story to the three of them. Alan knew some parts but Donte and certainly Amy had not heard it. I shared what Stark had told me, how he'd set me up, then raped my wife and killed my family.

"Ethan, you won't make it," Alan said. "If he's as evil as you say he's going to come looking for you. He can't and won't allow you to live. We have no element of surprise. He knows you and he knows you'll come after him. It will be a suicide mission."

"Perhaps, but I have no choice." Donte and Amy stood quietly, listening to our conversation.

"You always have a choice. Ethan, you risked your life to save Donte, and I assume this young lady, who I haven't had the pleasure of meeting yet, as well. You had a chance to go after Stark then. But you chose these people over your revenge. What does that say about your priorities?"

"You don't understand. He killed my family. He ruined my life." My voice was quivering. I was shaking and my eyes were welling with tears. The anger was pressing down on my chest. I'd never really dealt with my loss. I'd just carried my anger with me as fuel to keep me going. I woke every day, putting one foot in front of the other in an effort to find who killed my family and to make sure it didn't happen again to someone else's family. Now I knew, I knew who to direct my anger toward. I knew where he was. I just needed to finish the job.

"I do understand. I get it. But you have people here. They are alive, not ghosts of the past. You have me, you have Donte and I'm guessing you now have this young lady who I still don't know." He smiled at the last statement.

"Alan, this is Amy. Amy this is Alan. She was also an unwilling guest of Stark's," I said. "Amy this is Donte. I'm guessing you two never met."

"No we didn't. First, let me say it is a pleasure to meet both of you." She shook both Alan and Donte's hands. She turned to me and said, "Thank you. I don't know how much longer I could've gone on there. I am forever grateful to you," She stepped across the room, reached up and threw her arms around my neck. I bent to make it easier for her. She kissed my cheek and whispered, "Thank you," into my ear again. The warmth of her touch and the feeling of her skin against my cheek felt good. It had been so long since I'd had that feeling. But it also felt wrong. In my mind I was still married. It felt like I was cheating on my wife. I gently pushed her away.

"Ethan, I know I don't know you very well but it seems you've found a new family. Clearly these two consider you family, and if the three of you will allow me to join, then the three of us will call you family. That should count for something. "

Her argument was compelling and the tone of her voice had a melodic quality that made it hard to argue with. But I was still stinging from the revelations that I had just learned several hours before. "I'm going to have to think about my next step. Your next steps are easy to figure out. We need to decide how to get you out of here before they come looking. We need to figure out where you are going and how you are going to get there without getting caught. The longer we wait the more organized the soldiers are going to get in their search. Stark will want me bad. And my guess is he's going to want Amy back. This house will not be safe for long. We have too many loose ends, starting with Mr. Google. He'll roll over on us. As much as he agreed with what I was doing he'll cave to save his ass or for the right price. They'll figure out Alan helped me and they'll put two and two together. My guess is we have less than twenty-four hours to get you all out of here."

"What do you suggest?" Amy asked.

"Ethan, I ain't leavin' if you ain't," Donte said.

"Same goes for me. You know I won't run from a fight," Alan added.

"I can't be responsible for all of you. This is why I was a loner. I can't go through losing someone else. So this is my fight. You will leave and I will stay and that's how it's going to be." I was trying to sound convincing but I wasn't convinced myself that this was the right path to take.

"Look Ethan. You know me pretty well now. I've got nothing to lose. I'm in this all the way. You decide to stay then I'm staying. Your fight is my fight now. Unless you shoot me I'm in," Alan stated with clarity of conviction that was impossible to argue with. He was man who knew himself and knew what he was going to do and there was no changing that.

"Man, you think I'm gonna walk away now. You saved my ass twice. I owe you my life twice over. No way I can walk away. I'm in whatever you do. You go I go. You stay, I stay," Donte said with the same conviction as Alan's.

"Count me in too. You've saved my life as well. I owe it to you," said Amy.

"All right, all right. I need to think this through. Let me sleep on it. A few hours sleep will do all of us some good. We're all still amped up on the adrenaline from tonight. Everyone get a few hours in the rack and then we'll see where we're at. Okay."

Chapter 21

I woke a few hours later. The sun filtered in and out of the patchy clouds. The wind was blowing hard outside. I swung my feet over the edge of the bed. Every muscle in my body ached. I felt like a bus had run me down the day before. In some ways it had. An emotional bus. I had so many conflicting feelings. I hated Stark with every fiber of my being and I wanted to tear him apart piece by piece. But the words that my newly found friends had spoken last night were resonating against my hatred for Stark. I had risked my life for Donte. Alan had risked his for me. And then there was Amy. Amy was the deal breaker. I'd known her five hours but I already felt the prehistoric need to protect her. I would join my new friends on the run and I was already beginning to formulate a plan as I stood and stretched.

I took a hot shower for what I guessed would be the last time for a while. I stayed in the water for too long letting the heat soak into my tired muscles. The hot water seemed to wash away any last doubts about my decision. I dressed and shuffled down the hall to the kitchen. Amy, Donte and Alan were already up and eating breakfast. Alan was cooking eggs and they smelled heavenly.

"Let me guess, you have a chicken coop out back."

"Hey Ethan. Good Morning," Alan said cheerfully. The others chimed in with good mornings as well. "No, no chickens. Egg Beaters. Had them frozen in the deep freeze. Grabbed a bunch from the local market right at the beginning of the riots. Good source of protein in a small package." He tapped his head to indicate he'd been thinking.

"Nice. Well I've reached a decision," I announced. "I'll be joining you on the run."

Alan stepped over and shook my hand. Donte and Amy lined up and gave me a hug. We ate quietly and quickly. We were all too hungry to talk.

When we finished I leaned back and looked at my little army. A sixty-year-old Vietnam Vet, a fourteen year old kid and a pretty, petite twenty-seven year old blonde. I smiled. It was a tough group I thought. Battle tested. I chuckled out loud.

"What?" Amy said.

"Nothing, I was just thinking about what a group we make, different but the same. We fit. I was also thinking about what we need to do next. Every scenario is going to involve transportation. We have to get out of California. The state is locked down and under Martial Law. We don't have any travel papers and we can't just walk into the local garrison and ask for permission to leave. We need a vehicle and we need a point of exit, a path of least resistance. Where we go after that is open to suggestion."

"I think I can solve the first problem. Follow me," Alan said and began walking toward the back. We went out through the back door into the backyard. Across the yard was a detached garage.

"Don't tell me you've got a working car in there," I said incredulously.

"Ahh, not just any car. Wait and see," Alan said beaming. He reached into his pocket and took out the key ring that he'd taken the fence key off of earlier and unlocked the padlock on the garage door. He lifted the door, which gave out a groan as it swung up. In the middle of the garage was a car covered with a blue fitted car cover. "You ready?" Alan asked, still beaming.

"Yes," we said in unison. He peeled the cover back to reveal one of the finest examples of 1970's American muscle car. It was in pristine condition.

Donte whistled, "Damn. That's a 1970 Dodge Challenger. Is it original?" he asked.

"Yup," Alan replied. "Bought it when I got back from Nam. I'm the second owner. First guy lost it to repo. It sat on the lot because it was used and almost the price of a new one. In '71, when I got back, it had been sitting for over a year and the dealership was eager to get rid of it. It only had about a thousand miles on it when I got it."

"360cc V-8. Four barrel carb, flow master exhaust, original Plum Crazy paint," Donte said. I looked again at the paint and realized for the first time that the car was bright, gleaming purple.

I stared at him. I didn't expect the kid to know anything about cars.

"What, you don't think I know about cars? Shit, I read everything and anything that had to do with cars. This is one sweet ride." Donte said defensively.

"It's purple." I said.

"Very purple," Amy added.

"Naw it's Plum Crazy. That's the original color," Donte argued.

"Purple," I said flatly. "That won't stand out too much," I said sarcastically. "But it's better than nothing. Does it run?"

"Does it run?" Said Alan. "Hell yes it runs. I take it out and run it every few months. I can tell you from experience it will easily outrun a Humvee. Done it

161

twice." Vehicles were outlawed under martial law. It was too easy for roving packs of looters to move around so the military outlawed their use. "It'll do 140 without breaking a sweat," he added.

"What about gas?" I asked.

Alan moved to the cabinets on the far side of the garage. He opened the doors to reveal seven ten-gallon gas cans. "All full. I've got a siphon so we can pump the gas out of the cans. I'm not sure we can fit them all in the trunk but we can siphon gas out of abandoned cars along the way. The hose is long enough to reach into the bottom of the big tanks at the gas stations too. There's usually some gas left at the bottom even if the surface pumps won't pump it all out. The intake is above the bottom so that the sediment doesn't get into the tank. I installed two fuel filters in the hose itself so that any crap I pump out with the gas doesn't make it into my car."

"You must've been a boy scout when you were younger," I said shaking my head. Alan was the most prepared man I'd ever met. He thought through every angle and was ready for almost every contingency. He was a valuable asset.

"No, just a Marine my whole life. Dad was an ex-marine and he ran the house like it was a Marine unit. He taught me to be ready for everything. I hated it as a kid. My mom did too. She never let on but as I got older I realized she resented his inflexibility. I really didn't know anything else, nor did I think I had much choice so I enlisted as soon as I turned eighteen. It stuck with me just like it did him. I guess that's why I never married. Too set in my ways and I saw what the life did to my mother. Didn't seem fair to do that to another woman."

"Your readiness turns out to be a valuable trait given the set of circumstances." I said. Donte was circling the car, sliding his hand over the smooth paint. It was such a kid thing to do. Amy just stood and took it all in, trying to get a sense of us.

Alan re-covered the car, closed the big door, locked the garage and we stepped back inside.

"Next question. If we make it to the border how do we get across and where is the best chance to do that?" I asked.

Donte and Amy looked at me and had no answer. Alan held up a finger and left the room. He returned a minute later carrying a book. He dropped it on the table. It was a U.S. Atlas. I just looked at him and shook my head.

We opened the book to the California maps. It was divided into two parts, northern and southern California. There were dozens of highways and roads out of the state. There were many smaller roads that crossed from the north into Nevada and Oregon, but that would mean traveling six to nine hundred miles within the state. The smartest move was to exit on as straight a path as possible. Southern California is separated from the tip of Nevada and all of western Arizona by the Colorado River. A river meant bridges. Bridges are easier to defend and more difficult to cross. There were obstacles in both directions.

"I favor the direct route. We'll never make it in a loud purple car to northern California without being stopped. The major highways will be impossible. They'd use those for troop movement and will be heavily guarded so let's forget trying to cross on I-40, I-15, I-8 and I-10." I ran my finger down the map starting at the tip of Nevada and all the way to the southern edge of the state and started back up. I passed I-10 and stopped my finger about halfway between I-10 and I-40. There were two small towns across the river from each other: Earp on the California side and Parker on the Arizona side. Sister cities connected by California State highway 62, which, after crossing the river, turned into Arizona State highway 72. "Here. This is the place to cross. It may not be guarded at all, or at most lightly guarded. I doubt they'd put more than a squad on what amounts to a tollbooth. What do you think?"

"Makes sense to me," agreed Alan.

"I'm good with that," said Donte.

Amy just shrugged her shoulders.

We spent the next hour packing essential items: food, water, weapons, blankets, sleeping bags and clothing. Alan grabbed a toolbox in case we broke down. We all packed what few personal items we had. I felt bad for Amy. She had only the clothes on her back. I made a mental note that the first chance we had we would have to go 'shopping' for her. She deserved better.

We'd placed four of the gas cans from the cabinet into the trunk. It would've been nice to have all seven but we needed room for the other supplies. We figured the trip to the border would be about three hundred miles. The Challenger had a full eighteen-gallon tank. Combining that with the four cans gave us fifty-eight gallons of gas. According to Alan, the car got on average about ten miles to the gallon on the highway. With the gas on hand we would have enough to go about five-hundred and eighty miles, more than enough to get us out of California and well into Arizona. It even gave us enough to detour if necessary or if the ten mile per gallon figure was too high. I felt we would be able to find some gas later on if the need arose but it was safer to have it on hand.

Amy and Donte were waiting in the garage, ready to go. In fact, they seemed eager to go. They couldn't wait to get away. Donte seemed fearless. Youth would do that. His lack of hesitancy was evidence that he was oblivious to the dangers we might face on our run. Amy just seemed eager and cheerful no matter what. We hadn't had much time to get to know each other and I was looking forward to that time. She made me curious. It was a feeling I hadn't felt since I first met my wife. It was that feeling you had right after you'd asked the girl at school for a date and she'd said yes. You were excited and scared to death at the same time. There was something, beyond her beauty, that stirred those feelings in me.

I went back inside to double check that we'd packed everything. I was going from room to room and found Alan standing in his den with his back to the door. He turned when he heard me. He looked pensive.

"Everything okay?" I asked.

He looked down at his shoes. "Yeah. It's just that I've lived here for almost 40 years. Bought the house shortly after I got back from Nam. Used the G.I. bill to get it. I'll miss it. I'll miss some of the things in it."

"You still want to go? You can always stay."

He answered immediately. "It's a house, just wood and plaster. Things are things. There is one thing this house doesn't have and never did have. People. You and Donte and Amy are my people. Where you go, I go. Simple as that."

"Amy and Donte are ready. Do you want a few more minutes?"

"Nope, I'm done moping. Time to move on. Time to find our freedom."

Chapter 22

We climbed into the Challenger, Alan behind the wheel, Amy on the driver's side in the backseat, Donte next to her and me riding shotgun, literally. At my feet lay the PPsh-41 submachine gun and both of Alan's semi-automatics, all fully loaded. I had my .44's holstered. Alan fired the car's engine and it roared to life and we pulled out of the garage and down the driveway. The power of the engine rumbled the seat.

Getting from the house to freeway was going to be one of the trickiest parts of the trip. The city streets were littered with remnants of the riots. Collapsed buildings, burned out and crashed vehicles, and a host of other objects were a possibility. The freeways would be clear. The military would use them as supply lines and those would be kept free of obstructions. The second thing that was going to make this part of the trip difficult was Stark's men. We had been at Alan's for almost eight hours and Stark had had time to regroup and begin the search for us.

The street was clear. He punched the gas and we tore down the street. I watched Alan's as we drove away. He never even glanced in the rear view mirror.

Only once did we have to stop, back up and detour around an obstacle on our way to the freeway, and there was no sign of the soldiers. The eastbound onramp was clear and we rolled up the ramp gaining speed as we climbed. There were no patrols in sight and the two outside lanes of the freeway were clear as far as we could see. Ruined cars and trucks were piled against the k-rail in the inside lanes. It looked like a gigantic snowplow had come along and tossed the vehicles in a pile on the side of the road like big piles of snow. There were sections of the freeway where we saw no cars piled and then we would hit stretch where they were piled up by the dozens. Alan had wound the car up to just over a hundred miles per hour. He kept it at that speed as long as we had a long straight section ahead of us. He would drop to about eighty when a curve approached.

In the first thirty minutes we rolled through Hollywood, past downtown Los Angeles, and into San Bernardino County. We were cruising on I-10 and were going to stay on it until we got about halfway across the Mojave Desert. There we would take highway 177 out of Desert Center to avoid the possibility of running into patrols as much as possible. We said little. It was hard to hear over the din of the engine and the wind whistling in the open windows. It was a glorious feeling. It felt like four friends out for a Sunday cruise.

Outside the windows we watched the surreal landscape as we passed. The last time I had been on this drive Los Angeles had been a massive metropolis teeming with people. Now it was a burned out wasteland. Once glorious landmarks were charred piles of rubble. The familiar landmarks of Hollywood were gone. Even the Hollywood sign had been ripped down. The hordes of rioters had been bent on destroying everything. The gleaming glass towers of downtown were all blackened hulks. They reminded me of spent roman candles. We occasionally saw a person or two along the roadside or off on the streets below shuffling along aimlessly. We never saw another moving vehicle.

Since we didn't get on the road until late afternoon the plan was to drive until dusk and then find a place to hole up for the night. It was too risky to drive the roads at night. Our headlights would be seen miles away in the darkness but we would only be able to see several hundred feet ahead. We couldn't keep it a manageable speed without streetlights or sunlight. We hoped to leave the city and into more open country before dusk. Being away from the city would provide some measure of safety. Our goal was to make it past Palm Springs and into the desert outside of Joshua Tree National Park.

As we left the last of the city and began to climb the grade over the San Jacinto Mountains into the Palm Springs area the car was suddenly awash in floodlights from behind. A siren began to wail. A vehicle was pursuing us about a hundred yards behind us. The glare from the lights prevented us from seeing exactly what or who was chasing us. I needed to see what we were dealing with.

"Alan, reel them in, drop it down a bit."

"You sure, I know I can outrun them," he said.

"Yeah, if it's a Humvee then I know you can, but it might not be. We don't really know what's going on with the jurisdiction out here. Things might've changed." He gradually dropped the speed until the headlights were about ten car lengths behind us. "Keep an eye out for an off ramp."

"Stop your vehicle immediately." A voice boomed over a loudspeaker. "Pull over now or we will be forced to stop you." That told me volumes. It had to be military. Civilian police would never use that phrase. The military would. Now we needed to know what vehicle they were driving. Top speed for a Humvee was about ninety miles per hour. This vehicle had kept up with us when we were going one hundred. I had no idea how quickly they had closed on us. That would tell me a lot about the top speed. We were going to need a visual. I wasn't aware of any standard vehicle the Army had in its possession that would be able to keep up with the Challenger.

"We just passed a sign listing an exit two miles ahead and then another three miles after that," said Alan.

"Okay, Donte and Amy get down on the seat just in case." They complied immediately. "Alan, get off at the first exit and put a little distance between us and them as we go down the ramp. Then turn left at the bottom and go under the interstate. I should be able to get a visual broadside as they make the same turn. Then we'll know what we're dealing with. Get back on the Interstate on the off ramp on the far side. We'll drive on the wrong side until we get to the next exit and then reverse the process. When you get back on punch it. We'll see then what they have to work with."

The exit came up quickly and Alan did as I had instructed. He made the turn at the bottom of the ramp slowing to about forty; we had enough distance to see the car make the turn. It was a commandeered Highway Patrol cruiser. The ironic thing was it was the reissued modern version of the Challenger. It was going to be a duel between old school and new school. The doors had been painted over and I could see the faint outline of the white five-pointed Army star on the doors. It was too dark to make out the color but I guessed they probably had sprayed the car olive drab. The new Challenger would be tough to shake. It was a fair race. Top speeds were comparable. The newer version would have better handling.

Alan turned the Challenger up the ramp and stomped on the gas. The V-8 roared and we tore up the grade. The headlights behind us dropped away at first and then gradually began to creep up on us. We had a decent head start and needed to keep as much of it as we could by the time we reached the next ramp.

"Alan, give it all you've got. We need a good head start when we hit the next ramp. If we have enough of a lead you're going to drop me under the overpass. I'll cut 'em apart as they go by. If they don't follow you up the ramp turn around and come get me in a few minutes." He shook his head in agreement. I felt the car surge a little harder. I watched the odometer tick away tenths of a mile as we ate away the three miles to the next ramp. My eyes moved back and forth between the rear window and the odometer. The lights were slightly closer but I was fairly certain we would have enough space for me to bail out.

We made it to the ramp with at least a quarter mile lead. Alan took the turn at the bottom at reckless speed. We fishtailed a bit but he handled the turn like a professional race driver.

"Don't even stop. Just slow and I'll drop and roll." He slowed to about ten miles per hour. "That's good," I said. I grabbed the submachine gun, hugged it to my chest, opened the door, fell out the door and rolled as I hit the pavement. I did one somersault and popped to my feet in a dead run. Alan hit the gas causing the door to slam shut and the tires to lay rubber on the pavement. I headed for the base of the bridge abutment and dropped into a prone shooting stance. Our Challenger turned up the ramp just as the other came off the ramp and made the right. I leveled the gun at the car and let loose with several bursts. The right side headlight went out. I heard one of the front tires explode and the car responded by careening to the left. The driver over corrected to the right and the car spun, hit the shoulder on the left and rolled over coming to rest again on its tires but perpendicular to the road. The front of the car was almost head on to me. I fired a burst through the front window. I fired another burst through the front grill and the radiator fluid began to spill from under the car like a beast bleeding out. Steam hissed from under the hood. I approached the vehicle from the front. Stood for a moment as the glare from the left headlight shined in my face. I fired one more burst and the lens of the light shattered. I walked up to the passenger door, placed my hands on the window and leaned in for a better view. I could now see the two occupants clearly. The roof on the driver's side had collapsed and the driver's head was leaning to the left at an impossible angle. He was dead. The passenger was unconscious. He was pinned in and wasn't going anywhere soon. I felt bad. I had only wanted to disable the car but the driver had made an unfortunate overcorrection. I really didn't want these guys hurt. They were just doing their job. In a sense though they were casualties of war. A war I hadn't started and a war I didn't want. Still the remorse weighed heavily on me.

About three minutes went by and I could hear the whup-whup of the big cam in the Challenger's engine as it rolled down the ramp. Alan was taking it slowly. He turned and illuminated the former police car. It was olive drab. The car had been hastily painted with spray paint. Definitely not a professional job. The vehicle was a wreck. The front axels were broken and the whole car was rounded off from the roll over. I climbed back in the front seat and we left the wreck behind.

Chapter 23

We found a place to camp about twenty miles outside of Indio, well down the road from where we'd left the wreck. There was a dirt access road that led away perpendicularly from the highway and then curved behind a small rise about a half-mile later. We would be hidden from the road and even a large campfire would be hard to spot. It was also an easy place to defend. If we heard a vehicle approach we could climb the rise and see back to the highway. There was a small stand of scrubby trees at the bottom of the rise in a little wash. We collected as many branches as we could and piled rocks into a circle to make a fire ring. We got the fire going, laid out the sleeping bags and pulled out some canned goods to heat over the fire.

The temperature had dropped dramatically as soon as the sun went below the horizon. A slight breeze added to the chill and the fire was welcome heat. We huddled around as close as we dared and soaked in the warmth. Cold tendrils of air ran down my neck and into the back of my jacket giving me chills.

Donte and Alan shared their histories with Amy while we ate and cleaned up. It was almost 10:00 by the time we were done.

"I know we are all bone tired so I hate to say it but we should have someone on watch all night. I'd love a whole night's sleep but it's safer if we keep an eye on the fire and an ear on the road." They all nodded in agreement. " We can break it into three hour shifts. I have no trouble waking up and going back to sleep afterward if you want me to take the mid shift. Alan, you're an early riser so why don't you take the last shift and Donte you can take the first shift."

"Um, hello, did you forget someone?" Amy asked feigning indignation.

"I figured." I said before Amy interrupted me.

"You figured what? That because I'm a woman I'm not capable of standing a post?"

"No, I just figured that of all of us you could probably use a night of uninterrupted sleep more." I said. I hoped it didn't sound scolding. I was impressed by her bravado and didn't want to quash it.

She blinked, swallowed hard and said, "Well, thank you. I appreciate the thought but include me in the watch. I'm part of the team so I should pull my weight."

"All right, fair enough. Let's cut the watches to two hours. Amy can go first, then Donte, me and then finally Alan. Agreed?" Everyone nodded their approvals. Alan only had two sleeping bags so we drew straws and Donte and Amy won. Alan and I would get the blankets for the night. We stoked the fire and Alan and Donte curled around the perimeter on the far side from Amy and I. We were propped next to each other, shoulders touching, against a large boulder.

We sat quietly for about fifteen minutes. I could already hear Alan snoring lightly and Donte appeared to have dozed off as well.

Amy caught me looking at them. "What about you? Aren't you going to go to sleep? I'll be okay on watch by myself."

"I know you will. That's not why I haven't laid down. You and I haven't had a chance to say two words to each other. I'm not that tired," I lied. "You know very little about me and I know even less about you."

"Let's see. I know what you're motivated by. I know the sadness and hurt you've experienced," she said. The flickering fire reflected off the blue in her eyes. They were mesmerizing. I studied her face as we spoke. It had a childlike quality about it. Her nose was small but perfect. She had a small crease off to the left side of her mouth, which gave her the appearance that she was smiling even when she was in a serious mood. Her strawberry blonde hair fell across her forehead in a natural way that looked styled even when it was messy. She had a wonderful smile, big and genuine, that got her whole face involved in the process. Her most striking features were her blue eyes that seemed so full of life. They flicked this way and that stopping to focus on a detail then moving on. Taking it all in. Processing it all. They conveyed intelligence and warmth. It was a pleasant combination. I was drawn to her.

"You start," she said. "Tell me more about you. I want to know you. We have the time now."

"You know the recent history so I guess I'll start at the beginning. I had an interesting childhood. My parents were pacifists. My friends used to tease me that they were hippies. I guess in a way they were. They were just a generation too late to be real flower children, but I have no doubts that had they been just a bit older during the sixties they would've made the trek to Woodstock. They took me off to protests every weekend. They were vegetarians as well. Funny thing is as healthy as they thought they were, my dad dropped dead of a heart attack at fifty-five and my mom died of lung cancer two years later when she was fifty-six. She never smoked a day in her life. I sometimes think I killed them."

"How so?" Amy asked.

"I never really bought into the whole 'hippie' lifestyle. When I became a teenager it all seemed sort of silly and insincere. I guess that's why I enlisted in the Army right after I graduated high school. I knew it would really aggravate my folks. My Dad died right after I completed basic training. My mom died right after I was selected to go to Special Forces Q-course. I always felt like maybe it just broke their hearts."

She leaned against my shoulder. I could smell the shampoo in her hair.

"You've had so much loss," she said softly. "Your parents so early and then your wife and son. I'm so sorry." She said the last with such intense sincerity. People say things like that normally because they have no idea what else to say. But this was different. I could hear the real empathy in her voice. It was such a remarkable feeling.

"Thank you. I know you are sorry for me. I appreciate that," I said. She looked up into my eyes. I wanted to lean down and kiss her. Kiss her harder than I'd ever kissed anyone. But I was afraid it was too soon and I didn't want to scare her away. "Tell me your story," I said to break the moment.

"I came from your average run of the mill Valley family. I guess you could call me a 'valley girl'," she smiled at the last statement, almost embarrassed she'd admitted it. "Dad was an accountant for the studios; Mom worked part time as a clerk in a legal firm. As a kid I guess I did all the things little girls were supposed to do, dance, soccer, even some child beauty pageants. Did the whole high school scene. I was a varsity cheerleader, prom queen, dated the star football player for three years. All the stuff I was supposed to do. Had all the right friends, drove the nice car, got everything I asked for from daddy. Everyone envied me, except me. I hated my whole life. It wasn't mine. Mom and Dad had met at U.S.C. and I was supposed to go there. I applied and got in. First semester's tuition was paid for in advance. That summer I packed a suitcase, left my folks a note and took off to see the country, on my own, and never looked back. It was selfish, but at the time I saw no other way to do it. It was like taking off a Band-Aid, just rip it and go. My parents flipped out. They thought I was brainwashed or kidnapped. They even had the F.B.I. convinced that I must've been kidnapped. I was picked up and questioned in Dallas by the feds. It was hilarious. By the time I was done with the interview they were satisfied that I just needed to get away and find myself."

"Why didn't you just tell your folks you were going to do that?" I asked.

"Did you ask your parents before you enlisted?"

"Touché. So how did you end up back in the valley?"

"After the F.B.I. interviewed me I agreed that it was pretty screwed of me to just take off and not keep in touch so I agreed to call every few days and let them know I was okay and where I was. I think they were so relieved that I wasn't dead somewhere that they just accepted that I was going to do this crazy thing for a while then I would come to my senses and return to the life they had dreamed up for me. Truth was that was never going to happen. After drifting all over the country for about four years I ended up in Florida. I loved the beach lifestyle. I was waiting tables, making a living and having a ball. I'd been there about a year. It was the longest I'd stayed anywhere in those four years. I called home one day and Mom was really upset. My dad had moved out. He wanted a divorce. He told my Mom that she'd driven his little girl away and he couldn't stand the sight of her. I drove home in two and half days to try and help mend things. I thought I could convince them to get back together. That it was really just me and not anything they did. Two days after I got home the riots started. You know how quickly that came to our neck of the woods. Unfortunately, our neighborhood was ransacked quickly. Looters shot my Dad because he tried to defend the house. Mom and I ran but we lost everything. The house was burned to the ground so we had no home, no car, and no valuables or cash to even buy a ride out. We went from being really well off to totally homeless in a matter of hours. We ended up at the mall because the military promised they would take care of us and eventually help relocate everyone. We believed them." She shivered as she recalled this.

I put my arm around her shoulder and held her a little tighter. She leaned her head on my shoulder and nuzzled her chin under mine.

"The next year my mom died of an infection. We begged the military for aid and they said there was nothing they could do for her. It was the kind of thing you could go to a doctor for, get a prescription and be back on your feet in a day. They just ignored us. They loaded her body on a truck and took her away." She began to sob. Deep heaving sobs, letting out so much pain and hurt. I wanted to fix it right then. I wanted to make it right. But I couldn't and that made my anger burn even brighter. I kissed the top of her head and just let her cry until she fell asleep in my arms. I never bothered to wake Donte for his watch. I just wanted to hold Amy and keep her safe. I sat there with her head pressed against my side with my arm around her and let my anger, rage and hatred for Stark store away in the back of my mind. Someday I will let it go and Stark had better hope he's not anywhere near me when I do.

Chapter 24

I slept for the two hours that Alan had watch with Amy cradled in the crook of my arm. It was the best two hours of sleep I had had in ages. I had no nightmares for the first time in two years. I woke as the sun was just peeking over the eastern horizon. My face was numb from the cold. Someone, I guessed Alan, had covered Amy and I with a blanket. She was beginning to stir also.

Her eyes fluttered open and she said, "Good morning," through a yawn.

"Good morning to you."

"Morning," Alan added. "You two sleep well."

"Great," Amy and I answered simultaneously. We looked at each other and laughed. Our laughter woke Donte.

We ate breakfast, packed up the gear and got on the road in under an hour. It was a quick twenty-mile drive to the turnoff for highway 177 in Desert Center. I remembered driving through here on a family trip as a teen. This little town had an interesting history. General Patton had established a training center here during World War II to train tank troops to fight the famed German armored General Rommel in North Africa. It had also been a mining town owned by Kaiser Steel. It was here that Kaiser first started taking money out of miner's paychecks to pay for healthcare in advance because the workers spent all their money at the local saloon. That made this town the birthplace of managed health care. What a luxury that would be now, I thought to myself.

The twenty-mile ride to the turnoff at Desert Center went smoothly. We stopped a half-mile from the turnoff and scanned the small town through field glasses. We were certain that the big V-8 in the Challenger would've alerted anyone to our approach and I expected to see some motion if anyone were present.

"What do ya think Ethan," Donte asked.

"It seems clear. No movement. Unless there is a well-trained force there I would expect to see some movement out of curiosity. It has to be pretty infrequent for a car to come through here. There's not much strategic sense for the military to have anyone stationed here either. I think we're clear. Let's just take it slow in case though."

We fired the car back up and slowed to about twenty-five as we neared the town. It wasn't much of a town to begin with. Two gas stations, both burned to the ground. An old trailer park was off to our left just after we made the turn. A few of the trailers were filled with hundreds of bullet holes. Someone had either been very pissed or they had just had fun unloading a lot of ammo. In either case the bullets had caused the trailers to list like sinking ships.

Another mile up the road we passed the entrance to the Desert Center airport. It had been used by the military for transport into and out of the Armored Training Center. Standing guard at the entrance to the airport was a M-47 Patton tank, set on a low concrete block like a giant statute.

"It would sure be nice if we had that to cross the border, " I yelled over the road noise to Alan.

"Yes it would. Let's check it out."

"Alan I'm kidding, I'm sure it's decommissioned and where would we get the fuel? They just set that hulk there as decoration."

"Worth taking a look at. Maybe some idiot parked it with a full tank of gas."

"Not likely," I said. "But what the hell."

Alan swung the car around and we doubled back to the driveway. We got out and scanned the terrain. Seeing no one we walked to the tank. Someone had knocked down the wrought iron fence that encircled it. I climbed up on the tank. The hatches were bolted shut. Alan circled around to the rear and peered through the vent shafts.

"Engine's here," he said.

"Hatches are bolted shut. Is it worth trying to open it?"

"Why not. We can see if there's any chance of firing the engine. We've got some time. Won't take us too long to get to the border. Sure would be nice to have a tank," Alan said. He grinned at the last sentence.

Amy trotted over to the trunk and brought back the toolbox. We all climbed on top of the old tank. Alan pulled a socket set out of the box, found the correct socket and gave a pull on the bolts. There were four of them holding the main hatch on the top of the turret shut. I gave it a try and couldn't budge any of them either. Donte gave it a shot with no luck.

Amy had jumped off the tank and wandered over to the fence. She came back with a four-foot long length of fence upright.

"You going to beat it open?" I asked mockingly, and regretted my sarcasm immediately.

"Men. All muscle no brain," she said with a half grin. "Watch as the little lady moves the bolts." She took the handle of the socket wrench and slipped it into the hollow end of the pipe. I knew immediately what she was going to do and she was right. The Neanderthals were going to be outwitted by a superior intellect.

She looked at me. "Hold the socket on the nut so it won't slip." She used the length of pipe as a lever to exert a much greater force on the nut and it spun loose easily. She loosened all four of the nuts then we removed them the rest of the way.

Amy looked very proud of herself. "Nicely done," I said. We cracked open the hatch and swung the lid up. Stale air wafted out of the hole. It smelled of old sweat and dust. I had Donte bring a flashlight from the car and I swung the light back and forth through the interior of the tank. It appeared to be intact. I pulled my head out and Alan gave a look.

"Looks good to me. I wasn't in Armored but I've ridden in a few of these things and it looks like everything's in shape," Alan said.

Donte and Amy took a look as well.

"Let's see if it starts," Alan said. He climbed through the hatch and down into the driver's seat. I shined the flashlight in so he could see. There was a simple panel with gauges for R.P.M.s, speed and fuel tank. A single lever controlled both the throttle and the steering.

"Here goes nothing," Alan said as he flipped the starter switch. And it was nothing. Nothing at all happened. "It could be the battery."

"Alan, this thing is dead as a doornail. They wouldn't park a functioning tank right out in the open, would they?" I asked. He climbed out of the tank.

"No, they probably wouldn't but the fact that the engine is still there and the interior is complete means there's a chance. I'd like to try a few things," he said.

"Alan, we can't stay here all day. Plus we have no diesel fuel."

"Well, that's one thing we do have. This beast runs on regular gasoline not diesel fuel. We've got gas in the trunk. I figure this thing without all the equipment and artillery shells will get about 5 miles to the gallon. We're about eighty miles from the border. That's sixteen gallons to get us there. If we pour two of the cans in we'd have enough to get there and do what we need to do. There's no way they are guarding a bridge in Earp with anything that could stop a tank. We could roll right across the river with the Challenger following and use our small arms through the portholes to get into town, ditch the tank and be gone."

"Alan, this is crazy. This is a sixty-year old tank. It's been sitting here in the desert for God knows how long. Hoses have to be rotted; the battery has to be shot. For all we know the engine is seized."

"I just want to look at a few things. Give me one hour. If I don't have it running or can convince you we can get it running we can leave."

"What do you two think?" I asked Donte and Amy.

"It would be nice to have a tank," Amy said.

"Hell, yeah it would," Donte added.

I lowered my head and stared at my shoes. This was insane but Alan was hell bent on trying to get the thing running. "One hour and that's it. What can we do to help?"

"There should be a hand cranked starter motor for cold starts. It'll look like a lawnmower engine. Try to find that. The crank will either be in here or through an

184

access panel in the back. I'm going to take a look at the
condition of the engine and transmission. We may
need to find some oil. Donte, can you help me with the
engine. I'll need someone to hand me tools. These
engine compartments aren't the easiest to get to. Amy,
if you can help Ethan look for the crank and then see
what we can do about oil?"

We all agreed. I reminded Alan that he only had an
hour. We found the crank right away. Alan was
headfirst inside the engine compartment. "We're going
to check some of the buildings at the airfield. Donte,
you need to keep one eye on the road. Keep the
machine gun with you at all times. Okay?" He saluted
in response. I waved back.

There were three buildings on the airfield. Two
appeared to be hangers and the third looked to be an
administration building with a short tower on top.
"Let's try the hangers first. There might be some
drums of oil."

We walked down the road towards the first hanger. I
don't really know if I reached over and grabbed Amy's
hand or if she grabbed mine or if we did it
simultaneously but I suddenly realized we were holding
hands like two school kids walking to school. I glanced
down at our hands and then up at Amy. She was
already looking at me with a little smile. It felt electric.

We got to the door of the hanger and it was swinging
gently in the breeze. The glass in the center was
shattered. White paint, yellowed with age was peeling
off the building in long strips. It looked like it was
shedding a skin. As we stopped to look in, Amy tugged
my hand and turned me to face her. She reached her
hands up to my face and pulled me down to hers. She
paused for just a moment to stare into my eyes, as if to

say it's okay, I want this too, then she gently pulled me in the rest of the way and we kissed the longest most passionate, hungry kiss I've ever had. I wanted to stay just like that forever. All the troubles of the world seemed to fade away and for that brief moment nothing else existed except our mouths locked in that kiss. Amy finally broke the embrace and gently pulled away. We stared at each other for a moment and then kissed briefly one more time. There was nothing to be said that the kiss hadn't.

We entered the hanger, which was mostly empty. There were no planes, no vehicles, just some random pieces of aircraft equipment. I saw several portable pumps for pumping gas. A few airplane parts littered the floor. There were no fifty-five gallon drums, which is what I was looking for. We walked out of the first hanger and over to the second. It was in the same condition as the first, peeling paint, unlocked and open door, broken windows. Inside there were two planes, both badly damaged. Over in the corner was a pyramid of oil drums. We eagerly trotted over to them. I began tapping on the sides of the cans. There were ten all together. The first six were empty. The seventh was half full. I unscrewed the cap, found a long piece of one by one wood nearby and used it as a dipstick. The oil was thick and heavy but it was new. I had been afraid it was used oil, which might've worked but would burn up easier. I replaced the cap and tipped the can on its edge and began rolling the can out the door and down the road. The road dropped away from the buildings on a slight grade so Amy stepped in front to keep it from getting away from me. It made a loud racket as it bumped down the broken asphalt.

Alan poked his head out of the engine compartment. He was covered in grease and grime. "Oil?"

I nodded in response.

"Good we're going to need it. Everything looks good but this engine is dry as a bone,"

"What is that noise?" Amy asked.

"I hear it too," said Donte. "Sounds like a swarm of bees."

Alan and I heard it at the same time, "Motorcycles, sounds like lots of them. Get in the car, quick!" Everyone jumped in, Alan fired the engine and we raced up the access road and pulled the car behind the first hanger out of sight of the road. In less than a minute a group of eight choppers being ridden by what looked like hardcore bikers rolled past. Most of the bikes had single riders but a few had two. We held our breath as they rode past. We waited a few minutes to make sure they were gone. Those were the first vehicles we'd seen since we'd been chased and the only civilian ones we'd seen at all.

"Alan, let's get back at the tank, but we really have to get moving. The longer we sit in one place the more likely we are to have trouble run up on us.

"I just need a few minutes to lube everything up and then we'll give it a crank."

Chapter 25

Fifteen minutes passed and Alan popped out of the tank and declared he was ready to fire it up. We cranked the manual starter and the more than sixty-year old engine tried desperately to cough to life. Thick black smoke belched from the exhaust. It coughed and rattled and died back down. We cranked again, it went through the same coughing and belching but this time it roared to life with a loud backfire. It continued to idle without choking off. Alan let it idle for a few minutes to get the oil flowing throughout the engine. We all stood, slack jawed and unable to speak as much from shock as from the roar of the engine. I climbed up on the turret and hung down through the opening.

Alan yelled at the top of his lungs, "I'm going to engage the transmission, cross your fingers." I stabilized myself on the top of the turret as he shifted into first gear. The tank began to shudder and slowly rolled forward. It was nothing short of a miracle. I waved Donte to the tank.

"Donte, you'll ride in here with Alan. Amy and I will ride in the Challenger. We're going to drive ahead and then circle back behind to keep an eye on things. Let's see how far we can get this bucket of bolts."

Donte nodded and then disappeared into the belly of the tank. I jumped down and Amy and I started the Challenger. We drove on ahead a mile at a time and then circled back, dropped behind a mile and then came back up. Alan was rolling the tank at twenty miles per hour.

Ten miles down the road the tank began to shudder. Alan guided it to the side of the road and the engine stopped. We pulled in behind the tank. Alan was climbing out by the time I was getting out of the car.

"What's up?" I asked.

"Damn I feel stupid. We're out of gas. I overestimated the gas mileage of this beast. We only got about a half mile to the gallon," he said apologetically.

I was dejected. Having the tank was such a long shot and when it actually ran I was elated. This was disappointing. I did some quick math in my head. We had seventy miles to go, and I estimated three gallons to the mile to be safe. If there were hills ahead we'd use much more gas than we had on the flat ten-mile run we'd already completed. It would take over two hundred gallons of fuel just to get to the border. We would need to almost fill the gas tank. There was no way we could siphon that out of old gas station tanks and old cars. We would have to leave the tank behind.

We secured the hatch as best we could just in case we found some way to return to the tank. We got back in the Challenger and started up the road in our original seats. The mood was heavy and quiet. I could see the disappointment on everyone's face.

"Listen guys. I know it sucks that we lost the tank. Alan, don't beat yourself up over it. You got the damn thing running. The reality is we don't even know if the border is being guarded. We might just roll into Earp and cruise across the bridge to freedom. Until we know what we're up against it does no good to hang our heads."

Everyone nodded and seemed to perk up a bit but there was still a cloud hanging over the car. I had forgotten the tank and was far more worried about the unknown. The bikers had gone up this road and should the border be closed I doubted they had clearance to cross. That would mean at some point our paths might cross. It was entirely possible that there were more than just the group we'd seen and that really would create a problem.

The road ran north for about ten miles and then at the junction of highway 62 turned due east toward the California/Arizona border. We passed through the town of Rice, which amounted to a few rotting buildings and an east-west-south railway junction. Fifteen minutes later we began to see roadside signs indicating that Vidal Junction was just up ahead along with the turnoff for north and south bound highway 95.

"Alan, let's stop at the top of the next rise and make sure the town is clear."

Alan pulled to a stop just before the car crested the low rise we were on. He and I stepped out of the car and crouched behind some scrubby desert bushes and looked down on the town. It consisted of little more than two gas stations, a trailer park, an old diner and an official looking roadside building. The lettering on the side said "California Inspection Station." The other buildings were unremarkable except for the two large fiberglass chicken sculptures on the roof of the diner. They seemed oddly out of place in the middle of the Sonora Desert. What I didn't see was any sign of people or more importantly soldiers or bikers. There were no vehicles or motorcycles in sight other than a few rotting hulks parked in the trailer park. Those hadn't moved in years. I couldn't imagine why anyone would choose to live in such an isolated and ugly place as this. The eastern California deserts, the Sonora and the Mojave, have to be two of the most barren, dry, monotonous and unsightly places on earth. Perhaps there were people who found beauty in this place or solace in its desolation but it was not for me.

"We should check those gas stations as long as the town is clear. We could bring these cans back and forth and keep moving the tank closer and closer if there is enough gas in the underground tanks to do it," said Alan.

"We'll check, but Alan, I really think you need to give up on the tank. Chances are we will not find enough gas and it will take us an awful long time to cycle back and forth with forty gallons at a time. Don't forget we killed a guy, injured his partner and wrecked their car not too terribly far back from here. There are going to be some pissed off soldiers coming around looking for us and very soon. We could get caught in a pincer between the border and those guys. And we still don't know what we're going to face at the border."

We got the car rolling slowly into town and there was no welcoming committee there to meet us. We stopped at the first gas station. All of us got out and stretched while Alan tested the underground tank with his siphon. The station only had two pumps, one for regular and one for premium. Both tanks were bone dry except for some water at the bottom. We walked across the intersection while Donte stood guard at the car. This station was a bit more modern and had two islands with pumps. Each pump dispensed three grades of gas. The pump on the far side of the station dispensed diesel, which would do us no good. The premium container held enough to refill one of the cans we'd emptied into the Patton. We got half a can combined out of the other two, hardly enough to move the tank five miles and certainly not worth doubling back to do.

We went back to the car and drove a few hundred feet down the road to the chicken topped diner and pulled into the parking lot. Glass was broken out of most of the windows and the interior was a shambles. Kitchens usually held some very useful utensils so I thought it worth giving it a once over. Alan and Amy stood watch and Donte came in with me.

"Look for anything useful," I said.

"That's kinda vague," he replied.

"Utensils, tools, or anything we can use as weapons. Just like we were doing back in the Valley. Use your sense. If you think it would be useful bring it out".

I climbed through the debris and into the kitchen area. Most of the drawers and cabinets were open and empty. Some pots and pans were still hanging on big stainless steel hooks above a butcher-block island. The kitchen smelled of old grease. Everything was coated in a fine layer of desert dust. Nothing had been touched in a very long time. I could see that none of the dust was disturbed. I took one of the large stew pots thinking it might come in handy but the kitchen itself yielded little. I brought the pot outside and was going to suggest we leave and then I remembered something from a job I'd had in high school. I had worked in a mom and pop burger joint. I took the job not so much for the money but because my parents were hassling me to get a job and I figured flipping ground meat would irritate them to the greatest degree. I regretted that now. They had been good people, well meaning, even if I thought they were a bit off. I missed them.

The owner of the restaurant kept a handgun on the top shelf of the freezer and a big fire axe just in case he ever got locked inside during a robbery. He said he would kick the shit out of any of us if he ever caught us playing with the gun or the axe. He was a big mean son of a bitch and probably would've carried out the threat. To my knowledge no one ever touched that gun or the axe. So, I thought I'd check the freezer here. Maybe it was common practice in the restaurant business. It was a long shot but worth a try. I found the walk-in freezer, pulled the door open and heard the fresh air hiss in once the seals were breeched. The fresh air pushed rancid stale air out. I gagged and almost lost breakfast. I pulled the lighter out of my pocket and swung the door the rest of the way open. I waited a moment until the stench cleared some. The lighter barely provided any light and I thought about going back to the car for a flashlight. The walls were lined with wire shelving which still held boxes of dried decayed meat, French fries and other spoiled fried delicacies just waiting for a dip in the hot oil. I swung the lighter back and forth as I made my way into the freezer checking up and down the shelves as I went. About halfway across the floor I stumbled over something. I regained my balance and moved the lighter down. I recoiled at the sight of a dead body in a state of decay halfway between recently deceased and skeleton. The freezer had mummified the body. It was still dressed in the whites of a cook, including apron. There was a perfect hole in the upper right of the apron and a dark brown stain that spread out below it. The white paper cap had slid off the rotting scalp and lay on the floor. The smell was overpowering. In the corpse's hands was a Mossberg 500 Pump Action Field Shotgun. Sitting on the floor next to the body was a box of shells. A few loose shells lay in his lap. Apparently this poor bastard had been too late to the gun to prevent getting shot. He must've gotten hold of the shotgun after getting hit and bled out trying to load it. The door had not been peppered with a blast. I peeled the gun from the corpse's hands, and it pulled loose reluctantly with a sickly wet sound. I picked up the box of shells and grabbed the three loose ones as well. I stepped out of the freezer and checked the box. It was still full minus the three loose ones in my hand. I double checked the gun and found it was unloaded. The best laid plans I thought to myself.

I came back into the lobby holding my treasure in front of me.

"Nice," Donte said.

"Let's go. There's nothing more here." We walked outside and I showed the shotgun to Alan and Amy. In the sunlight I could see the greasy marks where the gun had rested in the man's decaying hands. I shared the scene with everyone leaving the gory parts out for Amy's sake.

"Amazing no one had found it until now," Amy said.

"He was pretty far back in there and the smell was pretty bad. I guess the casual person would assume that any food in the freezer was long gone bad and just passed on going in the dark space." I relayed the story of my high school job and why I had gone in and everyone nodded his or her understanding.

We moved down the highway a few hundred yards to the California Inspection Station. These facilities were on most highways that entered into California. Their purpose had been to inspect every vehicle that entered the state so that no outside fruits or vegetables were brought inside the borders.

"What the heck is this place?" Donte asked.

"They used to stop every car coming in and ask you if you had any fruits or vegetables with you," Alan said

"Huh? What the hell for?"

"So crops here wouldn't get contaminated," Alan answered.

"Always seemed really stupid and futile to me," I said. "I never saw them actually searching a car. I really think it was just a cover to check for coyotes, the guys that were smuggling illegal aliens. But the things aren't ever right at the border. They're always like forty or fifty miles inside the state and by then you could have smuggled in an elephant. Maybe that's why the damn state had to declare bankruptcy. Too much waste on stupid things like these."

"I asked an inspection guard one time about it and she said they stopped tons of infected plant material every year. I don't know if that's true or not, just what she said," Amy added.

"Well let's see what's left of this one," I said. The building had a covered arch that funneled all the vehicles between a booth and the office portion of the building. The structure was a total wreck. Graffiti covered most of the walls. Both the inside and outside looked like it had been used for target practice. The inside was gutted. Even the drywall had been ripped off of the studs. Someone or many people had taken out their anger on the government here. At least that's what it felt like. Much of the graffiti reflected that sentiment.

A quick search of the building yielded nothing but trash and destruction. It was time to make the final push to the border.

Chapter 26

It was only fifteen to twenty miles from Vidal Junction to Earp and the drive seemed very long. We were all silent for the ride. It was now into the afternoon and even for wintertime the desert sun beating down on the car made it uncomfortable and stuffy. After ten minutes we passed a sign, full of bullet holes, telling us that the border was three miles down the road.

"Alan, we need to pull off in a mile or two and do reconnaissance. I have a feeling those bikers that passed by are up ahead. They didn't look like the types that would get a free pass across the river. I also want to assess the border control without the Challenger announcing our presence."

Alan pulled off a minute later and I climbed a few hundred feet to the top of the small hill that was off to the left of the car. I scanned the scene below with my field glasses. Earp wasn't much of a town. There were a few low boxy houses, a gas station, a convenience store, a cinder block post office, and a large RV park that was mostly empty save for a few more permanent looking trailers. The interesting features were the parallel bridges crossing the Colorado River. One held the road and the other was a railroad trestle with a single track that crossed about fifty yards north of the road bridge. We had noticed only the road crossing on the map. The road bridge was made of concrete slabs that were set on concrete piles. It was a simple structure. Flat concrete road with railings on each side balanced on the supports. The rail bridge was far more interesting. It had five Pratt Truss sections tied together, one after the other to span the three to four hundred feet of river. Only three sections of the bridge were currently over the water. A fourth section on our side was over dry riverbed and the fifth crossed over the road. On the far side of the road bridge, blocking one lane was a temporary structure that looked like a guard shack. Two military vehicles were parked on the other side just off the bridge in front of a warehouse. There was a Humvee and a Light Medium Tactical Vehicle or LMTV. The military loves acronyms and this was one of the absurd ones. The LMTV is nothing more than a stake bed delivery truck painted tan.

There were two soldiers in the guard shack and several others milling about outside the warehouse. There was no more than a squad guarding the bridge. It was both good news and bad news. The good news was that the force was small, the bad news was that there was any force at all. There would be no driving across the bridge without a fight and they had the superior position.

The last structure on our side of the river, set opposite the turnoff for the bridge, was a roadhouse saloon. The saloon was just a stone's throw from the bridge. My fears were realized as I scanned the parking lot. Eight motorcycles parked in front. Now we had two potential barriers: bikers and soldiers.

I scrambled back down the hill to the car and shared what I'd seen with the rest.

"What next?" Alan asked.

"You like that question don't you," I said. "The answer is I'm not sure. We have a potential problem. I have no idea if the bikers will be enemy, ally or neutral. I've got some ideas about how to assault the bridge but the bikers are an x-factor. We need to know what they'll do."

"How do you plan to find out?" Amy asked.

I paused for a moment. "Ask them I guess."

"What, you're just going to walk into that saloon and say 'hey there'?"

"Anyone else have a better plan?" Three people stared blankly at me. "I guess that answers that. We really have no other choice. We have three options. One is to go forward, not knowing about the bikers, which could create all kinds of problems. Two, we could go back but we have all kinds of pissed off out looking for us that direction or three, we can find out before we go in there, barrels blazing. Way I see it there is really only one option, going and asking. We'll wait until dark. That way I can make it unseen to the saloon and scout things out before I go in. I won't be unarmed. No choice."

We moved the car to within a mile of the town and pulled off on a dirt access road out of sight of the main track. We ate lunch and rested quietly. A few hours later the sun began to slip behind the hills to the west. I holstered my two .44's and put on my black hooded sweat jacket. I wanted to blend into the night without looking like I was creeping just in case someone stopped me.

"Wish me luck. I'll be back as quick as I can."

"Ethan, I don't really want to bring this up but how long do we wait until we leave if you don't come back," Alan asked.

"I'll be back." I shook Alan and Donte's hands gave Amy a hug and began to walk away. I didn't get twenty feet and heard footsteps behind me. I turned just as Amy jumped up and threw her arms around my neck.

She kissed me deeply and passionately. I could feel her tears running off of her cheek onto mine.

She pulled her face away and choked out, "You'd better come back."

I set her down gently. "I will, I promise." I meant it.

I made it the mile to the saloon in less than twenty minutes and without being seen. As I got closer I could hear music blaring from inside. There were electric lights on inside. A few streetlights in town still glowed. The town must've been on the grid with Parker across the river. Across the river where the world was still somewhat normal.

The same eight bikes were parked outside. I crept up to a side window and looked inside. The place looked like it was still open for business. The music was coming from an old jukebox that was lit up like a Christmas tree. Two guys were playing pool at one of the two tables in the back of the place. An older biker was playing barkeep behind the dark wood bar. Several stained glass lamps hung from the ceiling and threw colored light against the walls. Two guys and a woman sat at the bar. Two other men and another woman sat at a table in the center of the room. They had glasses and were drinking something clear in them. There was no beer to be seen, which is what I'd expect to see in a place like this under normal circumstances. Seven guys and two women. There were eight bikes out front and I'd seen three of those with someone riding double, which made it likely that we were missing a man and a woman.

I ducked down below the windows and moved across the front of the saloon to the far side. The back left corner was out of my line of sight from my first position. I looked in through the bottom right corner of the glass and stared back to the rear. There was a large booth in the corner with a table large enough for all of the bikers to have sat around. Sitting in the corner of the booth was an enormous man. I couldn't tell his height but I would guess he was about six and half feet tall. He had a huge barrel chest and I could see the very top of an amazing beer gut that disappeared below the table. He had a salt and pepper beard that had taken years to grow to its current length and thickness. It was tinged yellow around his mouth from cigarette smoke. He wore a white t-shirt and had a leather vest over it. The vest might've fit at one time but now looked like a child's size. I would guess his age at about fifty.

Dancing for him on the table was a woman about ten years his junior. She was the type of woman who had probably been striking twenty years ago. She was still attractive but gravity had taken its natural toll on things and they weren't quite where they should've been. She was wearing just panties, a bra and heels. The dance was quite seductive and I could tell from her moves she was well practiced. The big bear of a man stared at her lustily bouncing his head to the rhythm of the music.

The source of the clear liquid that everyone was drinking was at the back end of the bar. It was a homemade still. A copper kettle sat in a big rock fireplace. A wood fire burned underneath it. Steam was hissing out the top. A long copper coil snaked out of the lid of the kettle, out of the fireplace, and terminated at the top of a big glass jug. The tip of the tube was steadily dripping clear liquid into the bottom of the bottle. It was churning out moonshine.

All in all it was a party. Everyone seemed to be in a good mood. Problem was I was about to be a party crasher. Sometimes that went well, more often than not it didn't. But there was no time like the present.

I paused at the door. Took a deep breath and slowly swung the door open. I stepped inside. Every eye in the place came to rest on me immediately except the woman dancing on the table. It took her a few seconds to realize something in the mood of the room had changed behind her before she stopped and turned toward me. She made no attempt to cover instead just placed her hands on her hips and glared at me as if to say "How dare you interrupt my dance".

The older guy behind the bar reached down slowly. I knew he was coming up with a gun so I raised my hands before he even showed me what he had. One of the guys at the table next to me finally said, "Who the fuck are you?"

"My apologies. I didn't mean to interrupt the party. I'm passing through, heard the music and stopped to see what's going on. Been a long time since I've heard a party." The room seemed to relax a bit. "I'm actually trying to get across the river and I was wondering if you could share any insight into that." The big bear of a man shoved the table forward almost toppling the woman in the process. She put her hand down to catch herself. He stood. Standing he was even bigger than I had thought he would be. He reminded me of a Grizzly Bear standing on its hind legs.

"I'm the guy you want to talk to," he growled. "But first you gotta get back here to me." His guys knew exactly what he meant. The two guys at the pool table stood up straight and dropped the pool cues on the table. The two at the bar rose off their stools and the two at the table to my right stood and shoved their chairs back in one motion. The pool players stepped in

201

front of the Bear. I now had two on my left, two on my right and two in front. It was a challenge of toughness. I knew I could draw the 44's, drop the barkeep, and then drop the other six before they knew what hit them. But this wasn't about that. It was a test of manhood. That was how they operated. Most men would've turned and run out of the door and the bikers would've laughed at his expense all night. A smaller sample would've stepped forward and taken on the first couple of guys but finally would've had their ass kicked. The smallest sample would win six fights and have the respect of everyone in the room. Pulling the guns would be for pussies. I took a step forward. Several of the men looked at each other in surprise. The Bear stood at the back of the bar with his arms crossed over his massive chest, resting on the beer belly that had taken years of rigorous training to develop. Thousands and thousands of sixteen-ounce curls had built that gut.

"Who wants their ass kicked first," I challenged. It was an important moment. The room exploded into laughter. All but two were laughing nervously. One of those was to my right and the other was one of the pool players. One of the bar stool guys even took a step back when I stepped forward. I pointed to the confident laugher who had risen from the table to my right. "How about you?"

He pushed his sleeves up, spat on the floor, raised his fists and stepped forward. He was a solid guy, a little shorter but muscular under his t-shirt. His head was shaved, the only guy in the room without either a mane of hair like the Bear or a long ponytail. He stepped forward with a menacing snarl on his face. He was trying to look tough but I actually wanted to laugh at the sight. I fired off a lightning quick roundhouse kick. My heel hit him square in the jaw and his chin hit the floor with a loud crack. He went out as he was falling. The laughter stopped immediately. They now realized this was serious. I gave them an out, "Do I really need to beat the crap out of the rest of these guys just to talk to you?" I yelled back to the Bear. "I'd rather not. I really don't know any of you and we might even be friends some day. What do you say?" All but the one confident pool player were eagerly looking at the Bear to let them off the hook. The Bear paused and eyed me up and down then began to laugh the heartiest laugh I'd ever heard. It boomed and echoed through the room.

"Come on back here," he said as he waved me back with a big meaty hand. I got handshakes, pats on the back and high-fives as I made my way to the back of the bar. I looked back over my shoulder and two of the guys were picking the poor bastard I'd knocked out off the ground and dropping him into a chair.

As I reached the table the Bear had his hand extended. I reached out to shake and his hand swallowed mine. He shook firmly but not crushing as I half expected him to do. "Have a seat," he said pointing to the booth. The woman climbed off the table and was sitting at the far end. She had pulled a black t-shirt over her bra but still had no pants on. "Spider, bring us a round," he hollered. The older guy behind the bar nodded and moved into action. "I'm Gangrene and this here's my woman, Bad Mama, " he said hooking a thumb in the woman's direction. I reached over and shook her hand. She nodded.

"Ethan Ryder, pleasure to meet you."

"That big dude you just dropped is Ox. He's the toughest guy here, also the dumbest. We've had a couple of other gangs roll into town, had to push 'em out. I've never seen him get his ass kicked. He's been a good addition to our crew. He rolled in here a few days after we did. Put him to the test just like you. He's gonna be a little pissed when he comes around. Don't worry though. I'll calm him down. Ox knocked those two over there out when we put him to the test." He pointed toward the pool table. "That's 'Mad Max' and 'Dirty Dog',"

Mad Max had been the other tough guy in the room.

"That's Spider at the bar." Spider gave a nod to me when he heard his name. "'Taco' over there on the first stool. He's the only spic in our group."

Taco was the guy who'd backed up when I stepped forward. Spider placed three glasses of the moonshine on the table in front of us and walked away. I smelled it instantly.

"Next to him is 'Cowboy' and his girl 'Gypsy'." They both raised their glasses to me at the mention of their names. Over there at the table helpin' Ox is 'Candy Girl' and her man, 'Scumbag'. Everyone this is Ethan Ryder."

They all raised their glasses in my direction. I picked up my glass and saluted back then took a sip of the clear liquid. It took my breath away, burned like liquid fire and made my eyes water. I fought off the urge to cough and instead let off the heat with loud "Ahh." It was like drinking paint thinner.

"How you like our special house wine?" he asked with a wink.

"Smooth," I managed to whisper. He laughed again at the comment.

"Where'd you learn to fight like that?" Gangrene asked.

"Army. I was Special Forces."

"Was?" His face showed some concern.

"Yup." I shared a brief version of my army career right up to my getting kicked out.

"Stark sounds like he needs a good ass kickin'"

"He could use a lot more than that," I said.

A few of the others had pulled chairs up to the far side of the table and were listening in.

"So, Mr. Ryder. What brings you to our neck of the woods?" asked Gangrene.

I briefly shared the story of our mission to save Donte, and our run in the Challenger. I left out killing the soldier under the overpass and our attempt to get the tank running.

"Where are you headed?" he asked.

"We're trying to get out of California. This seemed like a good place to try and cross."

"Not so sure about that. I lost two good friends to those assholes on the other side of the bridge when we first got here. They gunned 'em down before we even got to the guard shack. Hell, if we'd had papers they'd've killed us before we coulda showed 'em. You said you were with some other people. Where are these other folks?" Gangrene asked.

"They are waiting for me about a mile or so back up the road. I wasn't sure what I'd find here and didn't want to put them in jeopardy."

"I'm impressed. Tough these days to find a man who puts his people ahead of himself. You're a good man Charlie Brown. We need to go get your friends and bring 'em back here. The more the merrier. When you get back we can talk more about where you're headed. Did you walk down here?"

"Yes."

"Cowboy. Take Ethan here back up to meet his buddies."

"You got it. I hope you don't mind riding bitch," Cowboy said as he waved me to the door. Ox was just starting to regain his senses as I passed by. He glared at me as I walked by but made no effort to stand. We walked back out into the cold desert air. Cowboy was about six feet tall, early forties, with a thick black moustache, the sides of which ran all the way past his mouth and under his chin. He had a skull and crossbones bandana covering his head. Short salt and pepper hair peeked out from under the cloth. He wore jeans, cowboy boots, a white t-shirt with a brown leather vest. The back of the vest said "Vultures".

"Is your gang 'The Vultures'?" I asked.

"Yeah, we had more guys. A bunch left after the two got shot down on the bridge. They were a buncha pussies anyway."

I nodded. We walked over to the next to last bike. It was a huge black Harley. He had leather saddlebags and leather fringe hanging from the ends of the handlebars. Airbrushed on the top of the tank was a steer skull.

"Did you get the 'Cowboy' nickname because of the bike or the bike because of the nickname," I asked.

"My dad called me 'Cowboy' from the time I was born. My given name is Steve but since I was little I never heard anyone ever call me anything but 'Cowboy'. Hop on."

He climbed on first and I climbed on behind him. I held on to the sides of the seat and leaned back against the bar behind me. I figured it wouldn't be too cool to grab or lean on him. We ripped up the road and I remembered why people love motorcycles. The feeling of freedom that comes with the wind blowing across your face, the power of the bike under you and the pavement rushing by just inches from your feet was exhilarating. We made it to the turnout in under a minute. Cowboy stopped the bike between the Challenger and the road. I saw Donte and Amy hiding behind the car. Before I could say a word I heard "Freeze" come from behind me.

"Alan, it's me. It's Ethan. Everything's good."

Alan came walking up holding the Mossberg pointed at the ground. Donte came walking out from behind the car and Amy came running up, threw her arms around my neck and gave me a huge kiss. "I was so worried," she said. I kissed her again to reassure her that it was okay.

"We heard the bike coming and didn't know what to think," Alan said.

"It was a good plan. Everyone this is Cowboy. Cowboy this is Alan, Donte and Amy."

"Hello everyone. Good to meet you. Let's get out of the cold and back to the party."

The four of us got into the car, Cowboy mounted the bike. I quickly caught everyone up on the evening's events and finished the story as the tires crunched over the gravel of the Saloon parking lot.

"Park the car behind the building. I don't want those guys across the bridge to see the car just yet. First off, they might have an all-points bulletin and there can't be too many purple muscle cars on the road these days. Second, I don't want them curious about new visitors. Don't offer up too much information to the bikers. I think they're on our side but we need to be careful. They were hospitable but they might have a deal with the soldiers that we don't know about. Follow my lead.

Okay?" Everyone nodded in agreement. Alan swung the car to the rear of the saloon. We quickly got out and walked around toward the front and reached the corner right as Cowboy did.

"How come you didn't park up here?" he asked.

"We didn't want anyone to ding the paint," I said. He just laughed it off and the five of us went inside.

Everyone was still in the same places. Ox was more coherent and tried to stand as I passed by. He wobbled as he tried to put weight on his feet and tumbled back into the chair. We made introductions all around and Gangrene invited us all to his table. Bad Mama now had a denim miniskirt on.

After Taco set us all up with a round of drinks Gangrene said, "Before you left you said you were trying to get out of California and thought this was the place to do it. Problem is the bridge. They have all the firepower. If you try to get across the bridge they just cut you down. If you try to swim across they'll cut you down. We just don't have the firepower to get across the bridge."

"What if you had the fire power. Would you try or is this home? There's worse places," I said.

"Hell yes we'd try. We talk about it every day. We just keep hopin' they'll drop their guard and leave the bridge unattended for a while. Then we're rollin' across. We've been here three months though. We've seen a good lot of the crossings out of California south of Nevada and this one is far less manned than any other. It was a good call to try here but they never leave that damn post. Two guys day and night."

"What kind of weapons do they have?

"Guns."

"I know guns but what type. Handguns, shotguns, carbines, machine guns? You've been studying them. What have you seen?" I asked.

"They shot our guys with assault rifles. Most of the guys have side arms."

"Have you seen anything heavier. Machine guns, shoulder rockets, anything like that?"

"No, only small arms," he answered.

I glanced at Alan, who glanced at Amy and Donte. We all nodded. "I think we could match them pound for pound," Alan said.

"Whaddya mean?" asked Gangrene.

"We've got a number of small arms in the car. We have about the same number of soldiers. If they have a squad then they have twelve. We have fifteen. Do you have any weapons of your own?" I asked.

"We've got a few handguns, two .38 autos, a .22 revolver and a Beretta. Took the Beretta from a cop who tried to roust us a few years ago." He beamed at the accomplishment.

"What about ammo for them?"

"We've got a couple of reloads for the .38s, a box of .22 shells. The Beretta has a full clip but no reloads."

"It sure would be nice if we had the tank," Donte added. Everyone at the table looked at Donte like he was crazy.

"What's he talking about?" Gangrene said to me. "A tank? Really? Can we stick to reality?" he said looking at Donte.

I thought about the answer and decided that truth was the best bet. "We have a tank." I said it bluntly. "Back at the airport at Desert Center. Do you remember the tank that's parked out front? It's an M-

47 Patton. Looks like it's on display? You drove by it earlier today. We saw you guys roar by."

"Yeah I know that place."

"Well, it's about ten miles up the road from there now. We got it running."

The room went silent. Other than the music all of the Vultures sat with their mouths open.

"No shit?" Dirty Dog said.

"Don't get too excited. We ran out of gas and I doubt we can find over two hundred gallons of gas in the next day to get it here," I said.

"What kind of gas?" Gangrene asked.

"Regular."

"No problem. Looks like we got us a tank."

Chapter 27

Gangrene assured us he knew where to find more than enough gas and we decided to head there in the morning. The party went on for a few more hours. The mood was outstanding and hopeful. Even Ox and I made up although I wouldn't think of turning my back on him anytime soon. Near 11:00 p.m. Gangrene waved me over to his table.

"There are plenty of trailers down by the river. No one in any of 'em. Find one you like and you and your lady enjoy the rest of the evening. You might want to take her shopping first though."

"Shopping?"

"Yeah, most of those trailers were summer places. The closets are all full of clothes. I bet you can find her some nice new clean clothes, maybe even some nice bed clothes," he said adding a wink for emphasis.

"I think I'll just do that."

"You let Donte and Alan know too. They can take any trailer they like. We're all stayin' up in the three houses right up the road. I'd have you stay there but there's no more rooms left. Plus I get the feeling seeing as that little lady of yours has been leanin' on you and huggin' you all night that you might want some privacy." He nodded and looked over at Amy as he said the last.

I got up and walked over to Alan, Donte and Amy and shared Gangrene's suggestion. Amy and I said our goodnights and headed out into the cool desert night. Amy had no jacket and I could see her begin to shiver immediately. I pulled off mine and draped it over her

shoulders and put my arm around her. We talked as we
walked down the road toward the RV park.

"Let's go find you some new clothes. Gangrene says
these trailers are full of clothes."

"Sounds good. I've had this dress on for four days
now. Stark only gave me two dresses. I had to wear
them for days on end." I saw her look down at the
ground. A sadness seemed to come over her.

"You don't have to talk about this if you don't want.
Trust me, I know what a bastard he is."

"No I need to. I want to let go of it and because you
do know you're the person I want to let it go with. I
know you won't feel different about me after you hear."

"If you're sure then of course I'm here for you."

"What I didn't tell you last night was how it started.
When my mom got sick I went to the military begging
for help. They took me from the mall to their base and
brought me to Stark. He told me that if I slept with
him he would get me the medicine. He wasn't shy
about it, didn't even try to be subtle. Just came right
out about it like it was something he did every day.
What choice did I have? And he knew it. That week he
sent his guys three times to get me." She paused and
began to sob. I pulled her to me and hugged her tight.
She gently pushed back. "I need to finish this. I need
to get it out. Every time he promised. I felt so cheap.
I felt like a hooker. But it was for my Mom. I would
do anything for her. After the third time he told me
that he didn't have any of the medicine yet. I begged
him to do something and he just laughed and told me
to go home and wait. I felt so stupid and cheap. He
didn't send anyone for me again. My mom died a few
days later. He used me and threw me to the curb. He'd
let my mom die. I was so angry. I just wanted to kill

212

him. I went to the soldiers the next time they came to the mall and demanded that they take me to Stark. I had a knife hidden in my bra. I was going to lure him into bed and then stab him to death. I was on top of him, played it perfectly, reached over my head grabbed the handle of the knife out of the back of the bra and was about to bring it down into his chest. I don't know how he knew but he sensed something wasn't right and he grabbed my wrists. That was it. He locked me in that room and raped me just about every way you can imagine. I'd been there a few weeks when you came to my rescue. All I could think about while I was there was how to kill myself or kill him, whichever came first." She let out a deep breath. She cried some more and I held her close.

"He'll get his. Someday he'll get his," I said. We walked on not saying much until we came to the first trailer. "Shall we take a look? Remember we're looking for clothes for you and a couple of trailers for us to bunk down in."

"A couple?" she asked. "Oh I don't think we need more than one, do you?"

"Not if you say so. You just let me know which one you'd like."

"This first one will do just fine," she said. We began pulling clothes off each other the moment we stepped inside and were naked and wrapped together by the time we hit the bed. We made love with an urgency and a passion I'd never felt before. We lay there breathing hard, spent in each other's arms, just staring into each other's eyes. As soon as we caught our breath we went again, with even greater urgency and passion than the first time.

We woke, naked, wrapped together, arms and legs entwined a few hours later. We kissed passionately for a few minutes and then untangled ourselves. We dressed and then went looking for some new clothes for Amy. Two trailers down we found a closet full of clothes that fit perfectly. She took several pairs of jeans, a few t-shirts, two blouses and a leather jacket.

In the bottom of the closet was a jewelry box. Amy hadn't had any on, taken by Stark for sure. While Amy was trying on the clothes I rummaged through the box and found a gold necklace with a beautiful topaz stone the exact color of Amy's eyes.

I walked to Amy and held up the necklace. "For you."

"It's beautiful."

And then I performed one of my favorite slight of hand moves and made the stone and necklace disappear, holding my hands up to show Amy it was gone.

"Hey," she protested with mock indignation. "How did you do that?"

"A little something I learned along the way. Magic is a little hobby of mine."

"Impressive. Now how about you bring it back. And not from my ear. Too corny."

"Ok," I said reaching into the front of her jeans, pretending to rummage around for a moment and then pulling out the necklace.

Slipping it over her head she held the stone in her hand for a moment, then leaned in for a kiss.

"Do you want to stay here since the clothes are here?" I asked.

"No, the first one is our trailer, don't you think? Why don't we go back there and you can show me

214

some more of your magic tricks," she said as one corner of her mouth turned up.

I found that little half smile sexy as hell. "Absolutely." We carried the clothes back to the trailer, dumped them on the dining table, returned to the bedroom and made love again, taking our time, getting to know every inch of each other. When we were spent we drifted off to sleep, tangled together as we had before.

Chapter 28

I woke as the sun began to filter in through the frosted glass window of the bedroom door. I stood and looked down at Amy still sleeping, naked and even more beautiful in the morning glow than I remembered. Her blonde hair was fanned out over the pillow and she had the most peaceful look on her face. I could've stood there forever just memorizing every inch of her, but as much as I wanted to do that there were things to do today. I padded out to the living room and looked out the window to the east across the river. The bridges were visible from here and several soldiers were going about their mundane daily routine on the other side. Little did they know that tonight, barring any setbacks, their routine would be greatly disturbed.

A few fluffy white clouds were blowing by and the rest of the sky moved from glowing peach at the horizon to brilliant blue directly above. The breeze was gently blowing the branches of the trees out front. The inside of the trailer was freezing cold. I dressed quickly then gently woke Amy with a kiss. She stirred.

"Good morning."

"Morning." She yawned. "What time is it?"

"About six. I'm going to head up to the saloon and see who's up. Come on up when you are ready."

"Wait for me. I'll get dressed quickly."

She put on a pair of jeans, a white T-shirt, and the leather jacket and looked spectacular. We walked hand-in-hand to the saloon. We opened the door and immediately smelled eggs and some meat cooking.

Gangrene was at his table along with a few of the others.

"Morning," Gangrene roared. "You all sleep good? You both look a lot better than last night." Amy and I looked at each other and the corners of our mouths turned up at the mention of last night. "A good night of sex will do that for you," he said with a wink. Amy blushed. I found it remarkably sexy.

I nodded in his direction. "I'd say we slept well," stealing a glance at Amy and smiling. "Something smells great." My stomach had begun growling as soon as the smell of the food hit my nose. Sex is good for the appetite as well, I thought to myself.

"Taco's in the kitchen. He's scrambling some eggs. We got some chickens we collected up at the house that lay pretty regular. He's frying up some cans of corned beef hash. Wait till you taste his homemade salsa, too. Grew the tomatoes, onions and peppers himself. Damn good, and spicy. It gets the blood boilin' in the morning."

The door creaked open and Alan, Donte, Cowboy and Gypsy all walked in together. Cowboy and Gypsy waved our way and sat at the table with two of the others. Alan and Donte came back and sat with us. Bad Mama came in from the back a few minutes later carrying big plates full of eggs, hash and fresh salsa. We all tore into it and the only sounds uttered until the plates were empty were the joyful sounds made as you eat something that tastes so good it defies your imagination. As simple as this was, it tasted that good. I didn't know if it was the fact that I hadn't had something like this in ages or if it really was that delicious. In any case Taco was a heck of a chef. One by one we finished, slid our plates forward and leaned back against our chairs completely satisfied.

"So Gangrene. Let's talk about gas."

He roared with laughter. "I think that grub was pretty good. Didn't give me any gas," he joked. We all joined in.

When the laughter died I said, "All kidding aside, you said last night you knew where we could find enough gas for the tank. We need two to three hundred gallons. Where are you going to get that?"

"Back about thirty-five or forty miles there's a turnoff that goes up toward the mountains. Ten miles up the road is the Iron Mountain Pumping Station. It's one of the big pump stations for the aqueduct that brings water from the river to L.A. But it's like a little oasis. Because it's so remote they built like a little town for the workers. Pumps run on electricity. What happens when the power goes out?"

"No water." I said.

"Can't have no water, right. So there's back up generators. Big friggin' back up generators. And there's a big storage tank that feeds gas to the generators. It's the back end of a tanker truck. Gotta be ten thousand gallons. That should run your tank." He leaned back in his chair looking very pleased with himself.

"I would say that would do it."

After everyone was done with breakfast we filled the Challenger's tank with the remaining gas in the cans. The Vultures had two ten-gallon cans and a five-gallon can. We could collect sixty-five gallons at a time. It would take three trips up and back to fill the Patton with enough fuel to do the job.

We loaded into the Challenger and the Vultures fired up their bikes and our convoy began rolling back the way we'd come. Our car, four passengers, eight bikes, eleven riders, our army had grown to fifteen. We passed through the scrubby open desert, past Vidal Junction, where I'd found the Mossberg still clutched in a corpse's hands, past Rice and then another ten miles to the turnoff. The road was paved and formed a "Y" where it met the highway. There was no gate, just a small sign, announcing "Iron Mountain Pump Station. Property of Metropolitan Water District. No Trespassing". We ignored the warning and started up the road. About a half-mile further the aqueduct moved parallel to the road, about a hundred feet off to our left. It was dry now. The pumps had long ago shut down. No power to run them and no one to operate them. Most importantly no desire to do so.

Another quarter-mile ahead there was a landing strip that ran roughly parallel to the road. It eventually met the road and the taxiway crossed just as we came up the rise and saw the installation up ahead. The road curved left and crossed the aqueduct and we came into the oasis. Here in the middle of the most arid and desolate place I'd seen this side of Afghanistan was a miniature town. Built during the depression. The architecture of the buildings screamed WPA. Newer buildings were mixed in with the original. Remnants of beautiful lawns and landscaping adorned every building. As we moved deeper into the town we came to a large central circle, which once held a lawn with benches. It looked like a central park you would find in any small town in the United States. At the far end about a hundred yard across the desert was the pump station abutting a large reservoir. The reservoir was still about half full but the water was now green and murky. Leading from the rear of the pump station were three massive steel pipes. They came together at a concrete building about halfway up the mountainside and vanished there. It was an impressive facility. Great care had been taken to create the illusion of a little town. Workers had either lived here or stayed for long periods of time. There were houses and cottages further around the ring road, sitting up against the mountainside. The last building on the curved road was a recreation center with a large pool, now bone dry.

We intersected the road we had come in on and turned left, followed the road past the central park again and took the road that led to the pump house. On the far side was a secondary structure. It looked like a gigantic carport. Four pillars held up a steel roof twenty feet from the tarmac. Slatted walls lined the back and two sides. The front was completely open. Inside stood four giant generators, each on it's own concrete footing, two in front and two in back. On the right, next to the front row of generators was a gasoline tanker trailer minus the tractor truck. The big tanker sat on the rear wheels and the front balanced on two spindly jacks.

We stopped the car and bikes next to the tanker, climbed out and stretched.

We walked over and joined the bikers. "This is an amazing place. Seems so out of place here in the middle of nowhere," I said.

"I stumbled across it one day when I was out blowing off some steam," Mad Max said. "Brought everyone back here. Didn't find the gas until the third time we came."

"Does it have a valve for getting the gas out? How have you been doing it?" Alan asked.

"We just open up the big four inch valve there on the side," said Gangrene, pointing a meaty finger at it the middle of the tanker. "Put a bucket under it and catch some. We don't need much for the bikes. Kinda messy and it wastes a lot, but we figured even being sloppy this would last us forever."

"I've got a better solution," said Alan. He walked to the trunk of the Challenger and came back with his siphon. "There are access hatches on the top. We can just snake this down in there and pump out what we need nice and controlled. Donte, would you do the honor."

"No problem." He scaled the ladder quickly. "There are four of them, which one."

"Start at the rear. The tank is compartmentalized so that if it's ruptured it won't leak everything. Let us know how full it is," Alan said.

Donte worked the latches and swung the hatch door open. He recoiled at the fumes. "Whew. That's strong. This one's almost totally full." He snaked the hose into the opening and stepped back. Alan placed the other end into the first of the gas cans, squeezed the bulb for a few seconds and we could hear the fuel begin to fill the can. A few minutes later we had sixty-five gallons of fuel in the trunk. It put a load on the springs. The tires were compressed into the wheel wells. I did some quick math in my head. I knew gas was about twenty five percent lighter than water. Water weighs about eight pounds a gallon so the gas is about six pounds a gallon. Six times sixty-five are three hundred and ninety pounds. It was like adding two big people to the car.

"Two of us that were in the car are going to have to ride on the back of the bikes. There's almost four hundred pounds in those cans. I don't want to break the axle or damage the rear suspension. Plus the fumes might get pretty strong. Alan and Amy, why don't you ride on the bikes."

We mounted up and headed back down the road, turned right on the highway and made it down to the tank in about twenty minutes. It was still there, parked where we'd left it. In the back of my mind I'd been a little worried that someone had made off with it in the middle of the night. I wasn't quite sure how that would be done. I just had an irrational concern.

We emptied all the cans into the gas tank and Alan climbed in and fired up the Patton. It coughed, and black smoke billowed out of the exhaust as it roared to life.

"Why don't we split up? Half of us can escort the tank up the road while the rest of us go back and refill the cans. That way we won't have as far to come back and will cut the time down some," Cowboy suggested.

"That's a good idea. Alan and Donte can ride in the tank. I'll go with Amy in the car. Gangrene, you decide where your guys go," I said.

Gangrene, Mad Max, Ox and Spider stayed with the tank and the rest followed us to the pump station. It took four trips, the last time we were chasing the tank towards Earp when we met up. We filled the car and the bikes on the last trip and used one of the ten-gallon tanks to fill the bikes that were with the Patton. We even had some left over in the trunk. It took three hours to make all the runs and it was now 1130. The desert heat was beginning to make the inside of the tank uncomfortably warm. Alan said he was feeling light headed and Donte looked wrung out. Amy said she would give it a try so she and I took over tank driving duty while Alan and Donte took the Challenger. We had thirty miles to go and the tank was inching along at about ten miles per hour. We switched back and forth every hour and by 3:00 p.m. finally reached the spot where we'd pulled the Challenger off the road the night before. We drove the tank behind a low rise, and piled some tumbleweed over the back end. The camouflage wouldn't hide the Patton if someone walked right up on it but from a distance it made the boxy shape of the tank blend into the background.

We drove back to the saloon and parked the Challenger behind the building again. I figured that the soldiers had probably seen us on the way out that morning but I still thought it was better than leaving the car out in front in plain view just in case. We all went back inside. Spider poured a round of drinks and we all sat around Gangrene's table.

"Okay. We've got a tank, we've got an arsenal and we have soldiers. Now we need a plan. Any thoughts?" I asked. I had a good idea of how we should approach this but I wanted to hear some other ideas before I tainted it with mine. Sometimes the less experienced have the most innovative ideas. They can look at a situation in a completely different frame of mind. Alan started to speak but I raised my index finger off the table and he got the hint to wait. He nodded in response.

Ox raised his hand like he was in school. "We need to employ some diversion tactics. Throw them into a state of chaos," he said with a clarity I hadn't heard him use before. Even Gangrene looked stunned by the idea coming from him.

"Yeah we do. Good idea, Ox. Obviously we have to make a frontal assault with the tank but it's a long way across the bridge and the more we can divide the attention of the squad over there the less frontal resistance we can expect," I said.

"It's too bad that the cannon on that tank don't work," said Scumbag. "Not much they could do with that."

"That's true. I have an idea that might create the same type of chaos and concern. Do you have some paper and a pen?" I asked. Bad Mama stepped into the back and came back with some paper grocery sacks and a pencil. "That'll work." I drew a crude map and mapped out my plan. There was general agreement and a few good suggestions. Half an hour later we had a battle plan. We decided to put our plan into effect that night. We'd begin moving the tank at 2:00 a.m. and commence our attack at 3:00 a.m., about twelve hours away.

All you need is the plan, the road map, and the courage
to press on to your destination –
Earl Nightingale, one of the 12 survivors of the U.S.S. Arizona

PART III – The End Of the Road

Chapter 29

We all agreed to meet back at the Saloon at 6:00 p.m. for dinner, a final mental walk through and to make the last preparations for the assault. Amy and I had returned to the trailer and spent the early part of the afternoon making slow, passionate love. I guessed that Amy felt the same as I did, that this might be the last time we would ever do this if things didn't go as planned, but those thoughts remained unspoken. Instead, we let our hands and our mouths and our bodies say what we dared not say out loud. Our lovemaking was exactly as it should have been if indeed we would never share the experience again.

Afterwards we lay together, in the heat of the small bedroom, and just held each other. Finally I broke the silence, " Let's get out and take a walk. My mind is going in a hundred different directions. You, the assault, everyone else's safety, I just feel like moving."

"Sounds good. I'm going a little crazy myself." We got dressed and headed down to the shore of the river. We were around a bend in the river, out of sight of the soldiers guarding the bridge. We walked arm in arm, stopping to take in the beauty of the slow moving water contrasted against the arid desert banks above it. As we came over a small rise in the bank and dropped down the other side several large waterfowl, startled by our presence took flight from the bank, did slow lazy circles in the sky and landed so quietly and gently on the water's surface that they barely made a ripple. We walked another half-mile and decided we'd better return and began the trek back. We crested the small rise where we'd seen the birds and were looking out over the water to see if they were still floating there. When we swung our gaze back to the trail we were confronted by two soldiers in full combat uniforms. They were pointing their service pistols at our chests.

"Mr. Ryder? You are under arrest for crimes against the United States and for the murder of numerous military personnel. Please place your hands on your heads."

We glanced at each other. My heart sank. I could see the terror and panic in Amy's face as well. But we complied. We had no choice. Perhaps the Officer-in-Charge would be sympathetic. It was all we could do. I hadn't even brought the pistols with me. I was unarmed. It was a stupid mistake and I was angry with myself for not being more cautious.

They patted us down and cuffed both of us with our hands behind our backs. They led us straight out away from the river toward the road through the brush single file, along a narrow trail, one soldier in front, Amy next, then me and finally the other soldier, with his pistol occasionally jabbing me in the back.

As we came out of the brush into a clearing I could see the olive drab American made sedan across the sandy open space. It was parked along the roadside on the shoulder. There was another soldier leaning against the far side of the car and smoking. When he heard the crunching of our footsteps he turned. It was Stark. He had found us. All hope of getting a fair shake was gone. Amy gasped at the sight of him and dug her heels into the sand and began to backpedal. The soldier behind me saw her begin to hesitate and kicked my feet out from under me and toppled me to the ground. He grabbed her by the chain of her handcuffs and pulled her to the ground roughly.

"Where do you think you're going?" the soldier asked.

They helped us to our feet but each man controlled us by marching us forward and holding our wrists with their free hands and pushing the barrels of their guns into the smalls of our backs.

"Well, well Ryder. You've been quite the troublemaker haven't you? First you shoot up my base, steal my plaything there, and then you kill a soldier while trying to escape. Tsk tsk tsk." He waggled his finger as he made the sound. "And Amy, I've missed you. I know you've missed me. I've thought up so many wonderful things for us to do when we get home." Amy turned her head and looked at her feet. I could see her chest begin to heave as she started to sob.

"Put them in the back. We'll take them across the river and stay the night there," he said to the soldiers. "And then we'll head home in the morning," he said turning and staring at us.

We were loaded in the car, one of the soldiers between us. Stark sat in the passenger seat while the second soldier drove. As we passed the saloon Gangrene was standing out front, leaning against a post, smoking. He was hard-staring the soldiers, trying to intimidate them. I imagined he did this every time a military vehicle passed by. Stark was looking out his window at the bridges ahead and paid no attention to Gangrene. I leaned to my left and pressed my face close to the window and mouthed, "help" as we passed by. Gangrene's arm paused as it was going to his mouth with the cigarette. His posture straightened and he nodded. He had seen Amy and I and knew what was up. We had some help. Maybe.

We were taken across the bridge, the guards at the far end allowed the car through with a wave. We pulled up to the big warehouse on the left of the road. Stark exited the car and quickly trotted up and into the warehouse. The two soldiers removed us from the car and led us up and in the building.

It was a steel pre-fab structure about half the size of a football field. Inside there were crates of supplies stacked head high in four neat rows. One end of the building held two neat rows of cots. The rest of the space was filled with the equipment that the warehouse had originally held. From the look of the tools it had been some sort of machine shop. Along one wall was a row of offices. They looked like boxes stacked next to each other. Only the far room had a window. The others just had a single plain door. The rooms hadn't even been painted. They were still just drywall; you could still see the lines of mud and tape that joined the panels together. I wondered if they even bothered to put a ceiling on them. On each end of the row of rooms was an exit with a sign in the middle indicating they were emergency exits only. Several soldiers were working on the far side of the big space. They glanced our way then went back to the mundane chore they'd been assigned to do. I took a quick mental photograph of the building as we were shoved toward the offices.

One of the soldiers stepped forward, pulled a ring of keys from his pocket, unlocked the door and shoved me into the room. I fell forward with the shove and managed to roll to my right and landed hard on my shoulder. It was better than my face but hurt all the same. I rolled over on my back and saw that the room did indeed have a ceiling. The door slammed shut and I was left all alone. I heard the door slam shut next door.

"Amy, are you over there?"

"Yes," she replied. I heard the lock click on my door. It swung open and one of the two soldiers rushed across the room and kicked me in the ribs. The wind rushed out of my lungs.

"Shut up. If I hear another word out of either of you you'll get much worse, murderer," he yelled. There was no need for him to go in the other room. He'd been loud enough for Amy to hear.

The room was almost completely empty. There was no furniture at all. The floor had a layer of grey, unpadded, cheap, indoor/outdoor carpet covering it. There was some loose papers and debris against the wall. The room looked like it had once been an office with the furniture hastily removed and with no time to clean up after the move.

I rolled to the rear wall, pushed my back against it and levered myself into a standing position. The rear wall was corrugated sheet steel and the other three and the ceiling were unfinished drywall. The studs were exposed on this side. Whoever built the room hadn't even bothered to finish the room off. Drywall might make a nice inexpensive building material that's easy to work with but it made for lousy cell walls. What made it easy to work with was just what made for a terrible holding cell. All it took to cut it was something sharp to score it and then you could just break unwanted piece off. Cutting a hole would be easy if there was something to use to score the wall.

I was just about to check the debris when I heard the lock click. I moved to the corner and sat down. I didn't want to appear as a threat. The door swung open and Stark stepped in. He closed the door behind him and walked toward me. He stopped in the middle of the room and squatted down so he was eye level to me. "I should've just killed you in Afghanistan. I had so many chances. Your luck is done my old friend. Tomorrow you will come back with me, you'll face a military tribunal for your crimes, you'll be found guilty, and then a firing squad will put four bullets in your heart. I'll be sitting there with a bag of popcorn enjoying the show. Enjoy your last night Ryder." He stood and walked to the door, opened it, stopped and turned back. "Oh, and your little girlfriend next door, she'll be coming too. I'll let her watch and then I'll take her back to my office, and well, I'm sure you can figure it out. Meanwhile there is a guard posted outside so don't try anything stupid." He turned to leave and I called out to him.

"Hey Stark." He turned back into the room. "So, was it the dash mounted camera or the palm prints I left on the hood of the car I shot up that got you here?"

"What are you babbling about?" he said.

"How did you know where to look? Was it the video or the palm prints? I wasn't sure if the video was damaged in the rollover so I figured I'd better leave you a bigger roadmap. That's why I left you the palm prints. I'm sure you put an all points bulletin out for me. The prints matched the bulletin. Then I guess you had enough brains to put my palm prints with the description of a purple muscle car. I knew you'd send out another bulletin looking for the car after you heard about the prints. You must've thought either you were the greatest sleuth or I was the dumbest guy. Not so. I got you here and I've got you right where I want you.

You did take an awful long time to get here though. I figured you had enough brains to pick up on the report much faster. Oh well, doesn't matter, you're a dead man any way it goes." He stared at me trying to put together what I'd just said, then began to laugh.

"You've got balls Ryder, I'll give you that. But I hardly think you're in any position to make threats. You just sit tight and I'll make your last day as good as I can." He walked out, shaking his head, then closed the door and I heard the lock click shut.

A few seconds later I heard the door open next door. I could hear Stark's muted voice. A long moment later I heard Amy yell, "Don't come near me you bastard." Then I heard the slap. I pressed my ear to the wall. I could hear Stark near the back of the room. I imagined him, leaning over Amy breathing in her face, telling her what he's told me, groping at her. A long moment later I heard the click of shoes walking across the room, the door open and close and the lock engage. Then it was quiet.

I listened for a minute then knew I needed to get to work. I got on my knees and began searching the floor inch by inch. I started in the area that had the papers. There must've been bookshelves or a file cabinet here once. The type of debris and amount of dust against the floorboard told me that there had been something heavy and difficult to move. A minute later and I had the tool I needed buried in a large dust bunny. It was a jumbo paperclip. I turned my back to it and felt around until I was able to pick it up. I unfolded it and bent the end into an "L" shape. I worked the short end into the lock of the handcuff on my left wrist and worked the paperclip back and forth. In about twenty

233

seconds the cuff popped open. I brought my hands around in front and undid the other cuff.

I went to the wall between my room and Amy's and began using the end of the paperclip to dig a scored line up from the floor against the stud nearest the corner about two feet. I dug in until the paperclip went in a little more than one quarter of an inch. I made a similar line in the corner against the other beam. Then I made a horizontal score along the bottom stud. I brushed the dust off the wood and into the carpet and whisked it around with my hand. The lines and the dust were almost invisible. I decided I would wait to make the horizontal score at the top until I was ready to go. The top horizontal line would be obvious if someone came into the room. My plan was to wait until after the sun was down to make our escape easier once we hit the outside.

I moved to the other rear corner and made the same score marks on that wall. Then I locked the handcuff to my left hand and looped the open cuff over my right wrist and sat down to wait. It had been about 1600 when we were first arrested and I guessed about forty-five minutes had passed since then. I closed my eyes, ran through my plan over and over and simply waited.

When the clock in my head told me it was about 1800 I loosened the cuffs again and began making my horizontal lines. Several times I heard footsteps outside the room and had to stop and slip the cuff over my right wrist. It took me about ten minutes to get both the score marks done and I was ready to go. I went to the wall between my room and Amy's room, laid down on my back, placed my feet in the square I'd scored with one foot in each corner and pushed. I was afraid to kick the square in. I thought it would make too much noise as it came loose. I pushed hard and finally the square gave. It cracked in the middle and tumbled inward. I quickly flipped around and stuck my head into the room, expecting to see Amy's shining face. The room was empty. Stark had taken her the first time he'd gone in the room. I knew the door hadn't been opened again. There was nothing I could do but get out and reformulate a plan. Staying would just get me killed. I was too outnumbered, not to mention unarmed, to go searching through the warehouse, if he even had her there still. I moved to the other side of my room. Popped a corner loose and worked my fingers into the small opening I'd made and pulled the square of drywall into my room. I poked my head out the hole, looked to my left, saw it was clear and pulled myself out. I replaced the square of drywall as best as I could and then I darted to the emergency exit to my right, pushed the crash bar in quietly, and opened the door. I winced waiting for the door alarm to beep but it hadn't been set.

I looked out the door from side to side and saw it was clear, then exited and sprinted for the edge of the river and the tall brush that was growing there. When I was several hundred yards away I stopped and looked back. No change. No soldiers running after me, no panicked or frantic activity. I turned and made my way through the underbrush and reeds until I got to the railroad trestle. There were a series of I-beam girders supporting the tracks between the river's edge and the road that ran next to it. I used the beams like a ladder and climbed up to the tracks and took off across the river at a sprinter's pace. It was the longest three hundred yard run I'd ever made. Not only because I was afraid that a sniper was drawing a bead on me as I was exposed but because I was so torn. My head told me that this was the best and only way I was going to save Amy. There was nothing I could do creeping around in that warehouse, unarmed against a squad of soldiers and Stark. But my heart made me feel like I was abandoning her. I felt like I was running away like a coward. It's just not in my nature to run from a fight. I always stood my ground and fought it out and it always seemed to work. I questioned myself all the way across that bridge. In the end my head won out and I completed the run across, and kept going until I made the parking lot of the saloon.

I burst through the door, startled the hell out of everyone, and then stood, doubled over in the middle of the room trying to get my breath, my heart hammering in my chest. My lungs were burning from the run and the adrenaline. Alan came up and put his hand on my back.

"Ethan, are you okay?"

I nodded my head, then changed my mind and shook my head, still gulping air.

"Which is it? You're scaring me. Gangrene said he saw you in the back of the car. What happened?"

"Stark…Amy," I managed to get our between breaths. I took one more deep breath. "It was Stark. He got Amy and me. I got out. He's still got Amy."

"Come over here and sit," he said. He led me over to a chair and I sat, caught my wind and shared the story or our arrest, the warehouse and my escape. "I don't know where he took her. She was in the room next to me but when I went to get her out she was gone. He won't leave without me. It's going to change things. As soon as he figures out I'm gone they're going to come looking for me. He knows I won't leave without her. We've got to ramp up our assault to now. We need to go get the tank and the car now and put things in motion before they come over here. We have no defenses. In fact we're sitting ducks in here. Get all the weapons out here, locked and loaded. Alan and Donte, you need to go get the tank." I was frantic and everyone knew it.

"Whoa. Slow down. Let's think this through. They have no idea where you are. They don't know you're rolling with us. For all you know they don't even know you're gone. We have a good plan. We need to stick with it. Let's put some surveillance on them and if the activity seems to change dramatically then we can react," said Gangrene with the calmness that only comes with leadership.

"You're right. I'm sorry. I do think it would be a good idea to put a sentry of our own on the bridge. If they do decide to come over here we can put a stop to it."

"I agree," said Gangrene. "Dirty Dog, take that submachine gun and find a position just this side of the bridge, out of sight. If they try to drive across unload on their windshield. Mad Max, go with him and spot. If something unusual happens come back and let us know. Got it?"

"Got it," they replied at the same time. Dog scooped up the gun and he and Max headed out the door. Dog had been in the Army reserves at one time long ago and had been trained on a number of weapons. After Alan and I he had the most field experience of any of us.

"This does change things though. We know we have a 'friendly' over there now. We can't be so reckless with the firearms," said Alan.

"Firebombs either," added Scumbag.

"Going to change my role, too," I added. "Pull that map out and let's get to work."

Chapter 30

Our original plan had involved a full frontal assault. We had superior numbers, greater desire, potentially more firepower, surprise and a tank. With Stark's arrival we'd lost numbers and surprise. Losing numbers increased our desire. It was no longer just about escape. It was now about escape, rescue and retribution. We had lost surprise and that had been our biggest ally. We still had a tank, and soldiers they didn't know about, but they were going to expect us to come back at them at some point, and some point soon. We needed a new approach and we needed it quickly.

As I sat in the bar vaguely listening to the others discuss our options my mind wandered to Amy and from there to my wife and my old life and my son. How terribly wrong things had gone, not only for me but for them and for Amy. Would things go wrong for my new friends too? Would I drag them to their deaths as well? How was I going to save them? How was I going to save Amy? How was I going to save myself? We needed a miracle. We needed some magic. Magic. Magic! That was the answer. We would pull the ultimate trick.

"I've got it!" I yelled. The conversation came to a screeching halt. I began to explain. "We are going to use magic." Everyone looked at me like I had gone over the edge. "Sleight of hand is the answer." I gave them a quick lesson on the basics of this. There were seven principals to slight of hand. Palming: holding something in an apparently empty hand. Stealing: this is self-explanatory. Simulation: to give the idea that

239

something had happened that really hasn't. Switch: to change one thing for another. Ditch: to get rid of something unneeded. Load: to secretly move something from one place to another. And Misdirection: to bring attention away from something else you don't want them to see. I outlined my plan, which had all the elements. In a sense the plan would be one big illusion. The problem is magic takes practice and we were going to have to pull this one off without it.

As we finished formulating the plan Max came back through the door.

"There's all kind of activity over there all of sudden. It was real quiet and now it looks like someone kicked over an ant hill."

"They just figured out I was gone. I'm going to take a look." I grabbed the field glasses from Max and ran out the back and across a hundred yards of desert. Ran up the gentle slope behind the saloon until I had a clear view of the base across the river. The last of the sun was slightly illuminating the scene. It would be dark in fifteen minutes. Even without the glasses I could see more activity than I'd seen in the two days since we'd gotten there. The soldiers were in pairs searching up and down the shoreline behind the warehouse. There were two more guys at the end of the bridge watching the road. Another pair was walking the perimeter of the warehouse. "They're going to get itchy when they can't find me and come looking. It's time to get going. Everyone knows what his or her job is. Grab your assigned weapon and head out. Give me five minutes head start and I'll send Dog back."

I grabbed the two .44's and headed out the door and down the road to Dog's position. I reached him and sent him back to the saloon and then worked my way down through the brush between the two bridges, climbed a piling and perched on top to wait. I went over every element of the plan in my mind trying to see if we missed anything. On paper every plan seems perfect until they go into action. Then you needed to be fluid, reacting to the ever-changing variables. A million things can go wrong. I had been on hundreds of missions and they never went exactly as planned. What kept you from getting killed was being able to think on the fly, to adapt and react. I felt strongly about my abilities, was practiced and battle tested. Alan would be fine. He'd already demonstrated his ability to adapt in action. It was the rest of my army that concerned me. So many things can happen. Someone can be late or get delayed in getting to their assignment. The untested can get spooked in the heat of battle and run or simply turtle up.

I chose the frontal assault originally because success depended on surprise and brute force. "Shock and Awe" had been the plan in Iraq and had worked brilliantly. We had overwhelmed the fourth largest army in the world almost overnight. We just plain scared the shit out of them. Poor bastards dug down in the sand with rifles older than their parents and we're rolling in with hundreds of M-1 tanks, stealth bombers and fighters and enough artillery to obliterate them. It was an overwhelming show force. The Iraqis just gave up. I hoped to do that here with the tank. Even though it couldn't fire we could hit them with Molotov cocktails from the sides, sniper fire from across the river and a tank down the road. Scare and confuse. That had gone out the window with Stark. I had miscalculated with him. I wanted to lead him to me when we were already across the river and on our way. I wrote a roadmap right to me. Then I would ambush him. He'd gotten the jump on me and blown the original plan. My fault. I had put everyone in jeopardy because of my selfishness. But that hate still burned in my belly and I couldn't let it go. Now our plan required precision and timing. It required that no one was late. Our success required that no one bail out at the first sign of trouble. It needed everyone to pull off their job and it needed the enemy to buy into a lot. We needed them to act in a way that we expected them too. Victory was a whole bunch of "what ifs" It was going to take a lot of luck.

The clouds had rolled in and helped to keep the river dark. A slight cold breeze was blowing from east to west. That was good for us. The wind would carry sound to us more easily and keep any noise we might make from traveling easily to them. The river flowed by gently below my feet, endlessly moving from the higher elevations and the dam to the north and on into Mexico where it's eventually diverted off into farmlands and disappears.

The frenzied activity had slowed some but there were still more soldiers out milling around than usual. I looked over to the railroad trestle and saw the black form silently moving across the bridge staying low and hiding behind the big I-beams as he went. I knew it was Spider. He had said he got his name for a reason. He said he could climb like a spider and had volunteered for the duty.

Shortly afterward I heard the roar of the bikes and the Challenger firing up. They spent a good minute revving the engines as loud as they could. I spun around to see what the reaction would be. Four soldiers rushed to the LMTV from inside the warehouse. Two climbed into the cab and two piled into the bed. The truck fired up, headlights snapped on and the truck took off across the bridge. Then I could hear the bikes and the Challenger take off, the car laying a long strip of rubber as it hit the pavement. "Nice touch Alan," I whispered to myself. I could see their headlights reflected off the sides of the hills as they raced up the low grade heading back to the west. About thirty seconds later I saw the lights of the truck swaying over the landscape as they gave pursuit.

Now it was time to wait again. Activity at the base had slowed. The two extra guards at the guard post left and returned to the inside of the warehouse. There was now one guard patrolling the shore on each side of the road. I spent time counting the seconds that it took the two guards to make their way away from the road and back. I was curious how far they were patrolling down the shore. I did some quick math based on the pace of their steps, counting a yard per step and waited until they returned. Their pace was almost identical. They had been told to go three hundred yards out and back. I guessed that Stark figured I was laying low on their side of the river and would try to get Amy on my own. So in response to that perceived threat he must've decided to place two guards to defend that tactic. It was a waste of manpower. Even if I was there I could easily surprise and overpower one guard. Stark knew that or he should've. They never reported to anyone after each circuit, and were out of view from the guards on the bridge so even if one disappeared no one would know it until it was time to change watch. Stupid.

Having the bikes and the car drive away was the first part of our sleight of hand. This was the simulation. We wanted to make them think we were running. They had anticipated that as I had expected they would. They already had the guys ready to go, they knew who was going and they knew what vehicle they were taking. Perhaps Stark thought I was going to go all the way back to the Valley and try another assault there, or was just trying to cover all possibilities. It didn't matter. What mattered, as it does with all magic, is that the audience bought it. They bought it hook, line and sinker. And they were chasing my guys right into an ambush.

A minute went by, then two, and then three, longer than I'd anticipated. Finally I heard it, faintly, the crackling sound of gunfire. By the time the sound waves tried to cross the river the sound would be gone. I needed to hear one more sound and then it would be time to move forward. A minute later it came gently and quietly. The sound of the big tank engine firing to life drifted through the air. It had made a distinct backfire sound every time we had started it. So quiet I wasn't even sure if I had imagined it. I had been straining so hard to hear it that I might have tricked my mind into hearing it. But I had heard it. I was sure of it. I couldn't chance waiting so I turned and began my long trip across the bridge.

I took a look down to the far end of the trestle bridge and could just see the dark lump of Spider against one of the beams. He was in position and ready. I started my trip. Someone at one time had added chain ink fencing along both sides of the bridge along the original railing to keep people from falling or jumping into the river. I used it to climb along foot by foot on the outside. My feet were resting on a concrete ledge six inches wide, five feet below the edge of the low concrete base and twenty-five feet above the water, my hands were shoulder high holding on to the fence. Just my shoulders, hands and head were visible above the solid concrete. I had three hundred yards to go.

A hundred yards across I wished I had started earlier. My fingers were already beginning to cramp and get raw, and my shoulders were burning. Every fifty yards there was a pier like the one I had sat on while waiting to hear the guns and the tank. I took a brief rest at each one, catching my breath, shaking out my arms and hands and then listening for any sound of the Patton. It wasn't until the sixth rest stop that I began to hear the tell tale sound. Not only could I hear the big engine but I could also hear the clatter and squeak of the rollers and treads as it rolled over the road.

I quickly pressed on and made it to the eighth piling. My arms were cramping badly. I was going to need them to recover quickly. Worse were my fingers. The second joints on the three middle fingers of each hand were bloodied and blistered. Those would not recover so quickly. I had to hope that they would not impede any shot I would have to make. The eighth piling was just past the last of the chain link. I could now haul myself up on the roadbed at the prescribed time. I peeked over the concrete and the activity at the base had calmed even further. I wondered if my guys had recovered a radio and had answered calls. We had talked about the proper response in Ten Code. Alan was familiar with the codes but each branch has it's own codes. I took a chance and felt it was likely they were using MP codes. Since they were essentially a police detail, guarding a road, it was a good bet. I figured they would get a 10-40; acknowledge call or a 10-14; your location? I told them just reply with 10-8, suspect in custody. That would satisfy them.

I looked across the open space between my spot and the railroad bridge and nodded to Spider. He nodded back. Then we waited. The faint sound of the tank lumbering along the road gradually grew louder. I checked the guards and there was still no reaction to the sound. It was still faint and seemed to be moving from south to north. A few minutes later the tank turned and started toward us. It was clearly audible now. If I strained hard I could hear the Challenger engine as well. I imagined the sight of the strange caravan. A LMTV followed by a Patton 47 tank, a purple muscle car and a string of bikers. The image was funny and for the first time all night I began to relax. It was an odd sensation for someone going into battle and hard for someone who hadn't been there to understand. You plan and think and work through scenarios in your mind. You worry and check equipment and prepare and organize. And then it's go time. All the preparation kicks in and you relax and your subconscious takes over and you're ready. I was at that place right now.

It was then that I heard the LMTV coming across the bridge. I could feel the faint vibrations as the vehicles began to roll across its length. The glare of the headlights washed down the concrete. This was the "steal" part of the sleight of hand. We had secretly taken the needed item. The guards would relax at the sight of the LMTV thinking it was still their own and its head and spot lights would blind and mask the vehicles behind it. The magic was working.

246

Chapter 31

Seeing the headlights, that was my cue. I climbed over the edge of the rail with my hands high in the air and yelled, "I surrender, I surrender". It was time for the "misdirection". The two guards came out from behind the sand bags, weapons pointed at my chest. I heard the truck. The guards never noticed that the headlights had slowed to a crawl. That was misdirection. They were so focused and surprised by my actions that they had lost all focus on the truck. The truck was supposed to be there, I was not. They stepped forward. They were forty yards away and moving slowly toward me. Behind them two other soldiers had stepped out of the warehouse door and were observing the scene. One paused and quickly ran back inside.

Headlights washed over me from behind and I could hear the truck just one hundred yards down the bridge. Behind the truck I could hear the clanking of the tank. I knew it was there, I could hear the sound but the two soldiers weren't expecting it, they were expecting a truck and the truck's headlights made everything behind them disappear. Plus their focus was still on the suspect who had just suddenly appeared on their bridge. Their lack of an aggressive move toward me was working in our favor. I could see them yelling but the truck engine was drowning out their commands, so I slowly lowered my hand and put it behind my ear and shrugged my shoulders. They continued forward. I stood my ground. The truck rolled to a stop fifty feet behind me. I heard the tank grind to a stop at the same time. I heard the doors snap open and the sound of two men dropping to the pavement. They were hidden by the glare of the headlights. I knew all the soldiers could see was the black silhouette of two men. They would assume it was their men.

Behind the soldiers I saw Stark come bursting out the door. It was then I knew that Alan had answered the radio call. He had given them the 10-8 code. Suspect in custody. The soldier had run back inside had alerted everyone that I was now on the bridge. Stark had said something like, "Funny, I never heard the truck," or "When did the truck get back," and the soldier would've said "No truck." There would've been a long pause, a moment of confusion, a feeling that something wasn't right. And then recognition would've set in and then the panic. I pictured Stark tripping over himself to get outside and make sure the soldier was wrong, or had misspoken.

Stark stopped when he saw the truck. I could see the relief on his face. He even looked over his shoulder to see if the soldier that had brought the information was standing there so he could chew him out. He looked back at us and I could see his posture relax. It was short lived. I quickly reached down behind my head and drew one of the .44's from the holster on my back. I pulled the gun, brought it down, leveled and fired the gun in one motion. I did it so quickly the advancing soldiers had no time to react. I had palmed the guns perfectly. Shown them the empty hands, then made the gun appear. Magic. Gunfire erupted behind me at the exact moment I drew and fired. I saw both soldiers drop in a spray of blood. The one to my right that I had fired at first was hit in the chest and the throat at the same time. I had no idea if it was my bullet or one my friends that had done the job. It didn't matter. His throat exploded out the back of his neck. Tissue, blood and bone flew from the back of his neck in a pink spray and he fell in a heap. The soldier to my left was hit in the face. I saw the neat hole in his forehead. The back of his head blew out and brain matter soaked the road. He stood upright longer than he should have. A part of his brain was working on autopilot, and then he crumbled.

I heard a bullet sizzle by my right ear. It couldn't have missed me by more than an inch. I hit the deck and rolled to the curb on the right. I looked back to see who might've fired the shot but I couldn't see any of the bikers. They must've moved after the shot. Careless.

I looked to my left. I could see the small flame in Spider's hand; he touched it to the cloth in the bottle in his other hand. Flame licked up, he reared back and heaved the bottle toward the entrance of the warehouse. Stark saw it coming and he turned and retreated into the building. The bottled floated end over end, hung in the air for a long moment and then crashed into the side of the building just to the left of the door. Flaming gasoline sprayed over the wall and door. It hit right as a soldier had begun to emerge from the door. He was doused with the flaming liquid. He ran in circles, slapping at the flames trying desperately to keep them from his face. Finally he was overcome and dropped in a burning heap. He thrashed for a moment then went still.

My eyes traced back to Spider as he was lighting a second bottle. He reared back again. There was a crack from below. Spider tumbled back, the bottle dropped from his hand, smashed on the iron bridge and shattered. He was immediately engulfed in flame. He tried desperately to jump over the railing but the flames overcame him. The bright flames leapt up fifteen feet. I dropped my eyes down to the riverbank. The soldier that had been on patrol was still sighting the bridge with his M-16 about thirty feet away. I took aim with the pistol, squeezed off a shot, and quickly brought the gun back down for a second shot, all in less than a second. Both shots found their target and the soldier fell back. Both shots had hit him in the chest. They weren't killing shots. They'd hit his vest. Suddenly, I was aware of Gangrene standing next to me. He was holding the Mossberg. He leveled it at the soldier, took a beat and fired. The damage was fatal. Gangrene turned and waved his meaty arm and the truck rolled forward. Mad Max and Dog were in the truck. The tank followed, rolling forward, clanking across the concrete. Alan and Donte were the tank crew. Behind that was Bad Mama driving the Challenger with the other women. Flanking them were Cowboy, Taco, and Scumbag, one on each side of the car and one behind. The invading army. Ox had volunteered to take my original role of sniper on the far side of the rail bridge. He said he had done a lot of deer and elk hunting growing up and felt confident he could make the shots.

We had thirty yards to the end of the bridge when soldiers began to spill out the emergency exit to our left. The flames from the Molotov cocktail were beginning to ebb leaving an eerie orange glow. The sheet metal siding of the building had obviously not ignited. The plastic exit sign above the door was dripping melted plastic in a neat stalagmite below. To our right the sentry came into view. Dirty Dog leaned out the window of the truck and dropped the sentry with a perfectly placed shot to the head. Five were down. That left seven from the original squad, plus Stark's two guys and Stark.

Every soldier who had rushed out the door took one look at the tank and froze. Max gunned the truck engine and rolled off the bridge. He skidded to a stop on the right shoulder. Max and Dog bailed out the passenger door and took up a position behind the bed. Dog now had the submachine gun in his hands. Max held the two .38 autos. They took aim on the soldiers.

The Patton continued to roll forward. It stopped next to the guard shack. Alan swung the tank to the left so that the barrel of the big useless gun pointed at the group of soldiers. The remaining seven guys from the original squad were pinned down by what I was sure they believed to be the business end of a 90mm cannon. Only Stark and his boys were missing. We had just completed a good portion of our magic trick. We had used a "load" to secretly move a 46-ton tank a mile across a bridge and make it magically appear at this end without being seen. Quite a trick.

I was standing at the guard shack. Gangrene was next to me. The shack was just a small hastily built wooden structure about eight feet by eight feet. It was sitting on the westbound lane of the road. The inside was Spartan. There was a small desk beneath the window. Several papers littered the top. On the wall next to it were two shotguns. Gangrene pulled the guns down and checked to see if they were loaded. He shook his head. I looked around the room for some shells. There was a crate below the desk. I opened the lid and it was filled with neatly packed flash grenades.

"No shells but how about these instead?" I picked up one of the grenades and tossed it to Gangrene.

251

"Hand grenades. These will come in handy."

"They're flash-bang grenades. These don't explode. They just produce a really bright flash and bang that blinds and stuns the enemy. Used mostly for crowd control." I scooped four out of the box and filled my jacket pockets. I handed Gangrene several as well. We exited the shack and moved to the side of the tank.

Alan popped out of the hatch, looked down at the soldiers and yelled, "Bang!" Several of them actually jumped. He laughed. "Drop the weapons." They hesitated a moment. "Really, you guys want me to lower this gun and use it?" They looked nervously at each other and dropped the guns. "Kick them over here," Alan said.

As the soldiers were about to comply the emergency exit flew open and Stark came out pushing Amy in front of him. The coward was using her as a shield. He held an M9 Beretta pistol to her temple. He hid his head behind her. His two guys, both with M-16's at the ready, flanked him. The magic had just run out and now it was time for improvisation.

"Pick up your guns you idiots," he yelled at the soldiers. They complied. "Ryder, you have a choice. Tell your crew to leave their weapons and go back across the bridge and you come out empty handed or I put a bullet through her head."

"Let me give you a counter offer. You have a only one option," I replied, stepping out of the guard shack. "You can let her go, let these people go on their way, tell your guys to stand down and you can have me." I saw Amy mouth "No" and shake her head slightly.

"Hmmm. Let's see. I can let everyone go except you or I can kill everyone, and get both you and her. I think

252

I'll go with the second choice," he said, his voice filled with sarcasm.

I began to move toward the front of the tank and closer to them. "All we've got here is a standoff. If someone starts shooting there's going to be lots of people dead on both sides. You can have what you want. Just let them all go. This is between you and I now." I took another step closer and noticed the black canister rolling to my left. It came to rest halfway between Stark and I.

The soldier on Stark's left moved his eyes down in response to the motion. I closed my eyes tight and heard him yell; "Gren…" and then I heard the bang of the flash grenade go off. I heard yelling. A shot was fired. I opened my eyes and took off on a dead sprint toward Stark who was frantically blinking, trying to regain his vision. Everything slowed to a crawl at that instant. I heard the slap of my feet on the pavement. To my right I saw Max and Dog run around to the front of the truck firing at the scattering soldiers. Cowboy and Taco were running from their bikes. Flashes of gunfire erupted all around me. I saw one of the soldiers to my right go down. I reached Stark and Amy a second later. I slapped the gun out of Stark's hand and I saw it tumble end over end through the air; hit the ground and skitter away. My right arm wrapped around Amy's waist and I ripped her from Stark, scooped her up and took off down the side of the warehouse.

Behind me I could still hear the sound of the gunfight going on. We reached the end of the warehouse and turned right. Twenty yards back was a stack of empty pallets. We slid behind and I set Amy down. We heard footsteps running toward us. One soldier passed the corner and kept on going, then a second and a third. They passed and kept on going. We watched as they disappeared around a curve in the riverbank. I looked back at Amy. I leaned in and kissed her.

"Are you okay?" I asked.

"Yes, I think so. I can see again. What was that?"

"Flash-bang grenade. You sure you're okay?"

"Yes," she answered.

"I've got to go back there. You stay here. Don't move. Take this," I said and handed her the fully loaded .44 from under my jacket. "Take one beat if someone comes around the corner and if they aren't friendly then unload on him. Don't hesitate. Don't think. Just do it. I'll be right back"

"You'd better be." I leaned down and kissed her once more. I looked back as I reached the corner then took off toward the firefight. I dropped down the bank and climbed back up where the bridge met the slope. I flattened on my stomach and looked over the edge of the bank. Alan had moved the tank forward and was firing from a gun port. Max and Dog had moved to the front of the truck and were firing at a point down the street out of my vision. In front of the warehouse two of the soldiers and one of Stark's guys were down. Cowboy and Taco were lined up against the side of the building behind a support pillar, trying to stay out of the return fire that was coming in bursts. The soldiers were spraying their return fire at any target they could. To my right Gangrene had moved behind the tank. Farther back I saw Scumbag on the ground. He had a gaping chest wound. Candy Girl was cradling him in her arms. She was calling his name over and over. The other two women were huddled behind the Challenger's trunk.

Smoke and the smell of cordite filled the air. I clamored up the rest of the bank and ran to the side of the warehouse where Cowboy and Taco were. I took up the last spot in the line behind Cowboy.

"How many are left?" I asked.

"There are two guys down the street. They are pinned down behind a low wall."

"What happened to Stark?"

"He ran into the warehouse as soon as you grabbed Amy. Where is she?"

"I've got her hidden. Let's take care of these guys and then I'm going after Stark." I raised my hands palms up. Everyone could see me from my current position. One by one they stopped firing and were watching me. The soldiers continued to fire out of pure panic. They weren't even aiming. Bullets were hitting all over the place. There was no rhyme or reason to the placement. It was panic shooting. I pulled two grenades from my pockets and held them up. Everyone nodded in understanding. Max, Dog and I were closest to their position. I pointed across to them, pointed to the grenades, covered my eyes then made a running motion with my fingers. They nodded in understanding. I pulled the pins on both grenades, waited for both soldiers to stop shooting, figuring that they were now trying to reload, I stepped out from behind the pillar and then tossed the grenades toward the wall. I dropped back and covered my eyes, counted two, heard the loud pop, pop, of the two grenades and took off running. Max and Dog took off at the same time. We dove over the wall tackled both men, and wrestled the weapons away from them. They both had

255

handcuffs on their belts. We removed them and cuffed the men together, then cuffed them to two different poles with their arms stretched out. We removed their shoes and tied their ankles together with the shoelaces. They weren't going anywhere.

Everyone began moving toward us. Their faces showed the stress and exhaustion of the battle. Although it seemed like hours had passed the entire fight from the first shot had lasted just over ten minutes.

Chapter 32

"I've got to go get Amy," I said. "Keep your eyes open. Stark and one of his guys are still unaccounted for."

I ran the length of the building and stopped at the corner. "Amy?"

"I'm here," she called back. I turned the corner and began to walk to the pile of pallets. I saw Amy stand. I was so relieved to see her. I had been worried that Stark might find her in the short time I was gone. We hugged and held each other tight. She buried her face in my chest. I took the pistol from her and holstered it.

"Let's get back," I said. I felt her nodding against my chest. We turned and started to head back to the front. Ten feet from the corner one of Stark's guards crashed out of the bushes and dove at us. The three of us tumbled to the ground. He held his grip on my neck and Amy rolled free. He had a choke hold around my throat. He was strong and I could feel him ratcheting down on the arm that was digging in to my neck. I was on top of him face up and he was using my own weight against me adding to the pressure in my windpipe. I was starting to get fuzzy from the lack of oxygen. I only had a few more seconds before I would lose consciousness. In my current position I couldn't get any leverage. I tried to pull his arm away to no avail. I couldn't' strike any vulnerable parts of his body with my hands, arms or feet. My head didn't have enough travel to butt him from behind. He had his left arm wrapped across my chest pressing my pistols in, which didn't allow me to get to the handles of those either. I was defenseless. I tried to roll but the soldier had splayed his legs making it impossible to turn him. I saw Amy pick up a large rock and run toward us. She was angling to hit his head, but it was under mine. I was trying to scream for her to hit his left arm, which had my arms pinned at my sides. I could free my guns then. I tried to scream but I had no air left. I knew I was about to go under. I tried desperately, one last time. I mustered all the effort I could and squeaked out the word "Arm". It came out in a hiss but Amy got the message. She slammed the rock down hard on the soldier's left arm just above the wrist. I heard bones crunch. He immediately loosed his arm. His right arm loosened the grip enough for me to gasp a breath. My right hand rocketed to the butt of the pistol on my left side. I drew it, reached over my neck, felt the barrel touch his flesh, rolled my head as far right as I could and pulled the trigger. The blast was deafening and the barrel burned my neck. I felt the warm splash on the back of my neck and head. The soldier's grip went slack immediately. I rolled off of him, perched myself on all fours and gulped in air. I coughed and spit and finally felt my lungs relax and stop spasming.

Alan, Max, Dog and Donte came tearing around the corner, guns in front. They had heard the shot in our direction and reacted.

"Holy Shit," Dog said. I followed his eyes down to the ruined head of the soldier. There was a neat hole where his left eye had been. The back half of the skull was shattered from the concussion of the shot.

"You all right?" Alan asked as I rose to my feet.

I nodded and added a raspy, "Yeah". My neck stung from the barrel burn and I had no hearing in my left ear. I figured my left eardrum was ruptured. My head was ringing as well. But I was alive. The back of my head was sticky and I could feel the cooling blood beginning to congeal on my neck. I bent over and puked.

We returned to the bridge. Everyone was with Candy Girl trying to console her. Dog was tending to Scumbag. As I approached I didn't need to be told but Dog made a slashing sign across his throat to tell me Scumbag was dead. He had a gaping wound in his chest. He was lying in a large pool of his own blood. We covered him. We didn't have time to even bury him.

"We need to get everyone on the road quickly. Stark is still out here and he's not going to lay low forever. Alan, we need to dump the tank. Drive it to the river's edge, put a rock on the gas and hop off. Let it roll out into the water and sink."

Amy filled everyone in on what had happened. Gangrene, Max and I went about collecting all of the weapons and gassing up the bikes and the Challenger. We checked the Humvee and found it full of gas as well. We added five working M-16s to our arsenal and enough clips to fight for hours if needed.

We watched as Alan fired the engine, spun the tank in place and began the slow drive to its death. At least it was victorious in its final battle. Alan stopped the tank twenty feet from the water's edge. Climbed out and drug a large river rock into the tank. The transmission kicked in and the tank rumbled forward. Alan scurried out of the top hatch and jumped off the back just as the tank touched the water. It rolled out into the river, and slowly began to go under. Thirty feet out the tank hit the deep-water shelf, tilted forward and seem to hang in that position for a while then it slipped under the water like a ship sinking in the ocean. Steam hissed off the top of the water as the hot engine slid into the water. Air bubbles floated up and drifted away and then a greasy black steak formed where the tank had gone down. It too drifted away and the tank was gone.

Alan, Donte and Amy loaded into the Challenger. Max and Dog climbed into the Humvee with Candy Girl. Cowboy and Gypsy climbed on their bikes and Gangrene and Bad Mama got on theirs. Taco mounted his bike. I stood there.

"Where's Ox?" Taco asked.

"He should be heading back here," said Gangrene.

"I don't hear his bike," Cowboy said.

"Taco take a run back to the other end of the bridge and see where he is. Let him know we're clear."

It went unsaid but by the look on everyone's face we were certain something bad had happened to him.

Taco fired his bike and roared off to the other end of the bridge.

"Let's go Ethan," Amy yelled from the backseat of the Challenger. I walked over to the window.

"I've got business to take care of. I'll meet you in New Mexico. This won't take long. I might even catch up to you before you get there. I know the route. You know I have to do this. He won't let us go. We can't keep looking over our shoulders forever."

"I know you do. And I know there's nothing I can say to make you come with us now. But I need to say this because it will make sure you focus and you come back to me." She paused and stared in to my eyes. I leaned in closer. "I love you Ethan Ryder. I love you."

I leaned in and kissed her.

"I'll be there, I promise."

I walked up to Gangrene, who was sitting on his bike behind the Challenger. "I'm going after Stark. I will catch up. You take care of our troops, especially Amy." He nodded and we shook hands. He reached around with his free hand and gave me a bear hug, patted me on the back, then let go.

Taco rolled back to the group alone. "He's not there. His bike is gone too."

Confusion rolled across everyone's face.

"You know he wasn't really a Vulture. Maybe he just pussed out and took off when all the shooting started. He knows where we are going. If he wants to he can show up there, if not so be it. No one could've got to him and if they did his bike wouldn't be gone. He ran."

"Most likely," I said. I wouldn't miss Ox. Something about him always sat badly with me. I was pissed that he took my Weatherby though. I had been to hell and back with that gun and it had served me well.

Gangrene turned and stared at me. "Kick Stark's ass," he growled. He fired his bike and everyone else followed suit. I watched as the Humvee pulled away, then the Challenger. Then the three bikes in a line, Gangrene, Cowboy, and Taco moved on. Taco gave me thumbs up as he passed. I stood in the middle of the street watching them drive away until they disappeared around a corner a half-mile down the road.

The road was now empty except for the bullet riddled LMVT, listing badly to the left on its ruined tires. Behind me stood Max, Dog and Scumbag's bikes. Max and Dog's bikes were clearly ruined with bullet holes. Next to them lay the shrouded body of Scumbag. It was eerily quiet now after so much noise. My left ear was still deaf but with the quiet I hardly noticed the lack of hearing. I had my two .44s, the Mossberg and all the spare ammo for each. It was hunting time.

Chapter 33

I refocused myself on the new mission. Everyone was away safely, on the way to Gangrene's brother's place in Tesuque, New Mexico, just north of Santa Fe. They had been headed there three months ago when they were stopped at the border. The way Gangrene had described it he'd made it sound like paradise. After the last two years anywhere but California would be paradise.

The last time I'd seen Stark was when he was running into the warehouse so I figured that was as good a place to start as any. I leveled the Mossberg, pumped a shell into the chamber with a loud 'clack'. I opened the door slowly and entered where I'd been brought in cuffs less than twelve hours earlier. I moved along the south wall keeping my back against the steel and looked down each of the long rows of crates. When I got to the wall on the east, I did the same, checking the short rows between the crates. I stopped after each row and listened for any telltale sound. It was difficult because my left ear had just begun to start ringing. It was the same sensation that I had experienced after a loud rock concert. The ringing was good though. It meant that some of the hearing was returning and the eardrum wasn't completely wasted by the muzzle blast.

I made it to the north wall and checked the rows of crates from this end. The main floor of the warehouse was clear. Unless Stark had packed himself in a crate this part of the building was empty. That left the offices. The first office on the north end of the row was the one with the windows. I looked through into the small room and it was empty. The door was open to the second one and it was empty as well. The third room, which had held Amy, was closed. I kicked the door in and stepped back, waiting for a response somewhere. The crashing sound of the door breaking echoed a few times in the metal building. When the sound cleared I heard nothing but my own breathing. I looked into the room and saw it was clear also.

That left the fourth room, the one I had been held in. This time I went around to the hole I had escaped through quietly dropped to the floor and thrust my shotgun into the opening followed by my head. I pulled them back out quickly. There was no response. I looked in again and the room was empty.

Across from the corridor from me was the last room. The bathroom. I went to the door, kicked it in and entered. It too was empty. Stark had slipped out of the building.

This was a problem. It left the whole city of Parker and beyond to search. I crossed the warehouse to go out the east exit, the only exit Stark could've taken without walking back into our group out front. I figured I would try to logically uncover the direction Stark might go in. I was about halfway across when I heard a car start up outside the east side of the building. I ran for the exit. The trunk slammed closed. Stark was going to follow the group. He had to think I was with them. I popped out the door. Stark was just opening the driver's door to the car. He wheeled around as I came out the door. His face was a mask of surprise. I unloaded the Mossberg in his direction. He dove down next to the car and the rear window exploded inward in a shower of glass. I started to come around the back of the car when he came back up with an M-16. I dove back through the emergency exit into the building. He began unloading the clip into the side of the corrugated steel building. The thin wall was no match for the rounds. Bullets were flying in every direction, ricocheting off the concrete floor, smacking into the crates, leaving beams of light shining through the airborne dust. I dove behind the first crate. The firing stopped as the magazine emptied. I took off running for the far door. I needed to take this fight out of Stark's turf and into a place I knew better than he did. I knew instantly where I wanted to draw him. I sprinted even harder. I heard the door swing open, and his footsteps begin to pound across the floor.

"I'm coming for you now. You have no help, no escape, no chance. I'll kill you!" he screamed across the warehouse, sounding like a madman, his voice rising with every word.

I hit the crash bar on the door and dashed into the early morning light. I ran to Scumbag's bike. I prayed that it hadn't been damaged in the fight as the other two bikes had. I knew the keys would still be in the ignition. Scumbag had been shot off the bike and would not have had time to remove the key.

It was there. I turned the key just as Stark came out the door. I stared him straight in the eye as I stomped on the starter pedal. The big bike roared to life. I goosed the gas hard, popped the clutch, and turned the handlebars hard to the left while I held the front brake in check. The back end of the bike fishtailed around, squealing and smoking. As I turned I saw Stark raise the M-16. He was breathing heavily, the barrel of the gun rising and falling with each breath. I released the front brake, the rear tire bit and I rocketed across the bridge. I heard gunshots and felt the sting of chunks of concrete kicking up into my arms and legs as the bullets riddled the concrete next to me.

I went up the rise and leaving the city behind I looked back to see the green sedan just pulling out from behind the warehouse. I had at least a mile head start on him, far enough ahead to keep him in my rear view mirror and too far for him to catch me.

Off in the distance behind me the sun was just breaking the horizon. The air was cold but also refreshing. It was cleansing away the events of the night. It was sharpening the edges of everything. I thought back to Afghanistan and the things Stark had done to me, to our squad and the people of that country. I raced on. I recalled my court martial and the shame that the army had made me feel, all brought on by Stark's treachery.

I passed Vidal Junction. I remembered the corpse in the freezer. It brought my thoughts back to my wife and child, smoldering on the porch, their deaths at Stark's hands. My anger was boiling inside. I no longer felt the cold. I saw the small green dot in the rear view mirror. I slowed to let him close the gap. To let him think he was going to win again. Not this time. I could feel the focus and raw determination welling into a singularity. I thought back to Donte and his capture. How I'd begun to feel a responsibility for him, for another human being. He'd brought me back from the dead in that way. He had made me care again. I remembered by confrontation with Stark in the school office.

I passed through Rice, and recalled the first time I saw Amy through the window of that school office, curled up on the floor. Put there by Stark. Raped and tortured. Another life scarred by the bastard. I pictured her face. I had a duty to her to make sure he would never touch her again. My plan focusing in my mind with each thought.

The turnout was ahead so I slowed to allow Stark to close the gap even more. He was about a half mile behind me. I didn't want him to miss the turn. I reached the access road and fired the bike up to top speed, racing through the open desert to the pump plant. A minute later I saw the green car make the turn. It kicked up a little puff of dust as it crossed from the highway to the road across the dirt shoulder.

As I climbed the grade to the station I opened up the throttle and was running at full speed. I could see the green dot getting smaller in the mirror. The end of the road was up ahead. Literally. One of us would not be making the trip back down. I owed it to all those people that Stark had touched with his evil to make sure he stayed here forever. I pulled into the complex, turned left at the first intersection and looped around the road, past the recreation center and the employee housing to the central administration building. I drove the bike through the ruined doors and into the lobby, jumped off and headed for the stairs at the end of the building. The Mossberg bounced against my back with each step. I climbed to the second floor and kicked in the door for the last office. From the window I could see clearly all the way to the end of the airstrip. Stark was just entering the complex. He was slowing to a crawl. He was looking side-to-side trying to take in the oddness of this little faux town in the middle of the desert and hoping to find some sign of me. He turned left on the same access road that I'd taken. I ran across the hall and kicked in the door to the office directly across the way. I went into the room and then to window. Stark made the loop, moving very slowly by the little houses in this area until he disappeared around the end of the building.

I went back to first window and saw Stark come out from behind the building. He turned left at the intersection and headed towards the reservoir and the pump house. As he made the turn I caught movement down on the road down by the airstrip. It was a motorcycle. I swiveled my head back to see Stark heading past the front of the pump house and onto the road that circled the reservoir. It would take him a few minutes to complete the circuit around the lake. I turned my attention back to the bike. "Who was this?" I thought to myself. I recognized the rider as Ox a few seconds later. Why was he here? Had he followed us? Did he know Stark was here? I didn't want him to stumble into Stark so I left the room and ran down the stairs and out into the parking lot. I cut diagonally across the lot on foot trying to reach the intersection before Ox drove right up on Stark. I was still trying to figure out why he was here. Perhaps he had caught up with the group and they sent him to help to make up for leaving the bridge or perhaps he'd been sent back with a message. Maybe the group had run into trouble. But how had he known I was here? He must've followed Stark. I quickened my pace. I reached the corner right as Ox crested the ridge and came to the intersection. I held my hand up both to greet him and to stop him. He pulled the bike over to the curb. He had my Weatherby rifle slung over his shoulder.

He stepped off the bike and gave me a nod as I walked toward him. "What's going on? Why are you here?" I asked quickly. "Stark is here."

"No worries," he said as he lifted the rifle off his shoulder and stepped up on the curb.

I looked over my shoulder to see where Stark was, and then turned back to Ox. He raised the rifle and pointed it at my chest.

"What are you doing," I said and swatted at the barrel. In one quick motion he swung the butt of the rifle up and across my cheek. I stumbled back a few steps, my face exploding in pain and fell back dropping the shotgun in the process. I shook my head to clear the stars. "What the fuck? This is not the time or place to make up for the ass kicking in the saloon. We can go at it later. Stark is here and will be coming up that road in two minutes."

"I know he is," he said and barred his teeth like an animal about to pounce. "Slowly reach up and take the .44s out and toss them butt first over to me."

"What do you mean, you know he is? What are you doing?" I was confused by everything that was happening.

"Shut up and give me the pistols. You all thought I was the slow one. How much more do I need to spell it out for you? Perhaps this will make it clear." He reached to his back pocket and pulled out a small two-way radio. He depressed the button on the side and raised it to his mouth. "Colonel, do you copy?"

The radio hissed and crackled. "10-4. What's the word, Jackson?"

"Colonel, I am 10-20 at the front of the installation. I have Ryder in custody."

The radio hissed and crackled again. "I'll be there in two."

"10-4." He looked at me. Pointed the Weatherby at my chest. "Last chance. Pull the pistols and throw them over to me. You still haven't figured it out yet have you? My name is Jackson. Sergeant Jackson. I've been working that side of the river undercover for two months. I've kept those bikers away the whole time. I've used them to keep everyone else away from the bridge. I was the head MP at that installation and I realized early on it was easiest to defend the bridge if no one ever even got on it. It was working until you showed up. Those were my men you killed back there. As soon as you showed up I radioed back to the base and had them contact Stark. I knew who you were from the A.P.B. Plan was I would let Stark know where you were and he could just arrest you and your girlfriend while I talked the rest out of the little revolution you planned. Figured I'd take a ride after you were gone and disable your little tank."

"Very nice you piece of crap."

"How do you think he found you so easily by the river? The plan was going just fine until you squirmed away from Stark. Then I had no chance to let my men know you were coming. Just missed you tonight on the bridge though."

I recalled the bullet that had whizzed by my ear.

"And now you are going to die in the place that you brought Stark to die in. There's no help this time either."

"Well done, " I said and clapped mockingly. "Well done."

He stepped closer, still holding the rifle on my chest. "Oh and by the way, I owe you one of these." He swung his right leg toward my head. He was slow and I was able to roll with the kick. It glanced across my cheek but I fell to my right and rolled over like I was truly injured. I glanced down the road and could see the green car making the last of the loop around the reservoir. I had less than a minute. The sidewalk was broken beneath my chest and I was able to grab a baseball-sized chunk of concrete. I slowly sat up keeping my right hand on the ground, wrapped around the rock and hidden by my thigh. It was time for one more bit of magic, a little misdirection. I reached up to my cheek with my left hand to rub it. Ox's eyes followed my left hand and at the same time I fired a fastball of concrete with my right. The chunk hit him edge on his nose. It exploded, blood instantly squirting everywhere. I sprang to my feet. He instinctively dropped the rifle and grabbed his face with both hands. I ran full speed and hit him like an NFL linebacker hits a receiver coming across the middle. I felt his ribs break as my shoulder hit him. We flew five feet, landed on his back with me on top. I smashed my elbow into his nose again. He screamed in agony. I rolled him over, grabbed his chin with my left hand and the back of his head with the right and gave his head a quick snap. His neck broke and he instantly stopped fighting.

I picked up the Weatherby and the shotgun, looked over my shoulder and saw Stark making the last curve before the street. I had just a minute. I dragged Ox's body up the curb and deposited it behind a line of bushes. Then I took off on a run for the administration building.

I made it up the stairs two at a time and into the front office just as the green car passed the far end of the building. I lifted the shotgun and took aim on the hood. When the car was directly under the window, about forty feet away, I pulled the trigger. Dozens of small holes suddenly bloomed on the hood and the front windshield shattered. The car came to a stop. I pumped and fired a second time. Steam rose from under the hood and fluid leaked from underneath the motor. I was killing the car. Then I swung the gun to the front tire. It exploded when the shot hit it. I repeated for the rear. Then I leveled the gun at Ox's bike. Hit the engine dead center. Oil and gas ran out and pooled under the bike. One more shot and the gas can became a sieve, the remaining gas spilling out like a waterfall. The only working vehicle on the base was now my bike.

Stark finally came out of the car with the M-16. He brought it up to his eye and laid a line of shots across the windows of the upper floor. I instinctively dropped to the deck. When he finished the burst I popped back up to see him running away down the street toward the central park. I calmly set the shotgun down and picked up the Weatherby. It was like an old friend in my hands. I chambered a round, took a shooting position against the windowsill. I glanced at the trees to gauge the breeze. Stark was just entering the park. He had slowed to a jog. He was about one hundred fifty yards away. Hitting a moving target at this range was a little more difficult but certainly not impossible. I began to slow my breathing, letting my heart quiet down. Stark was jogging directly away from me. By the time I was ready Stark had reached the front of the pump house about one hundred seventy five yards away. I squeezed the trigger slowly, taking the slack out it, making sure to pull straight back so as to not pull the rifle off line. I exhaled and made the final squeeze. I saw the muzzle flash and almost instantly saw the bullet hammer into the back of Stark's thigh. He fell, the back of his cammo pants beginning to stain dark with blood. He dropped the M-16 he was carrying and clutched at his leg. He wasn't going anywhere.

I shouldered the rifle, picked up the shotgun and exited the room. I climbed down the stairs and left the rifle and shotgun with the bike. I pulled both my pistols from their holsters and stepped out the doors. I walked south along the building. I felt like a man on a morning stroll. I wasn't worried about Stark. He wasn't going anywhere and wasn't going to shoot. His leg was ruined and he was in too much pain to think of anything but flight. I'd seen it many times before. Just like old times.

As I came into the clearing and entered the central park I could see the spot where Stark had been. He was gone. He couldn't have gone far with a ruined leg. When I got to the spot where I had dropped him I could see the trail of blood leading toward the pump house. The M-16 was still there in the grass next to the wet stain.

Following the blood was like following a trail of breadcrumbs. Stark was bleeding heavily. The trail led up the street and past the front of the pump house. It went around and into the generator building. I could see the trail led around the far row of generators. I knew from our past visits that there were no exits on the sides or back of the shed. I worked my way over the last generator and looked around the corner. Stark was lying on the polished concrete floor halfway back in the building. I stepped out from behind the massive piece of equipment. I had one .44 in each hand. Stark saw me as I stepped out.

"Please Ryder. Please." He begged. I kept walking. "Come on please. Let me go."

I laughed at the comment. "Really?" I asked. "You think I should just let you go. After everything? You really are delusional, aren't you?"

"Please, please, please. I don't want to die. I've got lots of money. I'll give it all to you. Just let me live."

"Do you think the guys in our squad wanted to die? That first shot in is for them." I raised the pistol in my right hand, aimed at the knee on the good leg and fired. The blast from the hand cannon echoed in the metal shed. So did Stark's shrieks. "That was for my wife. She didn't want to die either." He was now lying on the polished concrete, bleeding from both legs and whimpering. I took aim again, this time at his left shoulder. I pulled the trigger and his shoulder was destroyed. "That one was for me. For all you took from me. Do you think I wanted my life turned upside down, my family, my career taken?"

"Please, stop," he whimpered.

I took aim at the other shoulder and pulled the trigger. Stark's right shoulder was a ruined mess. "Is that what Amy begged you every time you raped her, you bastard? I'll let you live as long as it takes you to bleed to death right there." I turned and walked down the aisle, big generators on my right and the gas tanker on my left. As I got to the end of the row I looked back at Stark. His head was off the floor and he was watching me walk away.

"Please, don't leave me here to die," he begged.

I raised the pistol and fired a round into the side of the big tanker. Gas began to run out of the hole. I waited until a small pool had formed beneath the tank. I fired a shot at the concrete right next to the puddle. It sparked off the floor and the pool instantly ignited. I turned and walked away. As I reached the central park grass the tanker exploded with a thunderous roar. I didn't even turn to look. I could feel the heat on my neck. "That one was for my son."

Epilogue

The ride to Tesuque was uneventful and I arrived there just hours after everyone else. The solitude and the distance of the ride washed away everything I had left behind and I was excited for the future. The future was unknown and full of expectation.

I related the story of what had happened at the pump station to the group and explained that Ox had apparently been lying in wait for us in case we doubled back and had followed Stark and I. The group was stunned when I told them who he was and what he'd done.

In the weeks following, Amy and I got to know each other in every way possible. We spent hours on long walks through the woods around the ranch. There was snow on the ground and the world was still at winter peace.

We learned that most of the country was on the road to recovery and returning to normalcy after the riots. The big cities were starting to come back to life one by one. The farther you got from California, which had been hit the hardest by the rioting, the quicker the recovery. California would be last to get relief, if ever.

In Tesuque it all really didn't matter. The local market had the essentials we needed and the ranch gave us the rest. Gangrene's family welcomed us with open arms and was glad to have the help. There wasn't too much to do now, during the winter, but come spring we were assured that there would be lots of work to do. I looked forward to waking up each day and doing the hard ranch work with the sun on my back and the fresh air in my lungs. It was freedom and it made it a difference.

Alan and Donte bonded like father and son. Alan rejoiced and thrived on sharing all of his knowledge and skills with Donte, and Donte was like a sponge. He enjoyed everything Alan had to offer him. Donte was becoming quite a mechanic and went about repairing a tractor that stopped working the previous summer.

Mad Max and Dirty Dog were enjoying the rest but were chomping at the bit to get back on the road. They were young and still wanted to see the world from the back of a Harley. I couldn't blame them. My long ride here left me with the urge to hit the highway as well. Amy and I talked about taking an extended trip next fall if we could.

Cowboy and Gypsy found a local preacher and got married about a week after we arrived. Gangrene and Bad Mama were best man and maid of honor and gave them away. That was how we found out their real names. Gangrene's given name was Horatio Greenberg and Bad Mama was Belinda. They were married, which nobody had known. After the laughing died down we all agreed to never call him Horatio, at least not to his face. He took to ranch life like a duck to water and gave up his bandana for a black cowboy hat. He wouldn't wear white. He said it was bad for his image.

Taco had taken up with a woman he met working as a waitress at the local bar. He moved in with her right away but still stops by every day.

Candy Girl was sad and distant most of the time. The loss of Scumbag hit her hard. Amy and I spent a lot of time with her since we could both relate. She seemed to be coming around but it was going to take some time.

The bunch of us rarely talked of the events of that week again, choosing to move on and remember better times before that and planning the great times ahead of us. Our little army had turned into a family.

I stood on the porch about six weeks after we arrived just enjoying the breeze and the sun, looking at the first signs of spring in the trees, when I saw the plain, blue four-door American made sedan come down the road and turn into the long drive. The car pulled to a stop at the front gate. It had the white and blue license plates of a U.S. government car. There was just one occupant. Everyone stopped what they were doing and stared at the man as he stepped from the vehicle.

He wore jeans, white cotton short sleeve shirt with cowboy boots and a turquoise bolo tie. He had short, close-cropped salt and pepper hair. He walked straight up the walk to me and stood at the base of the steps leading to the porch. He had a manila folder, thick with papers under his left arm. He reached into his coat pocket and I instinctively straightened at the action. He pulled a leather wallet flipped it open and showed me his badge.

"Sir, I'm Captain Paul Alexander with the U.S. Marshall's office. Are you Ethan Ryder?"

"Why do you ask?"

He opened the folder. Stapled to the upper left corner was my military I.D. photo. It was ten years old now but there was no denying that it was me.

"Sure looks like you. Mr. Ryder I'm here just to talk at this point. Can we take a walk?" Amy came through the screen.

"Everything okay?" she asked. I shrugged and climbed down the steps. We walked across the front yard and down to the rangeland and followed a fence

278

line as we talked. I could feel everyone's eyes on us as we went.

"Mr. Ryder."

"Please, just call me Ethan,"

"All right, Ethan. You've had a busy few months or so I'm told. I'm not sure you're aware but the U.S. Marshall's office is now responsible for rounding up insurgents and leading rioters. We are trying to restore order to our country. You've created a lot of disorder. A lot." I started to speak in my defense. He held up his right index finger to hold me off. "I've spent that last six weeks on your file alone. You were a high priority. Basically destroyed a military base single handed, shot up a border crossing, stole a tank. Where is the tank by the way?" Before I could answer he said, "Never mind, we'll get to that later. You killed a number of soldiers, including a decorated colonel. At first I wanted to hunt you down and put the bullet in your forehead myself. But as I interviewed people and found people who knew you I began to get a picture of something different. While I don't condone what you've done I do understand it. There are some holes in my information and exactly what happened but I have enough to understand that Stark was a bad dude and especially bad to you. In these crazy times I guess I have some leeway in how we deal with these things. I really have three options as I see it. First option, I could walk away, but you killed a few very innocent soldiers, in particular, the soldier that you killed at the underpass. I can link you directly to that one. We have video, prints and eyewitness testimony. I can guarantee at least life in a Federal penitentiary if not a firing squad. The ones at the border can't be tied directly to you and it would be tough to make it stick in court.

Second option is to bring you in and let you stand trial. I don't think that would be justice in this case. But it depends on your response to option number three. You obviously have a set of skills that could be very valuable to what we do. I would like to trade your freedom for the ability to call on you occasionally when we need your help."

He let the idea hang in the air without adding to it. We walked a few steps farther and then we stopped. I turned and faced him. "So my choice is be arrested, take my chances at trial and face the possibility of a firing squad or work for you occasionally and have the whole thing disappear. Hmmm. Tough choice. How often will you call on me?"

"Just when we need you."

"Then I guess we have a deal."

THE END

Ethan Ryder will return in *Ryder on the Storm*

ABOUT THE AUTHOR

Brian Finley lives in Southern California with his wife, two sons and his dog, Gizmo. This is his first of many novels to come. He is a graduate of Cal State Northridge and has worked in the sport and recreation field for most of his life.

RYDER'S ARMY
October 2011

Published by BWGK Publications

This is a work of fiction. Names, characters, places,
and incidents either are the product of the author's
imagination or are used fictitiously. Any resemblance
to actual persons, living or dead, events, or locales is
entirely coincidental.

ISBN: 0615556825
ISBN-13: 978-0615556826

Cover designed by: Budow Design.
www.budowdesign.com